THE DIAMOND TIARA

TRUST NO ONE.

Vogue

Crown Jewelz Publishing

The Diamond Tiara
Part VI of The Diamond Collection
Copyright © 2022 Vogue

ISBN-13: 978-0-9888004-6-5

Cover Design by Vogue

Website: www.simplyvogue.net
Instagram: iam_carmendavenport

Other Works in The Diamond Collection

This book is dedicated to the memory of

Annie L. Gary Smith

Thank you for always supporting me and The Diamond Collection.
May you forever Rest in Peace.

1

Kenema, Sierra Leone

A small amount of light adorned the stairwell. Despite the lack thereof, a band of armed men moved down the steps without breaking formation. The only sound which echoed off the walls was the repetitive stomps of their black tactical boots. The noise ceased as they neared the last step. One of the soldiers opened the basement door. Light spread like wildfire throughout the space. The repetitive stomps roared back to life.

The band of soldiers poured into a room already occupied by another group of armed men. The same black tactical gear was upon their frames. The number 66 was plastered in azure blue on their backs. Both parties stood in a loop around a white gentleman who rested at their feet. His face was clear and untouched while his clothes were in shreds and stained with fresh and dried blood.

The group broke formation.

Out of their core, a man in a blindingly white suit appeared. Pearl-colored alligator loafers lined his feet, large gold and diamond rings laced his fingers. His countenance was different from the designer labels he wore. Surly was an accurate description. He walked towards the center of the circle where the gentleman laid. Upon reaching him, he knelt for a closer look. Familiar was an understatement. He knew the man's identity way before he entered the U.S. Embassy in Freetown. Nonetheless, he didn't place a tracker on Howard Grendel until he learned Kenema was his destination.

A little over a year ago, his second in command brought him a copy of *The Brookstone Times*. The front-page headline was all about how his biggest buyer had beaten another case. It was a win for all of them. After hearing the news, his first task was finding the man who helped his comrade obtain his freedom. His original plan was to anonymously bestow upon him a jewel of gratitude. The plan changed when he learned his buyer's saving grace was a part of a scheme within the U.S. government.

He remembered that day clearly. A yellow manila envelope arrived on his desk. The envelope contained several photographs of Grendel, which placed him in the city of Brookstone, New York. Previous photos he received showed Grendel outside The White House. The first photograph he pulled from the envelope was a shot of Grendel walking up the steps of a brownstone.

The second was a complete shot of the structure, a building inscribed with the words Blue Magic. The third photo was the golden ticket. In the photo was the owner of the establishment—a Puerto Rican businessman, Jay Santiago, who he supplied with some of the most exquisite diamonds known to man. He was walking up the same set of steps.

The pictures showed that Grendel was more than a random American who stumbled upon a surveillance tape. He had ties to Santiago. Evidence suggested that Grendel assisted Santiago on his case in exchange for one thing—him. The U.S. government believed Grendel was harmless and could enter Kenema under the guise of a missionary. They were mistaken. He was already ten steps ahead of them. It was the reason the man was at his feet half-dead. He knew what they wanted. It wasn't his diamond mines. It was the people who worked his mines.

America always wants to be the savior.

"Howard Grendel," he called. The man's eyes flickered open. "Ship him," he ordered. His directive was clear. He left the room just as the man was bludgeoned. Grendel was no longer his concern. His comrade was. The name Santiago was now a trigger. It was a clear reminder that even genuine partnerships were built off deceit.

2

Brookstone, New York

The clock hadn't even struck seven-thirty, yet the city of East Brookstone was bustling. While the area was not as populous as Manhattan, the current atmosphere showed something different. Crowds of people filled the downtown area. The majority was on foot; whereas others hailed cabs or utilized other forms of public transportation. The subdivisions had far less traffic, but that didn't mean it was any less hectic inside the homes. School may have been out due to the holiday break, yet it was business as usual for parents and child-less adults who were chasing a dollar.

The Washington household was no different. Located in one of the wealthiest gated communities in the city, the mansion was a far cry from Tiara and Malik's humble beginnings. Their home, a property that had graced the pages of *Architectural Digest*, was well over ten thousand square feet and filled with only designer décor. That morning, they moved circles around each other, both working on different things, but with the same goal—to get out the house. Malik had their four-year-old daughter, Robin, on his hip while his free hand worked on the morning coffee. Tiara, on the other hand, was packing Robin's day bag and ignoring her cell phone, which had been beeping every few seconds.

"Can you get that?" Malik urged. The noise had become an annoyance.

"Not if I want to get out this house on time," Tiara shot back. Her phone beeped again, which was all Malik needed to leave the Keurig alone. He headed to the other side of the kitchen and picked up her phone. Tiara saw him out the corner of her eye, yet she didn't stop what she was doing. They made an agreement there wouldn't be any secrets in their house. He was free to check any device she owned and vice versa.

"This will definitely get you out the house," Malik told her.

He held the phone at eye level. Numerous notifications were on the screen, mostly texts and emails. There were also two missed calls. "Why is Monifah at the gate?" he asked.

That question made Tiara drop Robin's bag. Monifah Harris, now Monifah Kane, was a mutual friend she shared with her longtime gal pal, Carmen Santiago, back in their high school and college days. Monifah left town shortly after the murder of her ex-boyfriend, Rakim (who just so happened to be Malik's twin brother) and popped back up as the new girlfriend (but now wife) of Carmen's ex-husband, Michael Kane, who simply went by Kane. Most people expected Tiara and Malik to be close to Monifah due to her connection to Rakim. However, they never spoke.

Tiara pulled her phone from Malik's hands to read the messages. Monifah was in the area and wanted to see if she was available to chat. "I don't trust that woman," Tiara admitted, throwing the phone on the kitchen's island. "It's too early to be coming over to someone's house. It's not even eight o'clock." Tiara went back to Robin's bag, double checking to make sure she hadn't missed anything. "What does she want to talk about?"

Malik pulled the bag from Tiara's grasp. "You'll have to tell her the gate code to see."

"No, you just want to know," Tiara joked. She picked up her phone and texted the code. "Look at you. You ain't even dressed." Tiara glanced at her phone again, checking the time. "I have to deal with her, you deal with that." Tiara pointed at Robin's hair. "You've mastered the bun."

Malik kissed Robin's cheek. "Tell Mama she ain't got nuthin' to worry about. Daddy is going to have you lookin' good."

"He better," Tiara said, leaving the kitchen. Once she reached the foyer, she peeked out a window to see if Monifah was there. A car was pulling in her driveway. Although she wasn't prepared to deal with her, she stepped outside. The energy between them was awkward for several reasons, which boiled down to one—Carmen.

And from the looks of things, it ain't gonna get better, Tiara thought.

Her mouth dropped open as Monifah stepped out her car. She hadn't seen her in a few weeks, but her former friend had blossomed into a pregnant woman overnight. "Wow," Tiara mouthed, walking towards her. "This is so unexpected."

Monifah had a large grin on her face as if she came to gloat. "The cat is out the bag," she shrieked. She did a Kenya Moore-inspired twirl so Tiara could see all sides of her bump.

"You and Kane are having a baby?"

Monifah stopped mid-twirl. "Who else would I be having a baby with?"

Tiara shrugged her shoulders. "No, it's just that I've been friends with Kane for years and I know he's…" Tiara didn't finish. It wasn't her place to tell Kane's business although a large part of her assumed he told Monifah he was infertile. "He and Carmen used in vitro to have Kristian, so—" Tiara was interrupted.

"And he did the same for me," Monifah snapped. "Why would I be any different?"

"No, no, that's not what I'm saying. I just…" Tiara had backed herself in a corner.

"I came over because this is all new to me." Monifah took a few steps closer to Tiara to close the gap. "I've been gone so many years. This is my hometown, and I don't have any friends. I thought this was a good time for us to reconnect. You're a mother, I'm about to be a mother. I thought you could be someone I could go to for advice."

Tiara tried not to show her emotions on her face. Monifah wasn't on Carmen's hit list, but she didn't know how Carmen would feel if she got chummy with her ex-husband's new wife.

"Silence," Monifah muttered. "I guess that's my answer."

"No, no, it's just…" Tiara tried to back herself out a corner again. "Come on, Monifah. We haven't talked in like twenty-something years. You walked back in our lives in the least way we expected."

"You can't be my friend because you're friends with Carmen?"

Tiara gave her a reminder. "You married her ex-husband."

"And she fucked your boyfriend."

Tiara was taken aback. What Monifah was saying was true, but she hadn't thought about Carmen's bad deeds in a long time. To her, it was all water under the bridge.

"Carlos Rodriguez," Monifah stated with a smile. "Puerto Rican drug dealin' bad ass, the underboss of the Santiago cartel, former best friend of Jay Santiago, and the man behind Carmen Davenport who helped her get her coins up to start one of the biggest fashion companies in America, Flame." Monifah described him as if she were reading a character bio for a reality show. "What do you get from being her lapdog? I bet she has you taking care of her fifty billion kids while she's on her honeymoon fuckin' underneath an island sunset."

"I'm actually about to drop my daughter off at *her* house so her maid can watch her."

Monifah came back with, "I bet you have to pay her to do it."

Tiara sucked her teeth. She did pay Fiona. The woman deserved to get paid. She cooked, cleaned, and watched after three children five days a week and sometimes the weekend, if needed. "Okay, you're pregnant, you hate Carmen, what else?"

"Damn," Monifah muttered as if she hadn't started the Carmen-hate train. "We used to be close, Tee. Yes, you were always closer to Carmen, but we were like sisters, too."

The memories flooded back quicker than Tiara wanted. The three of them were like sisters. People even mistook them to be when they would see them together. With their deep rich ebony complexions, similar physiques, and hairstyles, they were the same aesthetic.

"Maybe we can try to get back there," Monifah suggested.

Tiara shrugged her shoulders. "I don't want to be in the middle of you and Carmen."

Monifah looked away. "You will always be loyal to her. For what, though? I don't get it. That woman is evil. Didn't you see what she put Kane through?"

Tiara had heard enough. She knew Carmen wasn't a saint. Yes, her friend had done some downright dirty and disgusting things, but it was *years* ago. Her friend learned from her mistakes, matured, and was focused on being the best wife and mother she could be. Monifah couldn't see it because she hadn't witnessed Carmen's growth. All she saw was the Carmen of the past.

"I need to go," Tiara announced, a hint the conversation was over. "Hopefully, you'll find what you're looking for even if it's not here."

"I hope you find what you're looking for, too."

Tiara raised her brow, unsure of what Monifah was getting at. It was on the tip of her tongue to probe her, but Monifah was walking to her car. She hadn't left though, which meant the opportunity was still there. "What is that supposed to mean?" Tiara asked, following behind her. "What is it that you think I'm looking for?"

Monifah didn't respond as she opened her car door. She got inside and for a split-second Tiara thought she was going to leave her guessing. She thought it even more when she heard the doors lock. Then, the driver side window rolled down.

"A hand to pull you out the rabbit hole," Monifah replied.

Tiara became even more quizzical. She didn't ask for another explanation as it would prolong Monifah from getting off her property. Still, her mind wondered. Monifah believed she wanted to be out Carmen's shadow. Yet, Tiara never thought she was there. Other people did.

But was she?

Truth be told, Tiara had given her life to Flame, a company she barely owned any part of. If anything were to happen to her, Robin would only inherit five percent, although she served as Vice President for over twenty years of her life. *That is a problem,* Tiara thought. She was the one who made Flame what it was. Carmen only provided the financial backing and designs. She built the business while Carmen was locked up and handed it off to her once she was released. At the time, Tiara thought she was doing the right thing because Carmen owned Flame. However, a fair percentage of the company should've been given to her. Instead, Carmen sold twenty percent to her and three other execs.

The conversation with Monifah created dialogue in her head that only existed in spurts. The thoughts also never created any action. With Carmen temporarily away from the business, she could start putting together a proposal for a greater percentage of ownership. She didn't know how her friend would feel about it. Therefore, she made a mental note to discuss it with Malik. He wasn't one to hide his opinion no matter how much it hurt. He also would tell her if she was letting Monifah get in her head.

"No one is even out here."

Tiara heard Malik behind her. "She just left. I'm gonna check the mail."

"Cool," Malik replied.

Once he closed the door, Tiara made her way to the mailbox. She looked up the street for any sign of Monifah's car, but her ex-friend was gone. Tiara told herself the conversation they shared should be as well *or* at least for the time being.

3

Gros Islet, Saint Lucia

A radiant beam of sun warmed Carmen's face as she stepped onto the terrace. Despite the early hour, the temperature was at a raging high. To adjust to the heat, she donned only a kimono-styled silk robe over her deep melanated skin. There was little need for modesty when the property was tucked away on a hillside distant from the other villas. With privacy at her fingertips, Carmen didn't hesitate to untie the robe's belt from around her waist.

She moved about the terrace carelessly, taking in the beauty of the villa. Ocean waves crashed around her. Birds chirped in the distance while the scent of Mother Nature tickled her nostrils. As if those splendors weren't enough, an infinity pool laid below her, the bluish green water bleeding into the Caribbean Sea. The sight of it reminded Carmen why she was on the terrace in the first place. Swimming at the very edge of the pool was her husband of all of two days—Jay Santiago.

Let's see how attentive you are.

Jay raised his head from the water. She smiled at him although he hadn't yet noticed her presence. His mind was elsewhere, which she noticed when he disappeared underneath the water for another swim. She let him be, moving towards the lower level of the terrace. Once she reached the pool's edge, Jay raised his head again. This time, their eyes met.

"Someone finally decided to get up," he said with a smile.

Carmen sat down, allowing her legs to fall inside the pool. Jay used it as an invitation, pushing his muscular frame in between her thighs. Naturally, she draped them around his waist. "I was taking advantage of being able to sleep in. You know our days are numbered."

"You're taking advantage of more than that," he replied. Jay's fingertips traced the edge of the robe as a reminder she was nude.

"So are you," Carmen stated, motioning to his bare skin as well. Certain they had the same intentions, she slid the robe off, leaving it on the terrace as she eased herself into the water. "Is this breakfast?"

The only reply needed was Jay's lips on hers, his tongue pushing its way deep into her mouth. When their bodies became entangled, there was no turning back. Their pants and moans floated through the air unnoticed as if the villa were surrounded by soundproof walls. The moment was an everlasting peace until the peace became disturbed.

"I'm not answering," Jay whispered. His phone was ringing from a nearby lounge chair. He ignored it, as did Carmen, until the ringing failed to cease. The unwanted noise forced him out Carmen's arms. He retreated to the terrace to grab his phone. *Malik* was on the screen. His friend for the past thirty or so years, he knew something was brewing if Malik called him.

"This has to be about more than business," he stated. Multiple voices were in the background, which made Jay believe his speculation was true. "What's going on?"

The voices became silent as Malik spoke. "Tiara was trying to reach Carmen, but she wasn't getting an answer. When she dropped Robin off this morning, Fiona told her she hadn't seen Patricia. She called me to come over to help look for her."

Jay kept his back to Carmen. The memory hit him hard as Malik reminded him of a sin he'd left in Brookstone. Patricia Davenport was Carmen's mother and his latest victim. "Carmen's phone is in the house. We're at the pool."

Malik overlooked what he said. "I broke her door down. Patricia's cell phone was still in her room, her purse, everything. We searched the premises, the cameras, it's like she vanished into thin air. Roman said he hasn't seen her in a while, too. I know he lives with y'all."

Jay visualized Patricia's lifeless body behind the rosebushes of their multi-million-dollar estate. That was where he left her. "Are you sure y'all looked everywhere?" Part of the y'all he spoke of was Roman, Linx, and Gully, his three right-hands, who were at his house almost twenty-four seven. The latter, Gully, was also his first cousin.

"I wouldn't have called you if we hadn't," Malik told him.

A wave of confusion fell over Jay's face. Malik's words didn't make sense, but he couldn't tell on himself. Someone had moved Patricia's body, which meant his secret was known. "Look, I'll see what Carmen wants to do and call you back."

"This isn't looking good," Malik was saying as Jay ended the call.

"What is it?" Carmen asked once she saw him hang up. "Is something wrong with the kids?"

Jay shook his head. "No one's seen your mother."

Her face read what he expected. She was taken aback. As if she could rush off to Brookstone that very minute, she climbed out the pool and slid her robe on. "No one has seen her since we left for Puerto Rico?"

"From what it seems. Fiona told Tiara she hasn't seen her. Malik checked her room. All her stuff is there, but she isn't." Jay handed his phone to her in the event she wanted to call Malik. She didn't take it, so he draped his arm at his side.

"Did he check—"

"He checked everywhere," Jay interrupted.

"Why are you cutting me off?" Carmen's tone was now one of suspicion. "What does everywhere mean to him? Did he check the cameras to see if she left or if someone picked her up? Did he check the hospitals?"

"I trained my men to be thorough."

"But did you train them to check the city and ask around?"

Once again, Jay handed her his phone. When Carmen didn't take it the second time, he tossed it onto the lounge chair. "Just tell me what you want to do."

Carmen rubbed her brow. While she should've been hopping on the next flight to New York, she wasn't ready to leave Saint Lucia. She didn't want to rush back only to learn her mother had taken an unannounced vacation. It seemed like the right thing to do, but it wasn't what she wanted. Everyone knew her relationship with her mother was strained. In Carmen's opinion, no one should've been shocked if she didn't hop on the first flight to Brookstone. Still, with the clock ticking, she needed a plan of action.

"Call Malik back," she replied. "Have him go through my mother's things and do a check on all her accounts. I'll figure out what I'm gonna do once I see what he finds out."

Jay grabbed his phone from the lounge chair to do as she requested. She headed in the house while he made the call. "For right now," he stated once Malik picked up, "we're gonna stay here. Carmen wants you to go through her mother's things and see if you can access her bank accounts. Check to see if there are any debits."

"Gully did that. She had her passwords written down in her planner. I forgot to mention it. Patricia hadn't used her account in weeks. The debits made were automatic drafts and it wasn't many of 'em," Malik shared. "We also checked her emails and there wasn't anything suspicious there."

"Where's Linx?" Jay asked. He was trying to narrow down who could've moved Patricia's body. "Is Akaila there?" Jay mentioned his stepdaughter on purpose. She was the 19-year-old adopted daughter of Carmen and Kane, who was currently studying at Brookstone University. There was a possibility she saw something as she lived under their roof and was home all the time.

"They're both right here," Malik answered. "Do you want to talk to them?"

Jay parted his lips to say no, yet, it was Tiara's voice, which prompted his silence.

"We should call Kane," she was saying. "He used to work for an intelligence agency. He knows what to do. This is what he does."

The last suggestion Jay wanted to hear; he didn't hesitate to voice it. "Don't call him. I don't want him anywhere near my house. Do what I said and check the city. I'm gonna talk to Carmen and we'll go from there." Jay gave Malik a chance to respond until a new thought entered his mind. "You know not to contact the police. The last thing we need is them in our business."

Once Malik agreed, Jay hung up. As much as he wanted to toss his cell in the pool, he settled for throwing it back on the lounge chair. What he was currently facing was the result of him being sloppy with his crime. A rookie, he was not, but his actions deemed him to be. Now, he was stuck on an island facing the end of a marriage, which had only begun.

Or so he thought. The sound of his phone ringing caught his attention. This time when he answered, it was Linx on the other end. "Did something change?"

"No," Linx informed him, "everything's the same. You know I have your back, right?"

There it was. The information Jay needed. "You always have my back. That's why I'll always have yours." Jay looked towards the house to see if Carmen was eavesdropping. He didn't see her in earshot. "Neither you nor your family will ever be in need."

"How far are you going to let this thing go?"

Jay didn't have an answer, but he would have to find one soon. It wouldn't be long before someone else would suggest for Carmen to get the cops involved. He couldn't let the search get far, but he also couldn't tell Carmen what he'd done. He would have to play it all by ear. "I don't know," he said. "I'll figure it out along the way."

A loud sigh sounded out Linx's mouth. "I guess we both will."

***

Brookstone, New York

The morning dew was still on the ground when Tiara exited the front doors of the Santiago Estate. She left the mansion the same way she came, except, this time, Malik was in tow. Robin was inside eating breakfast with Rakim and Nyla, the youngest of the Santiago clan. In total, her best friend, Carmen, had six beautiful kids. The oldest, King, being 21-years-old, who she shared with Jay. Then, there was Kristian, who was born while Carmen was married to Kane. She was the same age as Akaila, who Carmen and Kane adopted along with Akaila's 16-year-old brother, Malachi.

They got adopted right when shit was hitting the fan. Tiara remembered everything about that time. After serving seventeen years in prison, Jay was released, came home, laid Carmen on her back, and out came Rakim, who was now almost five. The infidelity caused Carmen and Kane to divorce. The two reconciled only for there to be infidelity on Kane's part. That put Carmen back in Jay's bed where they conceived Nyla who was now four. More drama occurred, which led Carmen to remarry Kane, divorce him a second time, only to marry Jay, days ago, on December 25th.

What a time, Tiara thought. She exhaled, unsure of where she should be headed. Normally, her destination would be Flame. With Patricia nowhere to be found and her best friend living it up in Saint Lucia, Tiara felt she should be on a scavenger hunt.

"You know you need to call Kane," she told her husband once he walked past her.

"We heard what Jay said," Malik replied. He continued to his car as if he didn't want to finish the conversation. Tiara followed behind him until they were standing at his vehicle.

"So, we're just going to wait around to see if she turns up?"

"Jay hasn't given another order. Plus, I can't be here all day. I have a meeting with King in an hour." Malik wrapped his arm around her waist and pulled her in to him. He planted a firm kiss on her lips. "Do I need to get Robin this evening?"

"I'll get her," Tiara replied. "I want to stop by for an update."

Malik looked at the house. He understood his wife's concern, but he wasn't trying to take the lead on Patricia's disappearance. He was growing tired of handling Carmen and Jay's messes. It was one of the reasons he took a position at King Records. By breaking away from Jay's businesses, he expected to have less of his friend's problems in his hands. Unfortunately, expectations were just that, expectations. "Don't involve yourself any more than you have to," he responded. "Have a good day, baby. I love you." Malik gave her another kiss before getting inside his vehicle.

When his engine revved, Tiara made her way to her own car. She was already late for work and sticking around the Santiago Estate for a second longer wasn't going to do anything for business. She missed most of the morning rush and walked onto the executive floor of Flame right before the clock struck ten-thirty. Her intention was to head straight for her office, yet she was bum rushed by Carmen's receptionist, Jessica McClain. Their new employee was the widow of Carmen's former driver, Donnie. Her best friend hired her after Jessica reached out to her for financial help. While Carmen did gift her with a six-figure check, she also gave her a job. Carmen hired her previous receptionist, Cathy, as her personal assistant, and she got paid to do little to nothing.

"I'm not used to you arriving this late," Jessica stated.

"Me neither," Tiara replied, still headed in the direction of her office.

"A man came by looking for Carmen. I asked him for his name, but he wouldn't give it. I referred him to you, but you weren't in your office. He said he would come back."

Tiara stopped in her tracks. "No one should've come looking for her. Carmen rescheduled all her meetings. How did he get on the floor?"

"I told security to let him up," Jessica shared. "I was hoping to get some information from him so I could direct him to either you or Jerry." The latter was the Senior Marketing Director for Flame.

Tiara rolled her eyes. It was obvious Carmen's new receptionist had zero knowledge of her boss' background or that of her boss' husband. Security was tight around Flame for a reason.

"I can tell you this," Jessica continued. "He looked mixed, kind of like Carmen's husband, but without the hazel eyes. His hair was cut low. Does he sound familiar?"

Tiara shook her head. "I don't know. What was he wearing?"

"He was pretty casual, some black pants and a white button-up."

Tiara gave Jessica a strange look. "He isn't a designer if you said he was in something casual. I don't know who that could be. Hopefully, he'll come back."

"I hope he does. I want to know who he is."

Jessica went back to her desk while Tiara escaped into her office. Too much was going on for her to even comprehend. The worst part of it all was that she was stuck in Brookstone to deal with it while her best friend was living carefree on a sandy white beach. She cringed at the thought, although she shouldn't have. Carmen wasn't the one who made her mother disappear nor did she order some man to come to Flame looking for her. The timing was horrible, but it wasn't her fault. If anything, Tiara hoped Carmen cut her honeymoon short to help her deal with it. If she didn't, she would do the one thing Jay and Malik warned her against. She would contact Kane.

4

Three days after receiving the phone call that Patricia was missing, the decision was made to return home. The honeymoon was no longer enjoyable with the countless calls from Tiara who kept expressing concern over Patricia's disappearance. There was also the news that a man no one knew had shown up at Flame looking for Carmen. All of it changed his wife's demeanor. No amount of consoling or lovemaking calmed her anxiety. Therefore, Jay sent for his private plane. He expected to get a different attitude from her once they boarded the flight to New York, but even in the air, she was distant.

Carmen sat across from him with her eyes towards the window, her arms folded across her chest. She hadn't uttered five words out her mouth despite his attempts to strike up a conversation. A part of him wanted to let her be, while another part wanted to know where her head was. She had conversations with Tiara before they left, but Carmen didn't always tell him what they talked about. He wanted to trust Tiara because she was Malik's wife. It was hard to do when he heard her trying to persuade Malik to involve Kane. He hoped his friend was doing his job at keeping his wife at bay.

"Do you think you can work with Kane?"

More shocked at the timing of the question than hearing her voice, Jay allowed his eyes to burn into hers. He didn't respond because she already knew his answer. His history with Michael Kane was extensive. It started when he was twenty-seven and the former Triad agent inserted himself into an argument he was having with Carmen. Jay saw him again when Kane arrested them at his warehouse. If that wasn't enough, he learned Carmen carried on an affair with him while they were dating. Upon her release from prison, she married him. She was pregnant with King, who Kane ended up raising as his own. To add to the turmoil, after he gained his freedom, Kane never stopped trying to send him behind bars.

"It's not something I want, let's be clear," Carmen continued. "Tiara keeps talking about how we should be doing more and how serious this is. She doesn't think I'm doing enough."

Jay's eyes continued to bleed into hers.

"I know I'm supposed to be at home," Carmen admitted, "because it's my mother. At the same time, I feel like I shouldn't be sacrificing my happiness for her. My mother put me through so much. I would be lying if I said the love was still the same."

Jay didn't respond as a hint to Carmen he was offended by her question. His lack of words made her turn her gaze towards the window. Although he was being silent, there was a lot he could say. Most of it wasn't even about Kane. She knew her ex-husband better than he did. He didn't have to drag his name through the mud. When it came to her mother, there were things Carmen didn't know. She didn't know her mother hated her for turning Flame into something she couldn't or that her mother wished death on her. She also didn't know her mother had an extramarital affair with his father, which produced their only sister, Eleise Santiago.

"I should be enjoying my honeymoon, enjoying you," Carmen muttered. She threw her hands up out of irritation. "We'll never catch a break. If it ain't one thing, it's the other."

To calm her nerves, Jay took her hand in his. "Our lives have been like that. But everything that's been thrown at us, we've dealt with and got over. We'll get over this, too." Carmen gave him a nod, showing her understanding "Let my team handle everything," he continued. "Keep Kane out our business and *we* won't have any problems. I promise."

When she squeezed his hand, Jay knew he had gotten through to her. From that moment on, the idea of him and Kane working together was never brought up. As for her mother, the topic would never go away. They dismissed it temporarily. Once they were behind the walls of their estate, the subject of Patricia's disappearance reared its head. While Carmen sat in the kitchen with Tiara and Gully, Jay pulled Linx into the home office.

"Where is she?" he asked once the door was closed. Linx's eyes showed uncertainty. "Where did you put her?" Linx's expression didn't change. Confusion manifested itself in more places than his eyes.

"I didn't know there was a body. I thought you just roughed her up."

Jay put distance between them. Patricia's body was no longer behind the rosebushes. It was the first place he looked when they arrived home. Without the evidence of his sin on the property, he thought Linx's phone call was confirmation he'd covered his tracks.

"I heard you," Linx admitted, "the night of your bachelor party. You and Patricia were arguing. It sounded like y'all were fighting. I didn't want to witness, so I walked away. When I saw you right before we headed to the party, the way you moved, the sunglasses you were wearing. We both know you don't wear sunglasses. I figured you were trying to cover up the fight. Now, I know it was a *murder*."

"Well, someone else knows." Jay leaned his six-foot-five frame on a desk in the middle of the room. His mind raced. The question of *who* arose, but so did the answer. He thought of his ghosts. Their job was to protect his family anonymously unlike Linx, Roman, and Gully. They were supervised by his right-hand, Cesar, whose death he faked to keep him from a life in prison. If anyone knew what he did, it was them.

"No one knows anything," Linx voiced. "Roman thought we were going to be on the chopping block for losing her."

"No one is on the chopping block," Jay whispered. He reached in his pocket and pulled out his phone. *We need to meet*, he texted to Cesar. His voice changed to a normal volume when he realized Cesar was the person who had taken care of Patricia's remains. "Are you sure y'all didn't find anything on the cameras?"

"We didn't," Linx confirmed. "Unless Patricia's body is still in the house. There for damn sure isn't any footage of her walking outside."

Someone had gotten rid of the camera footage. If they hadn't, his right-hands would've seen him throwing Patricia over the balcony. They also would've seen who moved her remains.

Jay's phone vibrated in his hand. He looked at it to see a text from Cesar.

Give me until tomorrow morning.

"Did Patricia leave your bedroom?" Linx's voice took Jay's eyes away from his phone. His question was far from his mind. Typically, if he needed Cesar to make an appearance, he would tell him where he was. He lived in Canada, but if he wasn't there, he was in Brookstone. Cesar was telling him his hands were tied with other business. It just wasn't *his* business.

"I need to link up with King." Jay changed the subject on purpose as he stuffed his phone in his pocket. It was a lie, and it still didn't get Linx's mind off Patricia.

"She did leave your bedroom, didn't she?"

Jay opened the door to the office as a sign the conversation was over. His right-hand didn't push the issue because Carmen and Tiara were making their way to the foyer. Gully was behind them, but he headed for the front door. "Have you heard anything?" he asked Carmen.

"No," she replied, "but I gotta take care of something. I'm letting Fiona leave so she can get some rest. I gave her the next few days off. She won't be back until after the New Year. Can you hang around for a bit until I get back?"

"Sure," Jay responded, "Where are you goin'?"

Carmen pulled her cell phone out her pocket. "Gully and I are going to search the city."

While he knew Carmen and Gully had formed a bond, he didn't expect her to choose Gully over him. "Is there a reason you didn't ask me to come?"

"Well, I figured you didn't pay them to baby-sit." Carmen pointed her finger at Linx. "Besides, I figured you wouldn't have a problem watching your kids." She spoke of Rakim and Nyla as they were the only two who needed supervision. Aside from Akaila, they were the only two out of their brood who lived with them.

"That's not what I meant, Peaches."

Carmen's mood softened at the sound of her nickname. It was an instant reminder of her mother. From what she'd been told by her parents, while her mother was pregnant with her, peaches was the only thing she craved. Her father joked that when she was born; her skin complexion was the same pinkish yellow color of the fruit. Thus, they nicknamed her Peaches.

"They've already eaten," she said, allowing the image of her parents to fade from her mind.

"You know I don't have a problem watching them. I want—"

"I know," Carmen interrupted. "You know the routine. Give them their baths in an hour or so and they should be ready to knock out. I need to go." A quick peck on the lips followed to silence him. She then hurried towards the door.

Tiara, however, didn't move as fast. While Carmen's best friend should've followed, she didn't. Tiara stayed put as if there were words to be said. If there was, the words would have to stay unspoken.

"Have a good night." Jay's tone was directive as he was telling her to get out. He still had a sore spot from hearing her persuade Malik to contact Kane. Though he was certain Tiara didn't know he had an issue with her, she took the hint.

About to address Linx, the loud roar of an engine flooded the space. One glance down the hall and he noticed a toy Hummer charging at him. Rakim was at the wheel while Nyla giggled with excitement in the passenger seat. Their presence brought a joy to his spirit that had been lost the past couple of days. Their innocence reminded him of the desire he had to become a better man. They would never witness the cold person he used to be. That man would be a stranger to them as if he never existed at all.

5

Down the hall, someone closed a door. The sound was loud enough to send Jay's eyelids fluttering. He looked to his left to catch a peek at the time only to see the empty space beside him. Not only was Carmen absent, her side of the bed didn't appear touched. His eyes shifted to her alarm clock. The time was 6:48 a.m. She was the only one not in their bed. Nyla was at his side, her small arm wrapped around him. Rakim was in a similar position, yet to the right of him. Although he didn't want to disturb them, he pulled himself from their grasp. They stirred but didn't wake.

Clothed only in a pair of old sweatpants, he walked down the hall until he reached Patricia's room. The door was closed, but he could hear movement inside. He opened it to find Carmen. A journal was in her hands, which she closed when he stepped in the room.

"You slept in here?"

"Our bed was full," she stated with a yawn.

Jay climbed on the bed and pulled her in his arms. The journal slipped from her hands. "Our bed is too big to ever get full." He nibbled at her neck although his mind was on what she'd been reading. "You could've gotten in."

"Y'all were already asleep."

"What's with the excuses? Last night wasn't the first night we went to bed before you." Jay playfully bit her neck, which prompted her to face him. "Where did y'all go last night?"

"Everywhere," Carmen replied. "We didn't find anything if that's what you want to know."

It was what Jay wanted to know. Nonetheless, he wanted to know even more what she was reading. That information she hadn't yet dispelled.

"Tiara wanted to talk to you last night."

Jay narrowed his eyes as Carmen admitted something he already knew. He figured Tiara didn't have the balls to ask her question, so she put Carmen up to it. He already knew what was coming, so he went ahead and addressed it. "I don't have anything going on that would prompt someone to take your mother. I don't have any enemies. If I do, I don't know who they are."

He couldn't fault Tiara for having the thought considering what occurred with Kristian. He had bad blood with another drug dealer, Blu, and as a result, she was kidnapped. As if the weight of that brick wasn't enough, he had to live the rest of his life knowing Blu had stolen Kristian's virginity.

Carmen ensured he received proper punishment for the crime, a bullet to the head, yet Kristian still had to live the rest of her life haunted by a brutal rape.

"Well, thanks for that, but that's not what Tiara was going to ask you." Carmen ran her fingers through his beard. "The anniversary of the *King* collection is coming up. The board wants to do something different with the ad campaign. She came up with the idea of you and King being the face of the collection. We're shooting for a father like son kind of theme. I haven't spoken to King about it, but I wanted to run it by you."

Jay braced himself to hear the worst only to learn Tiara wanted him to model some clothes. "You know I'm not a model." Jay ran his fingers down the left side of his face reminding her of the battle wound he suffered in his late twenties from his fight with Carlos. The scar had only faded by about thirty percent and would still be visible even with makeup.

"Are you saying no?"

"No," Jay said, quickly. "I'm saying, I'll do it, but you know I'm not a model." He felt Carmen's fingertips on his face as she traced the scar. "What were you reading?" He hadn't forgotten about what he'd seen. He knew that whatever Carmen was reading had kept her from sleeping in the bed with him. She continued to trace his scar as if he hadn't said a word.

When her fingers massaged the back of his neck, he knew she was stalling. The spot was a turn-on for him. She knew how to use her touch to calm and relax his nerves. Her caress was his medicine, a peace to the destructive thoughts, which filled his mind. Even now, she fulfilled a need he didn't know he had. That was, until her fingers became clenched around his neck. He blinked. When her grip tightened, he felt suspicion. When her grip tightened again, she became a threat. A natural response emerged. He pushed her arm away from him, breaking the chokehold. Expletives were on the tip of his tongue, but all he gave her was a dark stare. In return, he got a sinister smile. Then, she rose from the bed.

"I need to shower."

She grabbed the journal, taking it with her, as she headed out the room. Once out of sight, he touched his neck. The slight soreness made him realize how blind he was to her strength. If he hadn't reacted, she would've done more damage than she had. While she didn't admit her suspicions to him, she was aware of what he'd done. Her actions spoke where her mouth was silent.

"Jay," he heard her call.

He climbed out the bed but went no further than the doorway of her mother's bedroom. When he peered down the hall, he saw her holding his phone out to him.

"A private number just texted you. Someone is waiting for you in the garden."

Cesar, he thought. The presence of his right-hand made him leave the doorway. He took his phone from her to see Cesar's number on the home screen. He quickly told her who it was although she hadn't questioned him. "I told him to come by."

"Cool, I'm hopping in the shower. You can use another bathroom."

"I wasn't gonna join you."

Carmen went in their bedroom and closed the door. *I won't be down for another forty-five. Grab some breakfast from the kitchen,* he texted Cesar. He switched his ringer to vibrate as he headed down the hall. Carmen was already in the shower when he entered while the kids were still asleep. He moved quickly, gathering clothes and toiletries before escaping to another bathroom. In exactly forty-five minutes, he was dressed and out the door.

Cesar was exactly where his text said he was. Jay entered the garden to find his right-hand dressed like the CEO of a Fortune 500 company. It was the exact opposite of what he was—a bodyguard who most presumed to be dead. As much as he wanted to joke with him about his attire, there wasn't time for small talk. Not when his wife was potentially hours away from learning he was responsible for her mother's death. Jay parted his lips. "We both know I rarely ask you to make a personal appearance."

Cesar reached inside the jacket of his navy suit and pulled out a USB drive. He handed it over, but Jay wasn't quick to take it. "All the footage is there," Cesar informed him. "This is the only copy." Jay stared at the drive in Cesar's hands. "I didn't get a handle on things until everyone was gone." Jay grabbed the drive now that Cesar admitted he was the one who moved Patricia.

"Where is she?" Jay asked.

"Long gone," was Cesar's reply.

Jay rubbed his fingers over the drive as he debated what to say. His right-hand signed on to be by his side, but his job description never included covering up his mother-in-law's murder. Cesar took it upon himself to cover his tracks. "We can't talk about this here," he replied as he slipped the drive into his pocket. "They'll be fewer ears in the pool house." He headed in that direction.

As if the morning couldn't get any worse, they walked inside to find Roman half-naked in the kitchen. Jay couldn't fault him as the pool house was his living quarters. If anything, he should've given him a heads up or knocked instead of using his key.

Clad in a pair of boxer briefs, Roman's back was towards them until Cesar slammed the door closed. "Coffee," Roman asked, pouring himself a cup.

Jay mumbled a low no while Cesar remained quiet. "Can I use this area for a few minutes? I need some privacy."

"Sure," Roman replied as he picked up his coffee. "It's your house."

The remark brought a slight smirk to Jay's face. He looked at Cesar expecting to see some uncomfortableness, but instead, his face was tight. When Jay looked at Roman, he noticed his gaze was on Cesar. The two men were staring each other down. A silent argument was taking place, which didn't stop until Jay cleared his throat. Roman headed up the steps. Once he was out of earshot, Cesar dropped his façade. His cool as a cucumber act was gone and in its place was a person battling multiple frustrations.

"This shit is different. I pulled Carmen's mother out a bush."

Jay looked at the stairwell to make sure Roman wasn't lurking. "That bitch killed my mother." The words, although spoken in a whisper, sounded like venom. "You know how long she let me walk around believing my mother killed herself? She smiled in my face from day one knowing what she did."

Cesar sat on the couch to soften the tension. "I understand your motive, but I am now in a difficult and delicate situation. Shit, it isn't just me. These people didn't sign up for this. They got hired to protect, but not like this. They watched you kill *your wife's* mother. They didn't know what to do. They had to call me."

"You don't think I know that? I'm in this situation more than y'all."

Cesar recalled the events. "We waited until everyone went to Puerto Rico before we moved her. We wrapped her up and took her to Jimenez Funeral Home. I know you have a good relationship with them. They cremated her for us. We tossed her ashes in the Hudson. So, like I said, she's long gone." Cesar's tone was growing calmer. "You need to figure out what you're gonna tell your wife. What does she think now?"

"I don't know." Jay thought back to his interaction with Carmen that morning. She choked him for a reason. She knew something. Whatever it was, it wasn't enough for her to kill him. She allowed him to stop her. "I have to…" He fell silent when his phone vibrated in his pocket. He pulled it out and rolled his eyes at the name on the screen: *Andrew North*. A part of the White House administration and Grendel's uncle, he thought he rid himself of the man months ago. "I have to figure something out," he continued, ignoring the call. "She's gonna keep digging." His phone vibrated a second time.

"Do you need to take that?" Cesar asked.

North was still calling. "I do. Mr. North," Jay greeted.

"Mr. Santiago, I have some news," North informed him.

Jay looked at Cesar although his right-hand couldn't provide any insight on what North was about to say. "Do I have a choice on whether I want it or not?" His mind raced back to his first meeting with Grendel. A year ago, Grendel stole a surveillance tape out the office of the late Honorable Judge McCallum. The tape earned Jay his freedom as it proved self-defense for a shootout that occurred at his restaurant, Blue Magic. To show his appreciation, he met with Grendel. He learned the man worked for Amnesty International and was looking to investigate whoever was controlling diamond mines in Africa. "What is it now? You want me to help with global warming?"

"Grendel is dead," North stated.

The news set Jay on his feet. "What do you mean he's dead?"

This time, Cesar stood on his feet. "Who's on the phone?"

Jay didn't respond as North filled him in on the details.

"He was…" North's voice trailed off as his emotions overcame him, "found," he mustered to say, "in a box at the White House. The clerks in the mailroom found him. Someone mailed him."

"Was he in one piece?" was the next question out Jay's mouth. When North told him no, Jay knew Grendel was killed to send a message. "Tell me everything," he ordered, sitting on the couch.

North cleared his throat. "He had gotten a team together to go to Kenema. They were posing as missionaries. He thought this would allow them to get close to the people. He wanted to get some firsthand knowledge of what was going on." North's voice cracked. "I was at the airport when they left. I gave them money to help with the project. I didn't know this would happen."

Jay put the call on mute. "These motherfuckers," he spat. Cesar still had a questionable look on his face. He should have elaborated, as it was his right-hand who went to Kenema to investigate his business partner. Cesar returned with vast knowledge of the army who controlled one of the largest cities in Sierra Leone. The army was the reason Jay hadn't conducted any further business with his partner. He also pulled back from working with Grendel and North.

Jay took the call off mute when he realized North hadn't stopped speaking.

"No one has been able to contact anyone on the team. They may all be dead." North sounded like a man who was horrified. "Grendel felt this could work. He felt he needed to do something. After you fulfilled your contract, he wanted to find another way in."

The expression of anger Jay once wore changed to one of confusion. According to his knowledge, his contract with the U.S. government was unfulfilled. They gave him the task of finding the Pink Sunrise diamond. The jewel was originally his, acquired through illegal means, then stolen from him by his wife when they were in their twenties. The Pink Sunrise was in a location only Carmen knew. He tried to find it years ago. The conversation ended in them breaking up and her remarrying her ex-husband. The relationship, of course, didn't last as she was now *his* wife. The drama of it all made the Pink Sunrise a topic he stayed away from. "I didn't give them the diamond."

"But your wife did. She turned it in so your charges would be dropped. The government was set on having you locked up. You hadn't made good on your promise. She didn't tell you?"

The phone dropped from Jay's hand. He had been annoyed with Carmen that morning, but now things had taken a turn. He knew what the Pink Sunrise meant to her. She knew what it meant to him. For her to turn it in, it was clear confirmation of how much she loved him.

"Take this," Cesar told him, interrupting his thoughts. He was now holding his phone.

Jay grabbed it from his hand as North was still talking.

"This should tell you that something is going on over there," North was saying, speaking again of Grendel. "They knew who he was, what he was there to do. If you ask me, they know about you, too. They know you're helping us."

"I haven't helped shit," Jay yelled. "Grendel's blood isn't on me. Y'all should've minded your business and stopped when I told you to. Yes, they know about y'all. That's why he was sent home chopped up in a fuckin' box. That's the shit I warned Grendel about. You don't send a lamb to the lion's den unless it's dinnertime. You send a fuckin' army with guns cocked."

"We have to know where to send them first."

"Fuck you," Jay retorted. Grendel and North were only concerned about what he could do for them, not the safety of his family. The blatant insensitivity made Jay hang up the phone. He knew what was coming his way. If his comrade had suspicions about Grendel, he was going to investigate. It was only a matter of time before his comrade would connect Grendel to him. "That damn surveillance tape," Jay muttered. It was the item that linked them together. Once his partner made the connection, he would be staring down a barrel.

"I can hire more people," he heard Cesar say.

"How many more motherfuckers do I have to pay?" Jay's anger went to another level. He left the drug game to give his family a better life and he still paid men to watch their back. They couldn't leave the property without being followed. The closest him and Carmen got without security was their honeymoon, but he wouldn't be surprised if Cesar snuck ghosts out there. *I can't even fuck in peace*, he thought. "After all these years, I finally got Carmen to commit to me. Now, I'm bringing something else home."

"Every inch of this estate is under twenty-four hour surveillance."

"Grendel didn't deserve that," Jay stated, overlooking what Cesar said. His phone vibrated again. He received a text message from North detailing Grendel's memorial that was scheduled to take place in Washington, DC. While North was extending an invitation, the nation's capital was the last place he needed to be. A target was now on his back. The memorial was also set to be held on New Year's Day. There was no way he was leaving New York, on a holiday, without Carmen.

"You know we got you."

A new voice entered the conversation. Jay peered up to see Roman, now dressed, at the bottom of the steps. With all the yelling he'd done, Roman couldn't help but hear. How much he knew, Jay didn't know. At that point, it didn't matter. "Something we can't see is coming," Jay told them.

6

It was normal work hours, but the last thing Tiara was doing was working. She was just a body at a desk. Her mind was everywhere except on the Excel spreadsheet, which contained the finalized budget for Flame's upcoming calendar year. *Am I going to tell Carmen, Monifah is pregnant? She hasn't even told me if she's going to file a missing person's report on her mom. Did I pack Robin an extra change of clothes? Akaila said they were going to be baking. She is going to be so worn out when Malik picks her up. I don't think I took out the steak for dinner. I might have to do takeout.*

"Tiara," a familiar voice called.

She blinked her eyes to see Jessica in her doorway. A gentleman accompanied her she'd never seen before. Automatically, Tiara assumed him to be the man who was looking for Carmen. Her best friend was in her office, so Tiara wondered why Jessica brought him to her. "What's going on?" she asked, rising from her seat.

Jessica moved from the doorway to allow the man entry. Tiara studied his features, trying to see if she could place him somewhere. He was of medium build and his skin had been dipped in caramel honey. *No wonder she brought up Jay when she mentioned him*, Tiara thought, reminiscing. He was average height for a male and his hair had been cut close. Handsome was an understatement, so she quickly reminded herself of the good dick she had at home.

The only thing about him she wasn't impressed with was his clothes. His style was average to be a person who potentially wanted to work with one of the most talented designers in the country.

"Carlton Rodriguez," the man stated, holding out his hand.

Tiara's mouth dropped open. She looked past the man at Jessica who was exiting her office. She wanted to yell for her to come back, but the words never left her mouth. She didn't know a Carlton Rodriguez, but she knew a Carlos Rodriguez and the names were similar enough.

"I know this is a shock," Carlton said, moving his hand to his side. "It took me a long time to get the courage to come. As she told you," he continued, pointing behind him, "I wanted to meet with Carmen."

Tiara apologized as she realized how rude she had been. She stuck her hand out and in return, he gave it a friendly shake. "Let's sit," she encouraged, sliding in her chair. "Carmen is in today so if she's free, you may get a chance to speak with her."

"Well, I wanted to meet with her. Perhaps, you're the person I need to be talking to."

A large rock sat in Tiara's stomach. Something about his words told her he didn't come to Flame for design help. This was something personal.

"You probably can see the resemblance," he added, "plus our names are similar."

"You're related to Carlos," Tiara guessed. He spoke of a resemblance, but physically, there wasn't one aside from their complexion. Carlos was ruggedly handsome while the man in front of her was the poster boy for pretty boys.

"I'm his brother, or as I like to say, the Ishmael to his Isaac."

Tiara's mouth opened without a sound. She closed it when she felt a hint of jealousy. If he was Carlos' half-brother, what did he want with Carmen? She was never Carlos' girlfriend. She may have sold drugs for him and let him hit it for a night, but he never took her seriously. If anything, Carlton *was* in the right place. He needed to be talking to her. *Well, there is one little detail. How did I forget? Carmen is married to Carlos' best friend. Jay killed Carlos and his father. No wonder he wanted to talk to her. He wanted to go through her to get to Jay. Well, he can go through me, too.* "You know Carlos and I had a relationship?"

Tiara wanted confirmation he knew. She wanted him to say something to make her at least feel as if she mattered in Carlos' world. While her ex had given her a title, he was never faithful. Carlos had ties to the Santiago cartel, his pockets were laced, and he worked every bit of his swag in the streets. Women all over the East Coast were opening their legs to him.

"I know you were the last girlfriend he had before he was murdered."

"I was," Tiara confirmed. She hoped Carlton would tell her the reason for his visit. It had been more than twenty years since Carlos' murder. She hadn't heard from anyone related to her ex. She hadn't even seen the son Carlos never claimed.

"I want to talk to Jay. I know it's not easy getting close to him. He would be leery of anyone related to Carlos."

He spoke truth. If Jay knew a member of Carlos' family was looking for him, he would be on the defense. "Someone will definitely have to give him a heads up," she joked. "What do you want from him? You wanna know what happened that night?"

"Well, that, and I want to bridge the gap between our families. The ties were broken when Jay killed my brother and father."

"Or when Carlos slept with his girlfriend," Tiara shared.

"You're talking about Carmen, right?"

The words had come out her mouth before she knew what she was saying. From what she'd been told by her best friend, Jay discovered her infidelity after finding a sex tape of her and Carlos. "I said too much," she admitted. "Look," she wanted to change the subject, "why don't we share info? I'll talk to Jay and see if I can set something up. I can give you a call if he's willing to talk. Or if he's not."

"I can roll with that."

Tiara picked up a notepad from her desk and handed it to him along with a pen. He scribbled down his information and in return, she gave him her business card.

"Carlos and I weren't close," he disclosed. "He was my brother, but we really didn't know each other. Do you think perhaps we could meet again so you could tell me about him?"

"Sure," Tiara stammered. "I'll try to recall as much as I can." She gave him another smile to show she was comfortable with the idea. Nevertheless, she was far from comfortable. He was still a stranger, and the name Carlos didn't necessarily bring happy thoughts. Her mouth had gotten her into an unwanted situation. Now, Carlton was expecting her to reach out to Jay. *I can do this*, she thought. *It's a simple conversation to have. What if Jay is ready to talk to someone from the Rodriguez family?* Tiara followed Carlton out her office. She remained in her doorway until a familiar face stepped in view.

Twenty-something years ago, Kane was the highest paid Triad agent in the U.S. To keep himself from going undercover, he took a job at the Brookstone Police Department as a detective and their resident agent. Nevertheless, the inevitable happened. He made a deal with Carmen and Jay to protect their freedom, which cost him his employment. Due to his lack of cash flow, he was forced to accept a job working security at his ex-wife's fashion company. The position didn't give him the six-figure salary the Triad used to cut him. It did keep the bills paid and showed his new wife he could pull his weight. Just his luck, he married another ambitious, successful woman. While Monifah didn't make as much money as Carmen, she did well for herself.

"Kane," he heard a familiar voice say.

He had been lost in his thoughts for most of his walk-through, he didn't realize which floor he was on. That was until he noticed Tiara standing outside her office. "Hey, I'm so sorry," he said with a grin. He headed over to her and gave her a quick hug. "Good morning, Tee. How are things?"

"Do you have a moment to talk?"

Her concerned tone told him something was wrong. While his friendship with the Washingtons' wasn't what it used to be, they were still cordial. "Yeah, I got some time." He followed behind Tiara into her office. Before he could ask her anything, she pointed at his nose.

"What happened?"

That was all it took for her to remind him of the scar he now wore. More than a week ago, he had an encounter with his ex-wife's then fiancé. It occurred after he told Carmen how Jay had cheated her out of millions with the Santiago Estate. In true Jay fashion, he came looking for him, gun in hand. "Jay," he responded. "I think that says enough."

"Have you told Carmen?"

"Come on, Tee, you know the answer to that. Is this what you want to talk about?"

"No," Tiara replied. She thought about Carlton but decided to keep him a secret. "I wanted to let you know Ms. Patricia is missing. I wanted to tell you a few days ago, but I was told not to. Carmen and Jay didn't want any outsiders involved."

"Outsiders?" Kane questioned. "I guess that's what I am to y'all now."

"No, you're not." Tiara sympathized. "I wanted to tell you. I knew we needed your help. You know I don't have a good relationship with my mother. Ms. Patricia was like a mother to me. I hate to say this, but I feel like Carmen doesn't care. She did try to look for her, but she didn't fill out a missing person's report or anything."

Kane scratched his head at the subject. "Look, Tee, I know you want my help, but Carmen and I are in a different place right now. Whatever she has going on is not my problem unless it involves three people—Kristian, Akaila, or Malachi. Other than that, I'm out of it."

"This could involve them. Look at what happened to Kristian. She was kidnapped."

"And I dealt with that, remember? That situation is one of the reasons I'm working here."

More disappointment appeared on Tiara's face. Nonetheless, Kane felt she should've known his hands were tied. "Carmen is married now. I'm married. Out of respect for my wife, my only interaction with Carmen will involve our children. My wife was present when this happened." Kane pointed at his nose. "I'm not putting her through any more shit when it comes to the Santiagos."

"I understand," Tiara mumbled. "But, if Carmen asked, would you help her?"

Kane knew he needed to tell her no, but he couldn't. A twenty-year relationship was the reason. Carmen had been the love of his life for a long time and although they didn't survive their rough patches, he felt obligated to help her. It just wasn't something he wanted to admit to. "There are other things I have to concern myself with," he expressed. "For one, my parents are getting their house renovated and are moving in with me. Number two," he continued, "Monifah and I are expanding our family."

Tiara was already planning to bring that up. "How could you?"

Kane's feet shuffled at her reaction. "What do you mean, how could you? We're married. We want something that has a part of both of us."

"Carmen begged you for years to do in vitro and you told her no."

"And Monifah had to beg me, too," Kane yelled. "The difference is, she doesn't have any kids. She's over forty. Her doctor advised that if she wanted to conceive in vitro was the best route. You know my situation. I thought I was beyond sterile at this point, but the treatment is a whole lot better than it was years ago. I was able to give us what we needed."

"You know this is going to hurt Carmen."

"And I should care because? Did you tell her that when she decided to have Rakim and Nyla? I dare her to say something about it. She can go fuck herself just like she fucked Jay and had those two babies—during our marriage."

Kane didn't give Tiara the chance to respond. He headed straight for the door and walked out. *How dare she try and make me feel guilty for moving on. Carmen moved on long before me. She knew I couldn't give her a baby and made not one, but two with her ex. Shit, that ain't even the half of it! She got pregnant two more times after that. Yes, those were miscarriages, but she still got pregnant! I'm only having one and I'm getting condemned for that.*

Kane's anger was on full display. His walk was more aggressive and the people who passed him made sure to give him extra room in the hall. Despite his nature, he stopped in front of Carmen's door. He assumed she wasn't in, but he got the opposite. The door was wide open and to his surprise, she was inside. Normally, he would see her on the phone, drawing or going through piles of paperwork, but this time, her head was in a book. The pages were catching her tears.

That moment confirmed his soft spot for her was still there. He couldn't pass her door knowing she was upset and not console her. Not with what Tiara had told him. Without asking her permission, he walked inside. He closed the door behind him and even locked it. The visit needed to be private, especially if Carmen's pain stemmed from her mother's disappearance.

"Carm," he called out. She raised her head to meet his gaze. Now with a much better view, he could see she was reading a journal. "I didn't mean to bother you," he said once Carmen rose from her seat. He took a few steps back as she neared him. "I was doing my walkthrough. I saw you and…" He lost his words when she fell in his arms. More than a year had passed since they had been that close. The connection was almost foreign to him. He allowed her to hold him because he knew it was what she needed.

Even after a minute or so had passed, Carmen still hadn't let go. To further show his support, he wrapped his arms around her. The embrace calmed her and a few moments later, her tears disappeared. Kane peered at her, staring at her head on his chest. *This is how it used to be. Whenever you were stressed with work or had a problem, you used to climb into my arms like this. I would hold you until we both fell asleep.*

Kane lost himself in the memory of their marriage. Without thinking, he kissed Carmen's forehead. "I got you," he whispered. "You know that." Carmen separated from him. Automatically, he felt he had gone too far. He uttered apologies left and right, but Carmen didn't want his regret.

"No, I'm sorry," she said, wiping her face. "I shouldn't have jumped on you like that." She wandered back to her desk. She closed the journal she'd been reading and stuffed it in a drawer.

"Do you want to talk?" he asked.

"I do want to talk, but not about these tears." She did a quick outline of her face. "What happened to your nose?"

"How about we talk about something other than that?"

"Monifah?" she joked.

Kane shook his head. "I think we need to talk about you."

Carmen nodded. "I want to say I'm sorry," she told him, "for everything. I know I'm the source of a lot of your pain. I want to apologize in the event I haven't before. I was a bitch to you. I was selfish. I made a lot of bad decisions, but I can't regret 'em. Those decisions gave me two beautiful babies. I know it hurt you, though. You saved me from a lot. I never gave you credit."

The last thing Kane expected was an apology. "Where is this coming from?"

Carmen wiped her face. "It's coming from me wanting to take accountability. I know our lives are different now. I married the man you hate, and you married a woman who isn't fond of me. That doesn't mean we have to hate each other. I want us to be friends. I want us to be best friends."

Kane's eyes became enlarged. He promised Monifah he would distance himself from Carmen and now she was asking him to be her best friend. "Look, I want to be here for you, but you're right, things are different. We can be cool, but maybe we need to talk about what our definition of cool is."

"I guess," Carmen said. "After what just happened, I thought it would be easy for us to do."

Kane could see how she thought that. He was holding her close to him and even kissed her. While the kiss didn't land on her lips, if she hadn't moved, he would've headed there next. "There is still a love there," he admitted, "and I got lost in it. I do have a wife to respect, and you have a husband. We both know Jay wouldn't want us being friends."

"You're right, he wouldn't," Carmen agreed. "But we need to be. I think it would be good for our children to see." Carmen paused for a moment. "Can I tell you what happened this morning?" She didn't allow him to answer. "I found Rakim in his room playing with his baby book. He's never paid attention to that thing. He was playing with it and a picture of you and him fell out. He couldn't form the words to really ask me, but he was curious about you. He felt something when he saw that picture."

Kane faced the opposite side of the room. He didn't want her to see his tears. Rakim was the reason for their first and second divorce. The first time, he filed because he discovered Carmen's infidelity, which Rakim was a product of. Before the divorce was finalized, he played a cruel game of chess. He faked his paternity results to show he was Rakim's birth father. The lie was the reason he and Carmen reconciled. Eventually, they remarried. It also was the reason Jay filed a lawsuit for paternity fraud. When the truth came out in court, Carmen requested a legal separation before filing for divorce.

"I wanted him," Kane cried. "I wanted him to be mine. I deserved him."

He turned back around, no longer ashamed of his emotions being on center stage. Carmen was holding the photo in her hand. Rakim was less than a year old in the picture, which had been taken in the living room of her old apartment.

"When I think about our children," she said, "all I keep telling myself is how we need to show them we can get along. We can't keep this hate in our hearts. We can't keep holding grudges. Life is too short."

"It is." Kane held out his hand for the photo. When Carmen set it inside his palm, a smile came to his face. "You want to be best friends?"

"We *need* to be," Carmen corrected.

Kane let out a playful chuckle. "Let's see what your husband says about that."

7

The only place Jay could go to be alone was the third floor of Blue Magic. The conference room had once been the meeting place for the Santiago cartel until he disbanded it. The room was now a place he could escape when he needed a break from his businesses, right-hands, and even his family. With the news of Grendel's murder fresh on his mind, he needed a place of solace.

There were a lot of decisions he needed to make in a short amount of time. The first conclusion he came to was that he needed to tell Carmen about his comrade in Africa. He needed to show her that his days of keeping secrets were over. He also needed her support, which brought him to his second conclusion. He was going to have to take his partner out. It would work to his benefit if he eliminated him as a threat. The next decision he had to make was who was going to kill him. Cesar knew where his comrade lived, but after their conversation that morning, he didn't want to be the clean-up man.

The blood should be on his hands, yet Jay didn't know how he would tell Carmen he needed to commit another murder. She knew he got baptized the morning of their wedding. They agreed they would start going to church as a family once they came back from their honeymoon. He even told her he wanted to get involved with a ministry. Killing a man who hadn't yet threatened his life wouldn't sit well with her. However, if his comrade struck, Carmen would pick up her own gun to put him down.

That thought sent him behind the doors of Flame. With his personal badge in hand, he swiped it across the card reader to signal for an elevator. Just his luck, the elevator car closest to him was already at the lobby floor. He boarded by himself and pressed the button for the executive floor.

It wasn't every day he showed up unexpected. He hoped Carmen wasn't busy or even worse, in a meeting. His new situation was the last thing she needed on her plate. Nonetheless, it was better for him to tell her than when bullets started flying through their dining room window.

"I made it right on time."

Jay noticed the mail clerk boarding the elevator. He had been so engrossed in his thoughts, he hadn't realized someone was joining him. He recognized him as one of the many clerks who would hand him his packages. "How is it going?"

"So much better now that the Christmas rush is gone."

"I bet," Jay replied. The clerk pushed a large mail cart onto the elevator. Tons of envelopes and packages were inside. When the elevator car started to move, he shifted his attention to the control panel. The mailroom floor was only a few levels up while the executive floor was the penthouse.

"Congratulations on the wedding."

Jay smiled at the mail clerk. "I'm on my way to see Mrs. Santiago now."

"I gotta get used to saying that. Every day I see Davenport on things." He spoke of Carmen's famous tag line, *Flame by Carmen Davenport.* "Well, take care."

Jay's eyes shifted inside the mail cart. This time, he noticed a package belonging to him. He yelled for the clerk to stop as he stepped in between the closing doors to grab it. He wasn't expecting anything, but when he pulled the box from the cart, the package's presence made sense. It was from his business partner. Diamonds weren't a gift anyone sent without pay. Whatever was inside was a warning. There was a chance the contents of the package matched what was received in the mailroom at the White House. Due to his suspicions, he didn't shake or open it despite being alone in the elevator. *I already know he works like me,* Jay thought, *nothing is in here, but Grendel's dick.*

The thought made him lower his eyes. He lowered his eyes even further when the doors of the elevator opened, and Kane walked inside. Although he was now on the executive floor, he didn't move. It was his first time seeing him since he pistol-whipped him. Both their scars, though not all physical, were still fresh. He watched as Kane pressed the button for the lobby floor.

"I like the tattoo." Jay pointed at Kane's nose. He saw the annoyance on his face. It became melancholy when Kane's eyes traveled to his hand. Following his gaze, Jay looked at his hand as well. Kane was staring at his wedding band. He held it up to give him a better look. "If this catches your eye, wait until you see hers."

"I did see it," Kane answered, finally speaking. "Where do you think I was coming from?"

Jay dropped the package at his feet desperate to show Kane they could go for a round right there. He didn't back down and they met each other chest to chest.

"You still see me as a threat," Kane snarled. He backed away.

They were nearing the lobby floor and it was obvious Kane wanted more time with him. He inserted his security key in the control panel to stop the elevator.

"When are we going to let this shit go?" Kane yelled. "Don't you have her now? Isn't she your wife?"

Jay didn't reply.

"I'm sorry. That's what you want, right? Do you want an apology? I'm sorry for taking your girl. I was wrong. I'll admit that. I won't apologize for doing my job because your cartel needed to go down, but I didn't have to get involved with Carmen."

A single word didn't leave Jay's mouth. Partly because the last thing he expected was an apology. It was twenty or so years late, but it was there. Now that he had it, he didn't know what to do with it.

"I'm sorry about King," Kane continued. "I was the one who talked Carmen into putting my name on his birth certificate. I know all of that has been undone, but I apologize. If I'm honest with myself, you brought out the best part of him. He became the man I always wanted him to be because of you."

That was another apology that was long overdue.

"Nothing," Kane probed. "You don't have anything to say?"

"You can be forgetful," Jay replied, aware there was one more thing on the table.

"What did I forget about?" Kane retorted. "You don't think you got shit you need to apologize for?" He looked at Jay sideways because he thought he covered his bases. Then, he remembered. "Rakim," he said. He didn't know how he had forgotten when he had been the main topic of conversation when he was in Carmen's office. "I was desperate. I made one of the worst decisions of my life. I shouldn't have done that to you, to Carmen, or to him. I just wanted her to know I could give her something she's wanted for so long. If I knew it was going to cost me my marriage, I wouldn't have done it."

His apology, sincere or not, made Jay think about his own actions. There was fault on his side as well. He was the reason their marriage fell apart. "You and Carmen would still be married if it weren't for me. Although I felt she was rightfully mine, I shouldn't have slept with her while y'all were married. I also shouldn't have gotten her pregnant." Tension started to leave his body. "I'm not apologizing for Nyla because y'all were separated when we conceived. I do know it wasn't easy for you to see her pregnant." Jay took a breath before he continued. "Thank you for what you did with King. He's also the man he is because of you. You laid the foundation I couldn't."

Kane nodded his head showing he accepted the apology. "Whether we like it or not," he stated, "we're always gonna be linked. It's time we show our kids we can be mature about the situation. Carmen and I agreed to do it. We're putting the past behind us."

Jay picked up his package. With it now in his hands, he looked at Kane. He needed to find someone who could see into it without opening it. His wife's ex had connections, but he wouldn't do him any favors. "How is your partner doing?" He spoke of Sanders, a former detective at the Brookstone PD, who put his investigative skills to too good of a use.

The question caught Kane off guard. Sanders was the last person he thought Jay would ask about. "He's good," Kane replied. "He's Agent Sanders now. He got a job at the Triad. He's like King Tech over there." Kane brought the elevator back to life. The car went to the lobby floor. While Jay's initial plan was to see Carmen, he walked off the elevator like it wasn't. Kane calling Sanders, King Tech, was all he needed. Even if Sanders couldn't help him, he could point him to someone who could.

***

Four distinct voices filled Carmen's office although she was the only one in the room. One of many conference calls of the day, Tiara and Jerry were currently going back and forth over the location for the *King* anniversary party. As if that wasn't enough, Leon, the Vice President of Branding, was questioning her about Jay and King being on board for the anniversary shoot. The fourth voice belonged to Tabitha, the Advertising Coordinator, who was reminding them that two conversations were going on. The extra noise paired with the stress of her mother's disappearance had Carmen at her desk with her hands covering her face. She wanted to tell them to shut up. When her office door opened and King walked in, she hung up.

Perfect timing, she thought. She leaped out her seat when she noticed King was carrying his son, Prince. "I called you yesterday. I wanted to see y'all," she squealed, pulling the baby out his arms. "What have you been up to?"

"Still trying to get this record label off the ground." King watched as she went behind her desk and sat down. She started playing with his son, bouncing him up and down in her lap. "I got your message. I figured instead of calling back, I would visit. I also wanted to give Coco a break." He spoke of his wife of less than a year. "That's why I have Mr. Fat Man with me. You know Coco doesn't let him out her sight."

"I knew she was going to be like that," Carmen expressed. "She had all these reservations about being a mother and now it's the only job she wants."

"Literally," King agreed. He picked up a picture frame on his mother's desk. He stared at the picture of Jay with his two youngest siblings. Now that they were married, he felt like his mother was starting over. For most of his mother's marriage to Kane, she only had him and Kristian. Now she was married to Jay and had Rakim and Nyla.

"Did you hear about Kane's dinner?"

Carmen looked up from her grandson. "Kane's dinner?" she questioned. "He was just in here. He didn't tell me about a dinner." King parted his lips but was cut off by the sound of her desk phone ringing. Carmen knew Tiara was calling so she could rejoin the conference. Instead of answering, she unhooked the phone. "What is this dinner about?"

"He had a dinner last night. Somehow my invitation got lost."

"Well, whose didn't?" Carmen asked.

"Kristian, Akaila, Malachi, everyone but me," King explained.

Carmen stopped kissing Prince's cheeks as she heard the pain in her eldest son's voice. "That sounds like a family dinner. Was Monifah there?"

"Why wasn't I there?" King asked, overlooking her question. "He gave this big announcement about how he and his shrink of a wife are having a baby, but you don't invite your firstborn? Why was I left out? I've never left him out."

The temperature in the room was at least seventy degrees, but Carmen became ice cold. Kane stood in her office crying over Rakim, but not once did he mention he was having a child with Monifah. Technically, there wasn't anything wrong with it, neither was it her business. She simply saw it as betrayal. Two years after Kristian was born, she asked him to do in vitro so they could have more kids, but he refused. He wanted to get her pregnant naturally. When it wasn't happening, year after year, she would bring up in vitro and he would refuse. He accused her of not being patient. Yet, with King's news, Monifah didn't have to be.

"His parents are moving to Brookstone," her eldest was now saying. "They're apparently doing some work on their house and need to stay with him."

Carmen didn't care about the latter, although she knew Kane's mother would eventually show up at her door. Beverly hated her since the day Kane announced their engagement. In her eyes, Carmen was a prison whore who needed to be doing any and everything other than marrying her son. His father, Arthur, never paid her much mind. His eyes were always on a football game.

"Why would he do me like that?" King was asking.

"I don't know," was Carmen's reply. "I don't want to speak for him, but I know he feels your relationship with him isn't the same. That shouldn't matter, though. He was the only father you had until you were seventeen." She handed Prince back to him. "I know where he's at. Do you want to talk to him?"

King told her no. "I would only say something I'd regret. I'll see him at church tonight. Are you going?"

"I'll be there. Jay and I agreed we need to start the New Year off right." Carmen led the way to her office door. While she didn't want to kick her son out, she was desperate to get to Kane. She didn't mind saying something she would regret. She wanted him to get every bit of her anger while it was fresh.

As they made their way to the elevators, Carmen practiced what she would say in her head. Colorful language made up most of the dialogue. She didn't know what angered her more, the secrecy or Kane giving his seed to another woman when he refused to give it to her. *And out of all people, you had to give it to Monifah*, she thought. She tried to contain her anger, but it was hard to do. She found herself balling and unballing her fists as she thought of the moment they shared in her office. Now she felt even more deceived.

"I'll see you tonight," King told her once they were outside.

"See you," Carmen replied. She reached out for him and pulled him and Prince into her arms. She held him longer than normal because she knew he was upset. While she couldn't heal his pain, she could at least try to mediate between him and Kane. "I love you," she whispered in his ear. King repeated the words back to her before breaking his hold. When he walked away, she didn't immediately head to find her ex. She stood there until King was at his car. Once he was behind the wheel, she made her way towards the parking deck.

The area was empty aside from a Hispanic woman who was walking out the front entrance of Flame. Carmen didn't recognize her but considering she didn't interview everyone who worked for her, she wasn't concerned. The woman became the last thing on her mind while the good cussing out she was about to give Kane became the first. Or at least that's what she thought she was going to do. When she spotted him coming around the corner on a golf cart, she bawled. The tears didn't let up, not even when he noticed her and helped her into the passenger seat. "You're having a baby?" Her nose was running, but she didn't bother to wipe it. Kane looked taken aback. He muttered the name, "Tiara."

"She knew before me?" Carmen asked.

"I told her before I came to your office."

The tears came even heavier. Tiara should've known that Kane having a baby was something she should've told her ASAP. "You know this hurts me."

"I do," Kane agreed, looking Carmen square in the eye. "You had two of 'em."

"Don't even try to compare the two. I begged you for another child and you told me no. You told me no for *years*. I never told you no."

"I didn't tell you no. I told you no to in vitro. I told Monifah no, too, if it makes you feel better."

"You think this is funny."

Kane started up the golf cart as he saw a group of people headed towards the parking deck. While Carmen was a hot topic in the gossip rags, she didn't need to stay there. "She deserved to have the experience," he explained, driving away. "I love her enough to give her that." Before she could say anything, Kane pressed his index finger on Carmen's lips. He already knew what her comeback was going to be. "I loved you that much as well, which is why I agreed to have Kristian. I also loved you enough to believe my faith and prayers would give us a child."

"But it didn't happen," Carmen cried. "Why couldn't y'all adopt?"

The golf cart slowed down.

"I don't have to explain anything I choose to do with my wife. Just like you don't have to explain why you're giving Jay another baby."

"You don't know what the fuck I'm doing," Carmen yelled.

Her angst made Kane put the golf cart in park. He knew his ex-wife. If he pushed her enough, things would turn chaotic. "I guess our plan to be best friends is over. That lasted what, thirty, forty-five minutes?" She didn't respond to him, still battling her tears. "I didn't do this to hurt you. You may think I did, but I didn't. I understand you're hurt, but you gotta move on. I had to move on." A new thought entered his mind. "I could fix this, I could, but it would only cause more problems. It wouldn't do us any good."

A lightbulb went off in Carmen's head. For the first time, a new tear didn't emerge.

"Giving you my sperm would be the worst decision for both of us. We both know you can't have my baby. We're married to other people."

Carmen knew he was right. There was no way she could start the in vitro process with him. If Jay even knew she was considering it, his anger would manifest in a way that would send her and Kane six feet under. "We can't," Carmen agreed, "but I did consider it. I always wanted more kids with you."

Her revelation made Kane feel something. He wiped the remaining tears from her face. "If anything were to happen, God forbid, I'll give it to you, but right now, I can't. Monifah is too far along for us to stop anything. I wouldn't do it even if I wanted to."

Carmen replied with a nod because she knew it was the truth. Monifah was pregnant and that was the end of it. If it were the Lord's will, Kane's new child would come in the world completely healthy. One of many changes in his life, she didn't know how he was going to manage all the new additions. His condo wasn't the biggest and he already had Kristian under his roof. He was about to face a financial strain even with the extra income from Monifah.

"Let me help you," she told him. He gave her a confused look and she remembered he hadn't heard her trail of thoughts. "You don't have room for a baby and your parents. I know you're not broke, but all these changes are going to cost. If you're going to have a baby, I at least want it to be comfortable." Carmen looked at her lap only to realize she had her purse. She had been so distraught she didn't even know she grabbed it. She opened it as Kane told her he didn't want her money. "You didn't get anything out the divorce or at least not the second one." She pulled out her checkbook. "You can at least get a new place, something bigger." She started to write him a check.

"I can't bring that home," Kane told her as she kept adding zeros to the number. "Monifah and I have a joint bank account. How do I explain that?"

Carmen ripped the check out her checkbook. "By telling her the truth," she responded. She handed the check to him, but he didn't take it. She set it on his lap. "Tell her it was from a friend."

8

Tiara opened her front door only for a slew of seasonings and spices to hit her nostrils. The lingering aroma awakened a hunger she didn't know she had. It sent her body gravitating towards the smell. Once in the kitchen, she found Malik at the stove and Robin at her kiddie table with her coloring books. "You have it smelling good in here."

Malik shot her a smile. "I did a little somethin', somethin'."

Tiara gave him a quick peck on the lips. "You did a lot of somethin'." She followed up her words with another kiss before heading to their daughter.

"I made you a picture," Robin squealed. She tore the page from the coloring book and handed it to her. "See all the flowers?"

"Aww, it's beautiful, baby." Tiara pulled the picture from her daughter's hands. While Robin had colored everywhere, but in the lines, Tiara knew the page would end up like the others, right on the refrigerator. "Did you have fun at Auntie Carmen's?"

"Yeah." Robin started coloring a new picture. "We made cupcakes."

"Ooh, I bet that was fun, well—" Tiara stopped mid-sentence when she heard the doorbell ring. She looked at Malik who was setting a pan of leg quarters on the kitchen's island. "Were you expecting someone?"

"I was about to ask you the same thing. The last time someone showed up here unexpected, it was for you, and we got a pregnancy announcement."

Tiara remembered what she'd done. She had gone back and forth over rekindling her friendship with Monifah. When she finally decided to do so, she invited her over. However, that was before Carmen ditched their conference call and went ghost. Her friend's disappearing act left them all having to work late. "I did invite someone," she told him. "I forgot."

Malik didn't look pleased.

"I thought about it, and I do want to be there for Monifah," Tiara expressed. "Not everything she said this morning was bad. She made me think about how I do need to get more ownership when it comes to Flame. I've put in a lot of work, and I don't have much to show for it." Tiara looked for any kind of reaction to what she said. Malik didn't do much aside from stirring the mashed potatoes on the stove. "Is thirty percent too much to ask for?"

"I've always told you to start your own company," Malik began. "Yeah, you can't draw to save your life, but when you got money, you don't need to.

There is a lot of talent out there and all they need is someone to give them a chance. That person can be you."

"I should leave Flame with nothing?"

"Last time I checked," Malik said as the doorbell rang again, "having experience and a ton of resources was a whole lot more than nothing. We both know I didn't get my job at King Records because I was a veteran in the music business. I got it because I spent years working at Sapphire, forming relationships, and learning from the people who are."

Tiara playfully rolled her eyes. "With the connections you have, you are the music business *and* the streets." She gave him a quick peck on the cheek before running towards the front door. By the time she reached it, the doorbell had sounded a third time. She opened the door, already apologizing before Monifah came in view.

"I was trying to get settled," she fibbed. "I'm sorry to keep you waiting. I know it's cold out."

"It's okay," Monifah stated, stepping inside the house. "I know how it is when you get off."

Tiara offered to take her coat. While her salary alone could afford a live-in maid, Malik was against the idea. He wanted to keep a level of modesty.

After directing Monifah into the lounge, Tiara ventured into the foyer to hang up her coat.

"Is this a good time to tell you Carmen is blowing up your phone?"

Tiara peeked around the closet door to see Malik in the foyer. He was holding her phone, allowing her to see her best friend's picture on the lock screen. The timing was horrible, but she hurried over. "I didn't do it," she stated before Carmen could say a word.

"You're right, you didn't," Carmen replied with an attitude.

"Ooh, what happened? You weren't this jazzy when we were on the conference call." Tiara didn't hear what Carmen said because right when her friend started talking, Malik announced he was going to fix her and Monifah a plate. By the time her focus was on Carmen, she was hearing curse words. "Wait, wait, hold up, hold up," she stammered, catching on to what her friend was saying. "You're mad at me because I didn't tell you?"

"All I'm saying is that you could've said something."

If Tiara could've gone in the closet, she would have. She wanted to say a lot to Carmen. At the same time, she didn't want Monifah to know Carmen was upset about the baby. If she knew, she would rub it in. Monifah would be petty about the situation. "I did think about telling you. I realized it wasn't my secret to tell. Fertility, paternity, and babies are sensitive topics for you and Kane. No one should get involved."

"Y'all get involved in everything else," Carmen replied.

"Well, it's time for a change."

The words came out before Tiara thought about what she was saying. She sounded like her husband. He was the one who wanted to wash his hands of Jay and Carmen's drama. She was the one who wanted to be there for them.

"Maybe, it is." Carmen huffed. "I guess we all need space."

The phone disconnected in Tiara's face. When she thought to call Carmen back, she couldn't. Monifah was now in the foyer, her expression mischievous.

"The peasant knows?" she asked.

"She's madder at me for not telling her than the fact that you're pregnant."

Tiara scowled. Too much had occurred in the past few days for her to find room to worry about something else. If anything, Carmen's attention should've been fixed on finding her mother. *She left Kane, got back with her ex, and wants to be mad at me because I didn't tell her he was having a baby? Girl, please.* "Are you ready to eat?" She changed the subject on purpose so she could take her mind off Carmen. It didn't seem to work because even when they found themselves in the lounge with plates in their hands, her best friend's name still came up. Tiara told Monifah about Carlton and how he wanted to talk to Jay. That whole conversation led Monifah back to one thing—Carmen.

"I'm so glad I wasn't around for all that," Monifah was saying. "I swear, after Kane gave me the lowdown, I would've ripped her apart for you."

In mid-chew, Tiara wasn't quick to respond. She never thought about how Monifah discovered Carmen's deception. She assumed she read about it in one of the articles that outlined Jay's trial. "I bet Kane has told you a lot."

"We've shared a lot of things with each other," Monifah admitted.

"Well, all that drama and nonsense is water under the bridge."

Tiara didn't say much else as she continued to eat. The subject wasn't one she wanted to partake in. She would rather eat than reminisce about her best friend's bedroom tales.

"Did you ever see the tape?"

Tiara dropped her fork. Monifah's question was concrete evidence of how much Kane had dispelled. He had never seen the tape, but he had brought it up to Monifah. "Let's not go down that road." The question made her lose her appetite leading her to set her half-eaten plate on an end table. "Let's talk about motherhood instead."

"Do you know who has the tape?"

Didn't I just say I didn't want to go down this road? If it weren't already there, Tiara hoped Monifah could see the uncomfortableness on her face.

"I could never see myself being friends with a person who slept with my boyfriend."

"He was my ex," Tiara corrected. "It was wrong, dirty, vicious, whatever adjective you want to use. I let it go. Carlos is dead. Besides, it's not like they were in love. Carlos was jealous of Jay and wanted everything he had. He wanted to hurt him."

Monifah wasn't going to let up. "And you have the power in your hands to take Carmen down. I would've sued her for Flame."

Tiara threw her hands up starting to think inviting Monifah over was a mistake. Monifah knew she couldn't get close to Carmen, so she wanted to get in her head to make her turn against her friend. Monifah wouldn't be satisfied until Carmen was left with nothing and no one.

"Can I get y'all anything else?"

Glad to hear her husband's voice, Tiara gave him a blank stare to tell him things weren't going well. Although he caught the hint, he didn't save her. He only helped prolong Monifah's stay. She knew Malik wanted to be polite, but when Monifah asked for a cup of tea, she expected him to say they were out. When he didn't, she made a mental note to tell him about himself.

"Motherhood," Tiara stated right as Malik left the room.

"We have plenty of time to talk about that. When do you want to get together again?"

Never, was about to come out Tiara's mouth. Instead, she brought up the *King* anniversary party. That topic ended up being a mistake as well. The *King* collection was connected to Carmen, which gave Monifah more ammunition to go into a rant. She tuned her out until Malik brought Monifah's tea. Now that she had something to sip on, Tiara figured she would have better control of the conversation. She fooled herself. Monifah was doing more stirring than sipping.

"Seeing Malik reminds me of how much I miss Rakim."

Tiara hoped Malik was gone. His twin brother was a sensitive topic. She respected his wishes to not discuss him. Malik blamed himself for his murder although he didn't pull the trigger.

"I will never forgive her for what she did," Monifah was saying, still stirring. Her focus was back on Carmen. Monifah blamed Carmen for Rakim breaking up with her. She also didn't like that Rakim died in Carmen's arms.

A new thought entered Tiara's mind. *I wonder how you feel about Carmen naming her son after him.*

"You can help me, right?" she heard Monifah say. "Perhaps, Carlton can help us, too. We can all make sure she pays."

***

The time on his watch was nearing closer to seven, yet Jay hadn't made his way out the backseat of his limo. His mind was racing. Most of it stemmed from the package in his lap and a USB drive, which he rubbed against his thumb and index fingers. Before he left Flame, he was seated in his limo. His fingers were at work trying to locate a phone number or address for Sanders. A phone number was easy to find. All it took was a search through the listings of their state's resident Triad agency to locate the contact information for their Tech department.

After a couple of exchanges with a receptionist, he had Sanders' business line. When he called him, a heightened level of fear was present in the man's voice. While Kane's old partner was responsible for revealing one of his biggest secrets, the man was more useful to him alive than dead. Jay said what he needed to earn his trust, and Sanders gave up the address of his independent living facility. Twenty minutes later, he and Linx were walking inside. From the outside, it looked no different than any other apartment building. On the inside, Sanders' apartment looked like the Mission Control Room at NASA.

Agent Sanders was apprehensive about the visit which was evident by the gun in his lap. Jay didn't overlook it, letting it be known he was there for answers and not blood. His words didn't make Sanders move the gun, but it allowed him and Linx to stay in the apartment. When Jay handed him the package, Sanders immediately put it inside his scanning equipment. A minute or so later, Jay had his answer. The package didn't have a bomb or a decomposing body part. The package was a wedding gift from his partner, which contained something Jay never purchased from him—rough diamonds. Grendel told him the government suspected he was importing rough diamonds, but Jay wasn't. Now, with the package he received, they would have proof he was.

With the package's contents now revealed, Sanders expected them to leave. However, they were only getting started. In one quick move, Linx jerked the man out his wheelchair. Sanders' gun fell to the floor. Weaponless and unable to defend himself, he was now at his mercy. A part of his plan all along, Jay ordered Sanders to locate his criminal file. Begging and coaxing ensued, but he let it be known he wasn't leaving without it. Sanders went as far as telling him he didn't want it. In response, Jay told him he didn't want the advice. Once Sanders agreed to cooperate, Linx sat him back in his chair. The agent unlocked the Triad's system and downloaded his file as well as his father's. The documents were on the USB drive, which he was still rubbing between his fingers.

Jay wasn't fond of using Sanders' fear of him to get what he wanted. That's why he and Linx apologized for the way they handled him. He gave him his gun back, but only after taking every bullet out of it. He also had Linx wheel Sanders outside the apartment so when they left, there wasn't time for stunts.

"Your stomach ain't rumbling," Linx asked, interrupting his thoughts.

If he wasn't concerned about the information on the drive or debating about what to do with the rough diamonds, Jay would've admitted it was. Instead, he didn't give a reply. Linx didn't take too kindly to being ignored so he wasn't surprised when he heard the doors unlocking.

"I'm not going to be sleepy and hungry, too."

This time, Jay smirked. He grabbed the package in his hand and got out the limo. The move was all Linx needed. Although Jay got out first, Linx beat him to the front door. His right-hand escaped into the kitchen while Jay headed upstairs after securing the package and drive inside the home office. When he reached his bedroom, he opened the door to find the lights dim and Carmen underneath the covers. She was staring into space, her expression troubling. Her countenance made him wonder if it was the right time to talk about the Pink Sunrise.

Instead of asking her about it, he stripped down to his boxers and got inside their California King. When he pulled her into him, she didn't shy away from his touch. They laid there silently, enjoying the embrace until his stomach rumbled. Her lips curled into a smile. "I guess this isn't the right time to ask if you cooked." The comment made Carmen face him.

"I didn't," she replied. "I'm cooking tomorrow, though. You'll have all your New Year's faves. Do you want me to order you some takeout? Do you want Jamaican or Chinese?"

"I wanna eat you," Jay admitted. He slid his hand between Carmen's legs only to feel a pair of khakis. It wasn't like her to be in bed in business attire. He wanted to ask her what was wrong, yet he knew the answer. Her mother was missing. A topic he didn't want to bring up, his mind went back in the gutter. "You could've given me easy access."

"Did you ever meet Carlton Rodriguez?"

Jay cursed because the name sounded too close to Carlos Rodriguez. He cursed again because the question was coming from her. Plus, she made a detour from where he was trying to go. "Who is that?"

"He's supposed to be Carlos' half-brother," she told him. "He came to see Tiara today. Put that on the list of something else she didn't tell me. Jessica told me about him."

Jay sat up. Not only had he grown up with Carlos, he knew everything about the Rodriguez family. While his interactions with them had been nonexistent, he knew Carlos didn't have a brother. He was an only child or at least his parents raised him to believe he was. His own parents had done the same only for him to find out years later about the half-sister he shared with Carmen. Carlos was known to keep secrets when it came to drug deals and murder plots, but not when it came to family. "Carlos didn't have a brother."

"He has a brother."

Jay didn't bother to repeat himself. He climbed out the bed and grabbed his suit jacket. Once he pulled his cell phone out the pocket, he called the landline at their house in San Juan. Silvas, his butler, answered on the second ring. After greeting him, Jay posed his question. "Did Domino have any outside kids?"

"That's not a name you normally bring up," Silvas voiced with concern. "Did something happen?" Jay was quick to tell him no, but that was all he got out. The mention of Domino's name awoke a lot of pain Silvas needed to unleash. Although Jay wanted his answer, he allowed him to speak uninterrupted. It took a minute or two before Silvas finally said, "He only had one demon seed. That's all this world could tolerate."

"That's what I always knew," Jay replied. He didn't allow the call to linger, giving Silvas a quick goodbye and a promise the family would return to Puerto Rico. When he hung up, Carmen was now sitting up in bed.

"So, if he's not Carlos' brother, who is he?"

"Did you get a chance to see him?" Jay set his cell phone on a dresser and climbed back in bed. Carmen shook her head. "Tell Tiara to meet with him again and get a picture. If you get me that, I can find out who he is." An image of Sanders popped in his head. He thought about asking him to locate the man in the event Carlton was who he said he was. *I'll give Sanders a few days to calm down and corner him somewhere. I know he doesn't stay in that computer lab all day.*

"Will do," he heard Carmen say. He watched her as she set her alarm clock for nine o'clock. Watch Night was still on the agenda. With only an hour and a half to nap, Jay pulled her into his chest.

9

The sanctuary of the church was at seventy percent capacity. Carmen and Jay's presence didn't bring a series of murmurs, still, eyes and ears were on them when they entered. It didn't help that they were flanked by three well-built men who looked like they could pounce on anyone without warning. To add insult to injury, no one bothered to greet them. She couldn't blame them as most in the congregation were terrified of Jay. His reputation preceded him.

"Everyone is sitting in the third row." Akaila pointed at her sister. "See Kristian."

Carmen took notice of her daughter, not having seen her since her wedding. Their only communication had been by phone when she told Kristian, her grandmother was missing. *I wonder why she didn't tell me about Monifah. She lives with her. She knew from day one.* "I see," Carmen griped, also spotting Kane and his wife. King, Coco, and Malachi were also on the pew. Kane and King were sitting next to each other, giving the impression they worked out their differences.

Speaking of differences, Carmen bit her lip as Tiara walked towards them. Robin was with her, trying her best to keep up with her mother's quick strides. Nyla, on the other hand, who had been asleep, came to life. She climbed out Carmen's arms and ran down the aisle to meet Robin.

"Well, I guess we know where she's sitting," Jay stated, holding a sleeping Rakim.

Gully shared the same sentiment. "Let's just go sit with them."

Carmen gawked at him like the idea was harmful when it was harmless. He didn't know she was trying to keep her distance from Tiara. If she were honest with herself, the tension between them would be short-lived. Tiara was like her sister. Her friend wasn't on that time, anyway. Tiara approached her with her arms outstretched.

"You know we have to talk," Tiara whispered in her ear.

"Later," Carmen replied, not wanting to get into anything. Watch Night was not the place, especially when Monifah was a topic that could get her stirred up. When Tiara broke the embrace, Carmen gave her a smile, her pettiness fleeting. She even asked her if there was room on her pew.

"There sure is," Tiara said, happily. "You know these two want to be together." She pointed at Nyla and Robin. "Y'all are just in time, too. They're about to start the talent show."

"Sounds like a plan," Carmen gushed. She followed behind Tiara, trying not to look in Monifah's direction. There would come a day when she would see her baby bump. She simply didn't want to see it now. The wound was too fresh. Nonetheless, after the New Year had been prayed in, she was forced to see it. The moment Kane walked in the center aisle, it put Monifah on full display. Carmen had no time to react. Rakim shot by her and made a beeline for Kane. When Jay went after him, she intervened. She grabbed Jay's arm to stop him. Rakim and Kane embraced, which she knew was hard for Jay to see. She also knew Kane needed that moment.

"Jay, can I talk to you for a minute?" Tiara asked.

Carmen felt relieved until she realized Tiara wanted to talk to him about Carlton. It wasn't the right time, but if it put distance between him and Kane, she was with it. The con to the situation was that it left her with Monifah. From the size of her stomach, it was obvious she had been pregnant for a while. Kane was right when he said she was too far along for them to do anything.

Kane handed Rakim back to her. His entire face was lit. "Happy New Year."

Carmen replied in-kind. "See, he remembers you."

"He does. I needed that hug."

"Carmen," Monifah said, dryly.

Carmen grimaced. *Why is this bitch saying my name? She wants me to look at her. Well, bitch I have. Now, take your ass on.* Carmen kept her eyes on Kane, not paying Monifah any attention. He caught on quick and led his wife away. If he hadn't, Carmen would have given her what she wanted without delay.

"I got his number," Jay said, joining her. He held up a piece of paper with Carlton's contact information. "Tiara said he wants to meet with me."

"How many guns are you taking to that visit?"

"Don't ask me that in here."

Carmen covered her face in embarrassment. "You're right, I..." She noticed something odd. Halfway down the aisle stood Akaila and Roman, enthralled in a deep conversation. It wasn't unusual for them to be together, but the way they were positioned suggested something less platonic was going on. They were practically hanging on to one another. It wouldn't have been a big deal if Roman didn't work for Jay and if they didn't have a large age gap. Her husband's right-hand was in his late thirties. "Do you see that?"

"I do now," Jay said.

"Now it makes sense," Carmen voiced. "Every time I need someone to watch the kids, she's the first one to volunteer. Sometimes she asks before I can."

"She knows if she stays," Jay began, figuring it out too, "I'm gonna ask Roman to stay, too. She gotta have a driver." Akaila still had zero intention of getting her driver's license. Jay balled up his fist as he realized the problem Cesar and Roman had with each other. Cesar knew there was something going on between Roman and Akaila. Cesar also knew he wouldn't be down for any of his right-hands looking inappropriately at one of his teenaged daughters. "I'm gonna handle it."

"No, I'm gonna handle it. Let's go." She grabbed Rakim's hand. She took Nyla's in the other and made her way down the aisle. Once she reached Akaila and Roman, they put more space between them. "Look, I know this isn't the place—" She wasn't allowed to finish.

"Where are y'all headed?" Jay asked. "I need to stop by Sapphire to check on things."

In a flash, the focus of her frustration went from Roman to her husband. "You didn't say anything about going to the club. I thought we were headed home."

"I'm headed home," Akaila announced. "I can take them if you want me to."

Carmen raised her brow as her suspicion appeared to be true.

"That'll work," Jay stated, approving the idea. "I need your mama to come with me."

Carmen rejected the offer. "No, no, no, no, no, I'm worn out. That little nap didn't do anything. I'm going home and so are you. The last place you need to be is at Sapphire."

Jay pulled Rakim and Nyla from her grasp and handed them to Akaila. He then grabbed Carmen's arm. Her feet were planted so she didn't budge. "We'll be there twenty minutes top. I promise. Linx can drive them home and we'll ride with Gully."

"Do you see me?" Carmen shrieked. "I don't need to be going anywhere, but to my bed."

"I'll get you a Red Bull from the bar." Jay pulled her into him only to plant a soft kiss on her lips. "We won't be there long. I promise."

***

The air conditioner was working double-time in Sapphire, yet it couldn't cool the heat rising from Carmen's shoulders. Half-naked women were everywhere, their asses and titties bouncing like there was no tomorrow. That was only half the visual. The other half included the uncountable number of strippers who were fulfilling more than fantasies with the club's patrons. "Are you serious?" she yelled at Jay over the music. "Is this what you wanted to see?"

"I'll explain later," he shouted. "Get your Red Bull and meet me upstairs."

Carmen gave him a dirty look but did as he said. She hated moving through the throngs of people. One, she felt out of place and two, she looked it. She dressed for church not a strip club. She didn't know what Jay had to do that couldn't wait until his weekly rounds. *He doesn't even run his club. Nicholas does. All Jay does is collect his check and review the books.*

"Red Bull," Carmen told the bartender. "Put it on my husband's tab. You can give me two."

The bartender gave her a large grin before walking away to get her drinks.

This whole thing is some bullshit, Carmen thought, looking around the club. *How did we go from church to this? Now, I see how he got caught up at his bachelor party. All these surgically enhanced asses in his face.*

"You see the man going up the steps right there?" a female voice said beside her.

The man, of course, being observed was Carmen's husband.

"He owns the place," the girl continued. "My mom said she used to date him."

Carmen sized the girl up although she wasn't her mother. If the girl looked anything like the woman that birthed her, she could see why Jay would've dated her. She was at least a double D cup, had skin baked in brown sugar, and was dressed like her name was High Price.

"Girl, my mama said the same thing," her friend shared. "She said he got around."

It was no secret Jay was far from a virgin when they met. Matter of fact, he had a girlfriend. She just didn't expect for his past with women to be known. Now, even more, she wanted to get out the club. She turned away from them just as the bartender set two Red Bulls on the bar. "Thanks," she muttered, grabbing the energy drinks. She made her way through the crowd and behind the doors of Jay's office. He was seated at his desk, shuffling papers around, but not reading anything. It was impossible to do anyway. None of the lights were on. The office was lit solely from what was coming from the dance floor. "Are you finished?"

"Damn, Peaches, you haven't even opened a can."

She set one of the Red Bulls on the desk while she opened the other. She took a long swig hoping it would please him enough so they could get out of Satan's Paradise.

"Look, the strippers bothered me the first time I saw 'em," he admitted. "I made a lot of money at my bachelor party. I let Nicholas keep 'em and we've been pulling in those numbers every night, plus some."

Carmen took a second swig. "Two girls are downstairs saying their mothers dated you."

"Only two girls dated me, and I married one of 'em." He stood from his desk and walked around to where Carmen was. He grabbed the other can of Red Bull. "They might have fucked me. If they did, it was a one-night stand. They told them they dated me because it sounds better." Jay cracked open the Red Bull. "Why are we talkin' about this? You know what I used to do."

"The only one I ever had to look in the face was Tricia." She spoke of Jay's ex-girlfriend who was the birth mother of Akaila and Malachi. She was also the wife of the late Counselo DeGonzaza, Akaila and Malachi's father, a former member of the Santiago cartel. To add to the drama, Tricia dated Kane shortly before her death, which was caused by a drug overdose.

"You've looked a lot of 'em in the face," Jay countered. "They didn't say anything to you because they couldn't. They didn't date me. I told you, Carlos and I did the same thing every time Sapphire was opened. We would grab some girls, take 'em back to his place, and do our thing. It was sex and nothing else. I wasn't trying to let anyone get close to me. You and Tricia are the only women I've slept with more than once." He took a sip of his drink. "Get out your feelings."

Carmen knew he was right.

Jay broke everything down to her a long time ago. Tricia was the first girlfriend he had. He only dated her because he thought it was time to settle down. Months down the road, they met, and the rest is documented history.

"Why didn't you wear a dress?"

She frowned at his question. "Why did I need to?" A giggle followed. "We were only going to church. Until you made us come here."

"So I can do this," he replied.

When he reached for her crotch, Carmen moved out his grasp. It was the same place he was trying to go earlier when he came home. "Hell no," Carmen spat, figuring out why they were there. "Is this what you wanted?" A devilish smile formed on Jay's face. "You could've gotten your nut at home. You didn't have to drag me here."

"We can't be loud at home. Up here, we can be anything we want to be."

"Not tonight," Carmen responded. She put more distance between them, but it didn't matter. Jay only followed. They now stood in front of the office's wall-sized window, which overlooked the club's dance floor. She studied the scene until the twerking and gyrating became too much. "I know we talked about having another baby."

"Talked?" he questioned. "I thought we were trying to have another baby." He grabbed the Red Bull from her hand and set it on a table. "Isn't that what we were doing on our honeymoon?" He touched the metal clasp on her pants and undid it. His actions made her walk away from him.

"How many more do you want?"

"Seven," Jay said with confidence.

If Carmen had the Red Bull in her hand, she would've dropped it. "Did you say seven?" Jay nodded. "I can't physically give you seven kids. I couldn't even hold the last two. Let's compromise on one. We already have six kids and a seventh will make everything complete. We'll be done."

"I don't have six kids. You do. I have three."

There went another remark that would've made her drop her drink. "You don't count my other kids as yours?" The heat rose again from her shoulders. "You've never said that to me. You've always treated them like they were yours." Carmen shook her head in disgust until a smile emerged on his face. "Ooh, I was about to…" She marched up to him, pretending to slap him. It gave him the perfect opportunity to grab her. With one quick move, he was on top of her on the sofa.

His voice became muffled as he sucked on her neck. "You know I count them as mine. You're so sleepy, you can't even think straight."

"Come on," she told him, tapping him on the back. "We can do this at home." He acted as if he didn't hear her. She repeated herself, but it was useless. She could feel her pants sliding down and her own fatigue kept her from reaching down to pull 'em up. "Can you lock the door?" She asked the question because it was obvious Jay was going to get what he wanted. She simply didn't want anyone walking in on them.

"I'm about to lock your mouth." He rose a bit to unbutton his shirt. Once it was off, he brought his trousers and boxers down low enough to free his nine-inch pipe. "When you closed it, it automatically locked." He dipped his fingers inside her love box. "You love to play with me," he whispered as he massaged her pearl. "You already got a fuckin' rainforest."

If her eyes were opened, she would've rolled them. What he didn't know was that once she decided to give in, she prepared herself. It didn't take much when she had vast knowledge of how good his dick worked. Aside from the incredible length, he had the girth to match it. Her husband was blessed, and she got the reminder every time he entered her. She also gave him one, too. Jay was her first lover, teaching her much of what she knew. When they sexed, she showed him how much she retained. Even that night, she matched his rhythm and speed as their bodies went beat for beat.

It wasn't their first time sexing in his office. It was just the first time he openly admitted he wanted to make love there. She knew his reasoning came from their time in St. Lucia. The honeymoon allowed them to let loose in ways they didn't always have. It was on the island he regularly got to hear her scream. The sound did something to his ego. Every time they connected, he wanted to hear it. What he didn't know was that something so simple was going to take her there. The second she felt his phone vibrate in his pocket; her body went somewhere else. The vibration matched with their gyrations stimulated her ten times over. They never used toys and while his phone wasn't one, it enhanced the experience like no other.

"Don't," she moaned when she felt him grab it. "Please," she begged. She needed everything it was giving, and the vibration wasn't stopping. She didn't know who was calling him, but she didn't want them to stop or at least not until she couldn't go any farther.

Out of nowhere, the sound of something breaking sent Carmen's eyes open. "What is that?" She knew Jay heard it, but he didn't let up. The sound of bottles shattering filled the room while numerous yells bounced off the club's walls. It was followed by someone banging on the office door. She called Jay's name to get his attention, yet it came out more as a moan as their bodies contracted. His cell phone was still vibrating, aiding their plunge into orgasmic bliss. The fight below became an afterthought. Carmen couldn't do anything about it anyway. All she could concentrate on was the intense throbbing between her legs. Her soft pants became elevated until she gave him what he wanted. The piercing moan made his dick jerk inside of her and once again, he released his seed.

Although they were finishing, the fight below was still ongoing. An expletive flew out Jay's mouth as he pushed himself off Carmen. He fixed his pants and headed towards the window. He saw the mass hysteria and the responsible party—Roman. It was less than an hour ago he and Carmen discovered he was messing with their daughter. Now, Jay was watching him choke and punch the life out of Nicholas. Two of his bouncers were trying to pull him off, but even they couldn't break Roman's grasp. "This is some bullshit." Carmen was behind him fixing her clothes. "You won't believe—" His phone was still vibrating. He pulled it from his pocket so he could tell whoever was calling he would be down to break up the fight.

It didn't happen. His eyes grew large at the number of missed calls from Silvas and Cesar. To make matters worse, his right-hand texted him multiple times telling him Silvas was in trouble. He no longer hesitated in calling Silvas back. Just as the phone started dialing, the office door caved in. When Cesar and Gully stepped in the room, he knew more was happening than the fight below. It became evident when wails of fear came from the other end of the phone.

Immense chaos had him surrounded. Gully was yelling in his face, Carmen was in his ear, Cesar was handing him an iPad, and Roman was still a floor below trying to commit a murder. Out of the mayhem, only one clear realization was in his head. His business partner wanted him dead. He had sent men to San Juan expecting to find him when the only person at the estate was his elderly butler who couldn't defend himself. He didn't need an imagination to know how close to death Silvas had come. Nor did he need it to know danger still lingered.

Jay blocked out everything around him. He had to operate in steps and the first was getting Silvas out the house. He grabbed the iPad out Cesar's hands, which gave him a front row seat to the destruction. *This motherfucker shot up my whole got damn house.* The property damage was extensive, but when Silvas told him he wasn't hit, it made it minimal. "The security footage shows they're gone," Jay began, "but I can't promise you they are. Stay as close to the floor as you can. Make your way to the library." The line fell silent only to return with the sound of movement, heavy breathing, and faint tears. He heard a door open and then it closed. "When you get to the library, head to the bookcase on the right wall." Once Silvas told him he was there, he continued. "On the sixth shelf is a copy of *The Great Gatsby*. When you pull the book out, the bookcase will open. Keep the book with you and walk inside."

Silvas struggled to find the book, but eventually the bookcase opened. Jay directed him more. "The door will close on its own once you take a few steps inside. I know it's dark. My father designed it to where a particular step will alert a censor that will light the tunnel. Let your worries go. If you have that book, no one is getting through that door."

"Where are you taking me?"

The question reassured him that Silvas hadn't been harmed. "The tunnel leads to an underground garage. When you get there, you'll find a car. The doors are locked, but the keys are inside the book. Get inside and start it up. Once the car rolls forward, it'll hit a censor that will open a gate to another tunnel. That gate signals a pilot. At the end of the tunnel, you'll see an airplane. It will bring you to New York."

10

It was nearing three o'clock, but sleep was still a stranger. Based off what occurred in San Juan, Jay was unsure if he would ever get a good night's sleep again. If he did, it was because his hands held the remains of a person he once considered a friend.

That was your warning.

Those were the words on the text message he received from a private number. It had come shortly after Silvas confirmed he was on a plane headed to JFK Airport. The attack had changed his entire security operation and awoken the old man in him. He was now at war.

Before he could get to battle, he had to cease the fighting on his own turf. That meant dealing with Roman. He entered the pool house to find him sitting in the kitchen, icing his knuckles. The conversation was overdue as he spent most of the New Year accessing the damage at Sapphire and revising his security plan with Cesar. He hadn't even explained what caused the shootout to Carmen. There had been so much on his plate, he got her home without telling her anything.

"You already know why I did it," Roman stated.

Jay didn't sit down when he heard Roman's tone. He spoke to him as if the fight should've been expected. Most were aware of Nicholas' history with Akaila. They dated a few years back, which resulted in multiple pregnancies, which became multiple abortions. From what he'd been told, Nicholas didn't know about either for a long time. When he found out, he lost it, and made the worst decision of his life. Akaila still wore the scars of the incident. Now Nicholas wore the scars of Roman's wrath.

"Who told you, you needed to do anything?" Jay shot back. "He doesn't work for you. He works for me. You work for me."

"You should've handled him."

His comment made Jay take a seat. Roman seemed to have forgotten he and Nicholas had a parallel. "What he did to Akaila wasn't right, but I can't hold it against him. Not when the same charge is on my record." He and Roman met eyes. "The entire world knows what I did to my wife. Unlike Nicholas, I didn't get the chance for it to be a whispered secret. My shit is documented. It's mentioned every time I make a headline, good or bad." His face was tight. "Nicholas tried to make it right with her. Akaila didn't want his apology. She's not ready for it."

"She never told me that."

"You were there. Remember when I reopened Blue Magic?" Jay remembered the night clearly. It was one of the first events Roman worked. It was also the night he and Carmen announced their engagement. Roman was at the table when Nicholas apologized. If he didn't notice, it was probably because Akaila hadn't caught his eye. Roman said again he didn't know. "Look, you handle what I pay you to handle. You got me?"

"I shouldn't have fought at your club."

"You shouldn't have fought at all."

Jay rose from the bar stool. "The repairs for the club's damages and Nicholas' medical bills will be deducted from your pay. It won't hurt you. It ain't like you pay rent around here."

"I haven't touched her."

"Keep it that way," Jay replied. "You don't want your dick to bury you." He pulled his phone from his pocket to see Cesar calling him. Instead of answering, he gave Roman a heads up. "Sleep lightly. You're the newest entry on Carmen's hit list." Jay left him with those words as he made his way outside. His cell phone was no longer vibrating. He learned why when he neared the front door of the main house. Cesar and Silvas were making their way inside. He increased his pace, anxious to get to them. When he did, he wished he hadn't.

Silvas met him with a cold hard slap across the face. Despite all the mischievous things he'd done, his butler had never hit him. He hadn't done it when he was six and he caught him scooping handfuls of a freshly made cake in his mouth. Or when he rebuilt the Santiago cartel. Nor did he do it when he arrived in San Juan after serving seventeen years in prison.

With all the mistakes he made, Silvas always encouraged him and showed him love. It was obvious he reached his breaking point. There wasn't any physical pain associated with the slap. He had felt much worse from Carmen. It was the look of disgust and disappointment that broke his spirit. Silvas never made him feel like he failed him until that moment. A part of him understood why. He had left him defenseless. The estate in Puerto Rico didn't have a high level of security like the one in Brookstone. The estate was never under surveillance unless he and his family were visiting.

"Show me to my room," Silvas barked. With a shaking hand, he made his way up the steps one at a time. Long gone was the 22-year-old German immigrant who used to chase him whenever he needed a playmate. In his place was a man who was fragile and hurt.

"I'll take care of him," Cesar offered, his voice low. "Get some sleep."

Sleep wasn't an option. His emotions wouldn't allow him to sleep even though his body told him he needed it. Too much was running through his head. Although sleep wasn't on the agenda, he followed Cesar up the steps. He didn't head to his bedroom as he didn't want to risk waking Carmen. If he did, she would question him about what happened in San Juan. She deserved to know, but it was too much to explain at the hour.

Therefore, Jay opened the door to Nyla's room. A rocking chair was in the far-right corner. That became his spot for the next three or so hours. Sleep never came and he only closed his eyes to pray. He told God countless times he didn't want to revert to the old man. He wanted to give his family the husband and father they deserved. Somehow, every time things started to look up, another problem would arise. The problems only got bigger. The current one on his shoulder was the biggest. He would never voice it to his team, but they had met their match. While he had spent most of NYE trying to figure out how he would take his business partner out, the only conclusion was that he couldn't.

All he could do was give the people who could the golden ticket. The package of rough diamonds contained the information he knew the U.S. government wanted. It told them the who, what, and where. While his partner meant for it to be used as a wedding gift, it would now become his boarding pass to hell. Once the package was in the right hands, the U.S. military would take care of the rest. It kept him from committing another murder and having Cesar play the clean-up man. To put the plan into action, he would have to make an appearance at Grendel's memorial. It wasn't the right time for a trip, but if he wanted to keep his family safe, it had to be done. He only prayed his business partner didn't come with any more surprises.

11

Jay stepped outside his house only to see a concerned look on Cesar's face. His right-hand could see the lack of sleep in his eyes despite the fresh shower he'd taken and the tailored suit he wore. There was an hour and a half flight ahead of them to DC, but that didn't mean he could sleep. At some point, Carmen was going to notice he was gone and hit his line. He would have to explain the fight at Sapphire, the shootout in San Juan, and the trip to DC. He would admit his fault, promise her another good dick-down, and in a perfect world all would be well.

"I see you didn't take my advice." Cesar looked Jay up and down.

"There's too much going on for me to sleep."

Jay didn't say much else as they started the trek to the driveway. He snuck a glance in the direction of the pool house. Linx and Roman were huddled outside its doors. "One of 'em should've been at the car." He headed in their direction so they would know it was time to go.

"That's some wild shit right there," Roman was saying.

Jay could see they were watching something on a cell phone. Something told him it was a playback of the fight from the night before. Word had already gotten to him that several videos had made it to social media.

"Her titties were big back then," he heard Linx say.

Jay looked at Cesar, now confused by what he was hearing. "These horny motherfuckers."

Roman covered his mouth in disbelief. "Damn, he's working her ass."

"And it's time for y'all motherfuckers to get to work," Jay joked.

He thought they heard him coming until he saw the phone drop from Roman's hands. A startled expression was on his face. It told Jay something was wrong. He was going to ask what it was, but he was distracted by Cesar, who was pulling him away. He looked down.

A naked ass was on the screen, but it wasn't the nudity per se that made time stop. It was the fact that the naked ass belonged to a person who was once the closest to him. He was a man he would've taken a bullet for. He also was the man who allowed his jealousy to turn to betrayal. The second Carlos stuck his penis inside Carmen, the entire course of his life changed. He spent seventeen years trying to get the images of them sexing out his mind. He made the thought trigger-less. He forgave his wife and made peace with the past. Now, the memory was clear and present.

A tightness formed in Jay's chest. "We'll deal with this later," he heard Cesar say. He pushed Cesar away. He then bent down and picked up the phone. Enough adrenaline was running through him, Jay thought his grip would've crushed it. Somehow, the phone stayed intact.

"You like this?" Jay asked Roman. He held the phone up, the footage still playing. He increased the volume, allowing them to hear the grunts and moans.

Roman didn't utter a single syllable.

"You like it, right?" Jay's eyes were now on Linx. "Give—" Jay jerked the phone out Cesar's hand when he grabbed it. "Nah, they've been standing here watching my wife get fucked. They can at least tell me if they liked it."

Cesar tried to grab the phone, yet Jay held a firm grip. They were now standing chest to chest as Cesar tried to talk sense into him. "We have other shit to deal with."

Jay wasn't about to let up. He couldn't. The monster he kept buried had been given new life. His thirst to kill needed quenching. Someone needed to bleed. "Did you like it?" he yelled at Roman. "You like how he fucked her?"

Jay heard him apologize, but it wasn't a band aid for the wound. Roman had betrayed him twice in less than twenty-four hours. The worst part of it all was that he was referred by Silvas. His butler told him he could be trusted. Linx was no different, his right-hand who he met running the San Juan streets. His comment about his wife's breasts told him he looked at her in an inappropriate manner. From what the morning showed, none of his men were trustworthy. They were all like Carlos, waiting in the wind until they saw an opportunity to fly out his cage.

"Shut the fuck up and listen to me," he heard in his ear. The words brought him back to reality. He realized Cesar wasn't trying to control the phone in his hand, but the pistol. He didn't even know he pulled it out. He loosened his grip on the gun. "You have two sleeping babies upstairs. Do you really want to do this? You want them to see them dead right here?" Jay loosened his grip some more until the pistol slid out his hand. Cesar pushed him in the direction of the driveway until he was a good distance from Roman and Linx. "They made a stupid mistake, but they're not the enemy. The person who leaked that tape is."

His right-hand was right. Roman and Linx weren't the enemy. They were simply two men who allowed an explicit act to distort their judgement. The person who was the enemy had already paid his debt with his life. As for his wife, she paid with blood. She presented a peace offering when she bore him three beautiful children.

"I'm going to keep this," Cesar told him, sticking the pistol inside his jacket. "At least for a little while."

Jay's eyes were now fixed on his bedroom window. If Carmen was still asleep, she had no clue what was coming. He couldn't prep her for it as it would be one more thing that would delay him in getting to DC. Even when he realized he had to go back inside to retrieve the package of rough diamonds, he didn't go to his bedroom. It wouldn't have been beneficial for either of them. One look at Carmen and he would've seen Carlos on top of her all over again. The best thing he could do was walk out the door without a word.

***

Carmen didn't know how long she slept, but she wasn't ready to get up. When her ringer went off, she grabbed her phone to send the call to voicemail. Or at least that was the plan. When she saw Kane's name, she grunted. She grunted again when she saw it wasn't even eight o'clock. *What does he want? Flame isn't open. He could've waited till twelve. Ugh, this better not be something stupid.* Despite her annoyance, she answered his call. "Why are you calling me?"

There were a few seconds of silence.

"Kane?" she called. "Hello?" A few sounds came from the other end.

"Did you just wake up?"

"You woke me up." Carmen yawned. "What do you want? You know we didn't go to bed 'till late. It's the freakin' New Year. What's going on?"

"I've learned how to mind my business when it comes to certain things."

Carmen noticed the change in his tone.

"When it involves our kids, I have to get involved," he continued. More silence appeared. "Malachi texted me a copy of a tweet he received. It was a video. He was too scared to call you."

Carmen already knew where he was headed. They were living in the social media age where as soon as something scandalous happened, it was shared with millions. "There was a fight at Sapphire last night," she explained. "Look, I haven't talked to Akaila, but it's on my to do list. So do me a favor and tell Malachi I'm on it. I'll be calling him today anyway. I forgot to tell him what time dinner will be ready."

"You haven't checked your phone?" Kane asked.

"I told you. You woke me up."

A loud sigh emerged. "I thought you already knew." More silence, another sigh. "Someone leaked the video of you and Carlos. Now, for us, this is water under the bridge. I couldn't care less when it comes to me and you. When it comes to our kids, it's a problem."

Carmen knew she heard him, but at the same time she felt she didn't. What he said didn't make sense. It didn't seem real. It wasn't possible.

"Some kids are saying stuff to him. He's seeing stuff on the Internet," Kane continued. "I told Malachi to delete his social media, but you know that's how these kids interact nowadays. Thankfully, Kristian hasn't seen it. She's still asleep."

The phone shook so bad in Carmen's hand, it took her forever and a day to pull it from her ear. There had to be proof of what he was saying. She checked her inbox to see if she received a Google Alert. When she located it, she hesitated in opening the message.

"Who had the tape?" Kane asked.

She left the question unanswered. Or at least for the time being. She was still building the nerve to view the latest headlines regarding Flame. *It isn't me in the tape,* Carmen thought. *This is someone playing a cruel joke. Someone found out a tape might exist and got a look-a-like. No one has that tape. No one has mentioned that tape. Who would care after twenty years?*

She learned someone cared when she viewed the email message in its entirety. The first headline told her all she needed to know: *New York Fashion Designer Involved in Sex Tape Scandal.* She clicked the link, which directed her to a news article that provided context to the tape's existence.

"Do you see the video?"

The question sent her into a fit of tears. She didn't see the video. The article was on a credible website that would never show lewdness. What they did show was press photos of her and Jay as well as an old mugshot of Carlos. She closed the page and went back to the email. She scrolled through the rest of the headlines although she knew none of the sites would show evidence of her sin. She would have to go somewhere else to see what the world was watching.

"Who had the tape?" Kane asked again.

"I don't know," Carmen mumbled. That wasn't the truth, though. She knew Jay had it first. If he kept it in his possession, he moved it each time he changed residences. *I don't see Jay keeping that tape. That's not something he would want to keep.* The last time he moved was from his penthouse to her estate. All his belongings came with him except his furniture. Those items he left for Gully who lived in his penthouse. *Jay could've left the tape in his apartment. Well, who put it out? It couldn't have been Gully.*

"Who had the tape?" Kane asked the question a third time as if he didn't believe her.

Carmen told him once again she didn't know, but the words were barely audible. With a quick Google search of her name, she was able to locate a copy of the video. A loud shrill slipped from her lips as the initial image buffered. There was no more denial. It was her. The memory of the encounter had faded with time, yet the video made her recall everything.

"You see it now?" Kane asked.

She didn't need to answer him. The pain was in her voice as she cried. He told her to turn it off, but she couldn't. She needed to see it. She needed to see how much was out there. She muffled her screams although her embarrassment couldn't be silenced.

"Where's Jay?"

Carmen couldn't talk. She didn't even think she could breathe. The mere thought that Malachi had seen what she'd done made her gag. She didn't even want to imagine the look on his face.

Kane directed her on what to do. "You need to call Clement so he can start the cease-and-desist letters." Clement was Carmen's attorney. "Anyone who posted it needs to get paperwork. You can get a court order that will require them to take it down. I can link y'all with a Triad agent so you can find out who leaked it. File a lawsuit because you didn't give them permission to distribute it."

Carmen heard him loud and clear. She didn't say anything as she grabbed a notepad and pen. She wrote the name of the website that uploaded the video and the time. "You..." She thought twice about what she was going to ask. Kane had gotten her out of prison by hiding a fake pink diamond in Jay's house. There was a strong chance he found the tape. She could see him still being upset that she married Jay and wanting payback. "Did..." She didn't complete her thought.

"What?" Kane asked. "You wanna know if I did this?"

The thought was on her mind. She didn't want to admit it, but it was. Although they made up the day before, there were still years of pain between them. Considering the evidence, he should've known he was a suspect.

"You're not saying anything," Kane noticed. "You think I did this? Do you think I'm gonna wait twenty years to put a tape out? First off, out of respect for our kids, I wouldn't do it. You don't deserve that not even on your worst day. Look, I know I said this wasn't about us, and it isn't, but damn, Carm. You let him *do* you like that? This man was running sprints on your ass. Like, we both know we fucked the hell out each other, but damn, Carm. You rode the shit out of Carlos."

Yeah, I rode his ass. I was pretending it was your dick. I bet your stupid ass didn't know that. She didn't voice her thoughts. All she could do was hang up the phone. He was starting to make light of the situation like he didn't know all the things that were on the line. For one, she didn't know where Jay was. She could tell from looking at his side of the bed he didn't sleep there. If he caught wind of the tape, his mental state could spiral. Everyone knew he was diagnosed with bipolar disorder. Medication and therapy kept him together, but those two tools couldn't stop a bullet.

Her ringer went off again. Kane called two more times, but she let him get the voicemail. He then called again. This time, she answered.

"Is that really what you were thinking about?" he asked.

Her voice came out like a wail, "What are you talking about?"

"You said you did him like that because you were pretending it was me. Is that true?"

Carmen knew she thought it, but she didn't know she said it. It was obvious she had. "Yeah, I was," she admitted. "Those feelings are gone, though."

"We can agree there."

Thus came an awkward silence. It lingered longer than expected.

"What is this?" A female voice came on the line.

Carmen didn't need Kane to say anything. The second she heard Monifah's voice, she hung up. While she hoped he told Monifah about their new friendship, she didn't want to get him in trouble if he hadn't. Besides, she had enough to deal with. She wasn't done crying, but the tears would have to wait. It was time for her to take legal action.

***

Jay looked out the back window of his limo, thinking he heard a car. When he realized it was his mind playing tricks on him, he shifted his attention elsewhere. His demeanor had changed from earlier, which he attributed to Cesar. His right-hand talked him off a ledge. Cesar even requested for Gully to accompany them to the airport instead of Roman or Linx. They were now waiting for his cousin to show.

"What are you thinking?" Cesar asked.

The question came from his silence. About to reply, he didn't. His phone was vibrating. He expected to see a phone call from Gully, but the name *Malik* was on the screen. He figured he would get the conversation over and done with. "I already know," Jay told him. He looked at Cesar who was looking out the back window. He did the same, and this time, he saw Gully pulling in the driveway. "It's fucked up."

"It is fucked up. How is Carmen?" Malik asked.

Jay shrugged his shoulders although his friend couldn't see. "I'm on my way to handle some business," he replied. "I know you heard about the fight at the club. You keep your ear to the streets." Malik stated he had. "Well, what else are the streets saying?"

"What do you mean?"

He was about to elaborate when Gully stole his attention. Cesar gave Gully a quick update on the plans for the day and before long, the limo's engine roared to life. "What did you hear about the tape? I know you didn't watch it."

"I didn't watch it," Malik confirmed. "That's your wife."

"There's a whole lot of people talking about my wife."

"Dead all that noise," Malik advised. "You know what's going on in your house. You know that woman loves you. That shit was a long ass time ago. Whoever put that tape out is going to get theirs."

We can agree there. Jay was going to find out who leaked the tape. Whoever did it had broken in his house because he left the tape there. Once he had a name, his bare hands would handle the rest. "What are they saying about the video?"

"You don't want to hear that shit. You just want some ammo."

Truth be told, Jay didn't know what he was looking for. His ears were just burning to hear the talk. Roman and Linx had given him a preview, leading him to wonder if everyone else thought the same. "I do want to hear it," he admitted. "Tell me."

Malik didn't start talking right off. He talked around the topic, but Jay wasn't letting up. Eventually, Malik dispelled what he knew. "One dude told me his girl saw the tape and was like Carlos did his thing. Some other dudes were talking about how good Carmen rode him. It's bullshit, though. People talk crazy. Shit, some people didn't even know Carlos was dead. You got women out here trying to look for him."

"That is crazy," Jay replied, his attention focused elsewhere. A car pulled up outside the front gate. Cesar ordered his team to be ready to strike. Gully thought it meant the same for him because he put the limo in park and drew a weapon. "I gotta go," Jay told Malik. "I'll hit you up later." He hung up the phone just as Monifah stepped out the vehicle. "What is this bitch doing?"

Cesar ordered his men to stand down while Gully stashed his gun in the glove compartment. He put the limo back in drive before parking next to Monifah's car.

Jay grunted at her presence. "Y'all stay here, I'll deal with her." He unlocked his door and stepped out. From the way Monifah was looking, the visit wasn't about to be pleasant. She looked like she was ready to bite his head off. "How can I help you, Mrs. Kane?" He called her that on purpose. Her husband was his arch nemesis and although he couldn't kill him, Carmen wouldn't fault him if he sent a message through her.

"Tell your whore of a wife to stay out my fuckin' business."

Jay's face scrunched up. "What—" She threw something in his face.

"Get your bitch in check. Train your dogs."

"If you weren't pregnant," he threatened. She got back in her car. When she backed away from the property, he looked at the ground. He could tell it was a check, but he didn't get the full story until he pieced it together. Cesar joined him at the back of the limo.

"Put this in your back pocket. Let's handle DC first," Cesar advised.

"She gave that motherfucker two million dollars."

"He didn't get it," Cesar corrected. "It's right here in front of you."

Jay looked at the estate he shared with Carmen. The knife she stuck in his heart was now lodged. The last thing he needed to see was a check written to her ex-husband. The worst part was that the check was written only yesterday. She hadn't even respected him as her husband before she took from their household. It was like she had forgotten he was the head. He was going to deal with her, though. Until he could, his focus was Washington, DC.

12

It was below forty degrees. Every single chill or gust of wind was felt. Despite the temperature, it was still warmer outdoors than it was in Jay's heart. The flight to DC was only a playground for his mind. With nothing to do, there was room for his aggression to grow. Nevertheless, someone had to have a level head. Twenty minutes into the flight, Cesar advised it was time to handle business. By the time the plane was landing, there were contractors in place to repair the damages at the San Juan estate. There were also six new prospects for the property's security team. Work had been done, but there was still the main task at hand.

Twelve chairs were set in front of a monarch blue casket. Each seat was filled, however, none of the individuals were Andrew North. There were even more people on the outskirts. North didn't stick out amongst the crowd. It didn't help that Jay had never seen the man in person. All he had to go off was a photo he found on the internet. Jay studied each face until he located North several yards from his right. He signaled to Cesar. Neither of them moved, out of respect for the service, but they kept their eyes on him. When the service ended, they met their target.

North was in the middle of a conversation. Jay could tell from his reaction he was the last person North thought he'd see. Jay hadn't told him he was coming despite receiving the invitation.

"Mr. Santiago." North's tone was high-pitched.

Jay offered his hand, which he shook. "I need a moment of your time."

North excused himself from the other gentleman. He pointed towards a less crowded area where they could talk. "Welcome to DC."

"Thank you. I wish I didn't have to come under these conditions."

"I agree," North replied. A stretch of silence appeared until they were out of earshot of the other mourners. North looked back and forth between him and Cesar. "Our last conversation didn't exactly end with goodbye. I thought I was on your bad side."

"It ended with a fuck you," Jay reminded him. "Perhaps this one will give you that goodbye." He handed the package to Cesar so his hands could be free as he spoke. "That name you want," he continued. "I found a way for you to get it."

"It would help a lot of people." North's eyes watered. "We received the remains of the rest of Grendel's team. Their bodies had been shipped to various federal buildings."

Jay turned his gaze to Grendel's casket. "He shot up my house," he dispelled. "My butler was in it and that doesn't sit well with me. I look at that man like my father. He wasn't hit, but what could have happened is what matters."

"How can I help you?" North asked.

Jay knew he was about to sign his own death certificate. Not only for himself, but for his wife and kids. Still, it had to be done. For the longest, he didn't have any plans of giving his business partner up. He refused to say anything. One little hiccup on Grendel's part and his business partner had forgotten about his loyalty. He hadn't even called him to see what was going on. He suspected he betrayed him and used his suspicion in the worst way possible. He forced his hand. "I have something that will give you all the information you need."

"And in return?" North asked.

"I need the strongest military force you can find."

North looked at the package in Cesar's hands. "Is that it?"

"That's your golden ticket." Jay held out his hand and felt the package as it was set in his palm. "Can you promise me that?"

North pulled out his cell phone. "If you can promise me that what's in that package will give us what we need, you'll get that military force. They'll invade Kenema once the mission is signed off." He held up his phone. "I'll make the call right here, right now."

The deal sounded sweet. Pure sugar to Jay's ears. Now, it was time for North to make it real. "I need y'all to get this motherfucker." He handed North the package. The seams had been taped, but it was minimal to North. He used his keys to break the seal and once he looked inside, his eyes glowed. He pulled out the letter, leaving the stash of rough diamonds inside. He gave it a quick read. When North whispered the name, Jay responded with a nod. Like he promised, North kept his end of the deal. He made the call and an hour later, they left him for a flight back to Brookstone.

***

An expletive flew out Jay's mouth as he stared at the broken bottles and glassware. All of it had been swept into a large pile in front of Sapphire's main bar. The club's cleaning crew was adding to it with other miscellaneous trash. Their job description didn't entail fixing the scratches on the bar counter or the broken glass shelves on the back bar. Another vendor was needed for that.

Prior to leaving the club the night before, he left one of King's childhood friends, Phase, in charge of getting things handled. He was second in command at Sapphire, following behind Nicholas. He proved to be a good pick for the role. Aside from the cleaning crew, Phase had carpenters and electricians in the club to assess and repair the damage.

Until the repairs were made, the club couldn't be open for business. The brawl put both time and money on the line. Thousands of dollars would be missed. Jay depended on his businesses to keep money coming in and to keep his employees afloat as well. If one business went under, it wasn't just a loss for him, but also for those on his payroll. It wouldn't hurt his billionaire status, but he didn't like interruptions when it came to his money.

After making a mental note of the damage, he escaped to his office. His presence was known, which he learned from the conversation below him.

"That was the owner, right?" a male voice said.

"Yeah, that was him," another male replied.

"He doesn't talk much?"

The other man chuckled. "He talks. He didn't say anything because everyone saw his wife gettin' smashed. You know he just married the bitch."

The word *bitch* made Jay rise to his feet. He looked at the dance floor, but he couldn't tell which group of men were holding the conversation.

"You haven't seen it," the man continued. "I never really paid attention to her. I knew she had clothing stores. She definitely had me looking today."

Jay's eyes darted across the area only to realize the men were in a blind spot. He could put an end to the conversation, but that's what he *didn't* need to do. With the bar area already in shambles, it didn't need a coat of blood and guts.

"She knows how to ride a dick," the man continued.

The other man spoke up. "Damn, I gotta find that tape."

The comments had Jay feening for a bloodbath. He patted himself only to remember Cesar still had his pistol. It wasn't an issue as there were about a dozen more around the office. One search and he could have the men laid out. The only downfall was that it wouldn't stop the chatter. Millions of people were making the same comments.

If he needed to do anything, he needed to stop procrastinating. The day was over, and he hadn't confronted Carmen about the tape or even the Pink Sunrise. She had reached out to him, though. Fifteen missed phone calls and twenty texts were all from her. Not to mention, he received two phone calls a piece from their attorneys. She had taken the right steps while he was taking the wrong ones. His lack of communication was only setting him back.

Truthfully speaking, his fear was not in seeing her, but in losing control. He had done it once before and he promised himself, she would never see that side of him again. Still, he had to test himself. *Can't keep running. It's best to face these demons now.*

"He was making that pussy clap," one of the men said down below.

I make her pussy clap, Jay thought. *Carlos ain't do shit. He made her cum once. She's cum three times on my dick.* Fed up with the conversation, Jay opened the door to his office. He didn't leave the doorway when he saw Gully standing across the hall.

"You wanna get 'em now?" Gully asked.

His cousin was ready to ride out with him. "Nah, I need to get to my wife. We're gonna let 'em live. At least this time."

***

There was minimal noise when Jay stepped in the foyer. Now, by himself, he listened for any sound he could catch. Not hearing voices or movement, he made his way upstairs. The door to his bedroom was closed, which gave him time to gather himself. There was a lot he wanted to confront Carmen about. He also knew she would have a few things for him. He took several deep breaths before he twisted the doorknob.

He opened the door to find her in bed with the covers up to her chin. Every single light was on, which was unusual for the time. She wasn't sleep yet she was staring into space as if she were in a daze. Considering the circumstances, her current state made sense. If she didn't look distraught, he would've been concerned.

He closed the door behind him. The fear of losing control was still on his back. He waited for her to address him, but she never did. Her silence told him he had to make the first move. "I know today has been hard for us," he began. His voice prompted Carmen to turn over. Her back was now towards him. *That wasn't a daze.* He waited a few seconds to see if she would say something. "What did Clement say?" The question went ignored. "It took a lot for me to come home."

"Then, you should've stayed where you were."

Her response lit a match. "I would have, but everywhere I go, motherfuckers are talking about how good my wife got fucked." His statement was all it took for her to turn around and throw the covers off her.

"They wouldn't be talking if you hadn't of kept the tape."

"Kept the tape?" Jay yelled. "How did I keep a tape when I was in prison for seventeen years? What? You woke up and forgot about that? I did that time for you."

"For me," Carmen spat. "You didn't go to prison for me. You went to prison for you."

"I went to prison for every bitch who ate off me," he shot back.

"Oh, I'm a bitch now?"

Jay didn't voice his comeback. He thought it, though. The truth of the matter was that she wasn't a bitch. However, when she made him mad, she was the bitch of all bitches.

His hesitation allowed Carmen to have diarrhea of the mouth. "I've spent the entire day trying to deal with this shit. I've had to deal with lawyers, my publicist, my fuckin' board, the kids, paparazzi. All this shit could've been avoided if you'd gotten rid of the tape."

"You didn't hear one word I said."

"What—"

He cut her off. "How can I keep something I didn't have? Did I get the tape? Yes. I put it in our bedroom. I left the house, went looking for you, came back…" Jay realized what came next. He remembered dragging her down the steps. He remembered punching her. "You know what happened," he said instead. "Weeks later, we were arrested, and I was locked up for seventeen years. I didn't have shit."

"Well, soon enough we'll know," she responded. "Kane put me in contact with a Triad agent. He's looking into it. I should have a name in a couple of days."

Jay sucked his teeth. "You've been talking to Kane?"

"I have to talk to him. We have kids together."

That same ol' bullshit excuse. Y'all kids are grown. Jay reached in his jacket pocket and pulled out the remains of her check. He tossed it on the bed so she could see it. "That's what we're doing now?"

She picked up the pieces and tossed it in the trash. "It was my money."

Jay was on the bed before he realized he jumped on it. He wanted her to hear every word. "I don't give a flying fuck if your face was on the money. You don't take nothing out this house without running it by me."

Carmen huffed. "What control do you have over *my* money? I do what I want. I made it. I can decide how I want to spend it."

Jay climbed off the bed. The Carmen he didn't like was present. "You did make it. You made it the same way you got in this mess—lyin' and fuckin'." He caught the lamp right before it hit him. The lamp slipped from his hands, landing at his feet. "Throw somethin' else."

"Fuck you."

Carmen climbed out the bed and headed inside the bathroom. She slammed the door as if that would keep him out. He only followed her. When she sat on the toilet, Jay hoped she wasn't about to shit. "Why did you give him the money?"

"Because he needed it."

"And you thought it was a good idea to write a check for two million dollars and not tell me? I'm your husband."

"Do I have a husband?" Carmen started to pee. "Or do I have a husband in name? I got married, came home to a missing mother, a fight in your club, a shootout, and a fuckin' sex tape."

"Okay, okay," Jay stammered. "I see where you're going. You want to pin this all on me. Like I did all this shit. So, let me ask you, do you think I did something to your mother?"

"Don't bullshit me."

"Now we're getting somewhere. Is that why you choked me the other day?"

"Can I pee in peace?" Carmen grabbed some tissue.

Jay noticed she wanted to dead the subject. *She doesn't want me to admit it. If she knows what I did, why isn't she more upset?* He could linger on the subject, or he could move to the truth. He decided to do the latter. "That tape hurt me just as much as it hurt you. I had to relive that shit all over again. The last thing any man would want is to see the woman he loves being touched by someone else. It was a hurdle we got over, but the wound is open again. I even got a fresh one. I'm watching the world praise this muthafucka. He fucked my girlfriend and got the glory."

"You perceive it as glory."

"So, what do you call it? Everyone's talking about how good he fucked you."

"He's fuckin' dead," Carmen yelled. "That shit doesn't matter. He's dead. People are talking to be talking. They write a comment, they joke, they go on with their lives. We're the ones dealing with the real shit. I'm the one about to lose an international contract. There's a chance I could be suspended from my own company. But that ain't the worst of it. The worst is knowing your kids are scared to look you in the face. The worst is continuously apologizing for something only to have it thrown at you repeatedly. We haven't even been married a week and I'm already sittin' on a toilet, screamin' at your ass. That's the fucked up shit."

"The fucked up shit is watching someone be celebrated for something that ruined your life."

There came a deafening silence.

Jay lowered his tone. "The best thing for our marriage right now would be for you to take accountability. You want me to hold this one, but I can't. The tape wouldn't exist if you hadn't made a deal with the devil. The tape leaking had nothing to do with what I kept or had. We both know I didn't want that tape out there. Talk to me like you know me."

Carmen swallowed. "You should sleep in a guestroom tonight."

Her reply stuck another knife in his heart. She still wasn't going to take responsibility. She didn't even want to try and make it right. If she couldn't, he didn't know if he could ever lay next to her again. She needed to budge if he were to give any more fight. He couldn't be the punching bag for her wrongdoings. A lot of their past issues were on him, but this one wasn't. He only wished she would accept it.

13

The smell of fennel tickled Jay's nostrils. Still half asleep, it took a few sniffs before his eyes opened. The scent, now more present, reminded him of one thing—Silvas. Jay had been so consumed with his other troubles; he hadn't made amends with him. He figured they could have a conversation before the whole house was awake.

After being kicked out his bedroom, he ventured inside Nyla's room and slept in the rocking chair. It suited him the previous night but didn't show the same grace. His back was sore while his legs were stiff. He took his time standing up, feeling every bit of his age. He stretched for a bit, careful not to wake his daughter. From there, he ventured in Rakim's room. His bed was empty. That told him one thing. He was in bed with Carmen.

He saw for himself when he went in their bedroom. They were both knocked out, their bodies side by side in the middle of the California King. He moved discretely as he showered and dressed, careful not to wake them. He then headed to the kitchen where his butler was in full chef mode.

"Good morning," Jay greeted.

Silvas looked over his shoulder, yet he didn't speak. He continued kneading dough. Jay didn't take it personal as he knew his butler had gone through something traumatic. He would just keep at him until Silvas broke. "There was a lot going on yesterday. I apologize. I didn't help you get settled." Jay took a closer look at Silvas, and a slight smile formed on his face. Silvas was wearing his clothes. None of the clothes fit as his butler was about seventy pounds lighter than him. He figured Carmen had raided his drawers since his butler had come to New York with nothing but a copy of *The Great Gatsby* and a cell phone. "Let me take you downtown for a new wardrobe."

"Carmen is taking me."

Well, damn, at least he spoke. "I'm fine with that." He pulled out his wallet and grabbed his Black Card. "Make sure y'all take this." He set it on the counter. Silvas looked at it then resumed what he was doing. "I made a mistake," Jay admitted. "I apologize for what happened. I thought you were safe because you've always been safe. It was poor judgement, which is why we're fixing it now. I have contractors booked to fix the house. Interviews are lined up to get a whole team out there."

"You are your father's son, but he left you too early. You had more lessons to learn."

"Which is why I'm blessed to have you," Jay responded. "You can teach me."

Silvas dropped the dough onto a floured cutting board. "Why did you ask me about Domino? Why were you curious if he had other kids?"

Jay took a seat on a bar stool. "A guy named Carlton Rodriguez showed up at Flame. Tiara spoke with him, and he said he was Carlos' brother. Apparently, they have the same father."

"So, you know that's not true?"

"I don't know what to believe. I got his number, but I haven't called him. I haven't even seen him." Jay watched as Silvas grabbed a rolling pin and started smoothing out the dough. "You brought Domino up because you thought I knew something was going to happen. I didn't. The shootout had nothing to do with Carlton. It was a misunderstanding with a business partner. If he hadn't of came like he did, we could've talked it out. I had to make a move." He watched Silvas as he worked. "You know I need you."

"Judging from that argument last night, you do."

Jay could tell Silvas was trying to ease out a smile. "I love my wife. She just fucks with me sometimes."

Silvas added his two cents. "She knows she was wrong. Give it some time, it's not even eight o'clock."

"She spoke to you?"

Silvas shot a glance in his direction, which confirmed she had.

Jay lowered his head. Not because Carmen was open with Silvas, but at what he was feeling. "I've always been prideful. It was an effortless way to be because I was the one in charge. I always had people under me. When Carmen did what she did, I lost it. Like, how could someone get the same thing I got? He wasn't better than me."

Silvas started cutting the dough. "It had nothing to do with who was better. You may have been the ringleader, but you're nothing without a circus. It had everything to do with a woman who wasn't mature enough to handle what she'd been given. She's a lot younger than you. She wasn't raised in this life."

His butler spoke truth. Carmen's innocence is what attracted him to her. He looked at her as the person who could make him better. She did, but not after he paid for it with his freedom.

"Carlos is still haunting you," Silvas continued. "He was your brother, and it hurts you that you killed him." He continued cutting the dough. "You never mourned him because you couldn't get past the hurt. You can't mourn him now because you're reliving what he did. It's only worse because the world is your audience."

"The world is loving it."

Silvas grabbed another cutter and handed it to Jay. "Which is a blow to your ego."

Jay took it and joined him at the counter. "We had an offer on our wedding photos, but they pulled out. They think the wedding was a joke."

"What they think and what it was, is two different things."

Jay cut about four biscuits before he set the cutter down. He knew Silvas was working, but he pulled him into a hug. Regardless of what he was going through, his butler knew how to make him feel as if things would smooth out. While he and Carmen hadn't made up, a reconciliation was around the corner. He also knew Silvas had forgiven him when he wrapped his arms around him.

***

The second she heard her ringer; Carmen dropped the tube of mascara onto the bathroom counter. She rushed in her room, trying to get to the phone before it woke Rakim. The noise caused him to stir, but when she answered Tiara's call, he went right back to sleep. She hurried back in the bathroom, closing the door behind her. "Mornin'," she called.

"There's no good in front of it, huh?" Tiara replied.

"I had a rough night. Shit, a rough day, you know about it."

"I know," Tiara admitted. "Well, I was calling because I wanted to give you the heads up on what happened at the board meeting."

The tube of mascara was back in her hands, but she set it down. When she and Tiara had spoken yesterday, she learned an emergency board meeting was called. There was talk of suspending her until the sex tape died down. The board was conflicted on the idea because of the upcoming anniversary shoot and party for the *King* collection.

"The board was impressed with how quick you moved with the cease and desist letters. They also liked that you started an official investigation. It shows you're taking this seriously. They feel like this could all die down within a week." Tiara was presenting good news.

"What I'm hearing is that I'm not getting suspended."

"We never did an official vote," Tiara shared. "Suspension isn't on the table."

Carmen whispered words of thanks to God. She would've continued, but a loud beep in her ear notified her she had another incoming call. She looked at the screen to see Kane was calling her. She quickly told Tiara she would call her back. She accepted Kane's call and before he could speak, she asked for confirmation they were in the clear. "Your wife isn't lurking, is she?"

"Thankfully, she's in the shower. The same place she was supposed to be yesterday."

Carmen noticed how annoyed he sounded. Nevertheless, she knew it didn't come from Monifah interrupting their call. It came from her snooping through his things and finding the check. Carmen wanted to write him a new one, but she knew she had to go about it the right way. That meant having a conversation with Jay where they made the decision together. If he agreed, the next step would be for Kane to acquire a separate bank account so he could receive the funds.

"I wanted to call you," Kane continued, "because my friend was able to speak with the individual who posted the initial footage. It's not even a person we know. It's some man out in LA who stole the tape off an executive's laptop at Lucid Entertainment. That's like the biggest porn company out there. Lucid was going to contact you about distribution, but he took it before they could. He's an intern there. Well, he was. They fired him once the tape leaked."

"How soon can we get a meeting with them? We still don't know how they got it."

"He's supposed to be working on that today. Hopefully, I'll have an answer by this evening."

Carmen gave him her next plan of action. "I need that man's information. I'm suing him."

Kane gave her a word of advice. "You can sue him, but you're not going to get anything. This is a regular Joe. He doesn't have shit. Let's focus more on how Lucid got the tape."

A sigh slipped out Carmen's mouth. She didn't like the sound of that, but the day was starting off better than yesterday. Besides, there wasn't enough money in the world to take away her embarrassment or pain.

"How are you holding up?" Kane asked.

"I feel better, but last night was rough. I really fucked up."

"With what? With Jay?"

"I said a lot of things I shouldn't have," Carmen told him. "I was mad at him for not being here. He didn't answer my calls or texts. He left me to deal with this shit alone. Even his little yes men didn't tell me anything. He has them trained to do what he wants."

"Perhaps they didn't know where he was."

Carmen bit her lip. It was a possibility. Linx told her he was supposed to drive Jay to the airport, but plans got changed. If he did have additional information, he didn't share it. "That could be true," she replied. "We also got into it over the check. I was wrong with how I handled that."

"You have a different husband this round. See, with me, you were the breadwinner. Yes, our money went in an account together, but my coins was gas money compared to what you were bringing in. I struggled with saying anything every time eight boxes of red bottoms came to the house. I felt like it wasn't my place. You don't have that with Jay."

"Because I married a fuckin' billionaire."

Immediately, she regretted mentioning that detail. Kane knew most of Jay's wealth came from his days as the head of a major drug cartel. In the past, when their interactions were less than pleasant, he would throw it in her face.

"I'm sorry, Carm, I have to call you back," he said, finally speaking. "There's a U-Haul pulling inside my driveway."

"Uh oh, Monifah is leaving you."

"She ain't going anywhere. Let me call you back."

Kane hung up the phone as he looked out the window. Still confused, he opened the front door to see his mother step out the truck. She was the last person he expected to see. His parents were moving in with him, but it wouldn't be for another month or so. "Mom?"

"Great, you're up," she said, walking towards him. "You can help him."

Kane looked at the U-Haul. The man behind the wheel wasn't his father. "Where's Dad?"

"At the house, he ain't coming."

His mother grabbed him into a hug. He hugged her back although he really wanted to give her a good shake. The guestroom wasn't ready and the last thing he and Monifah needed was an extra person in the house when they were in the middle of an argument. His wife hadn't taken kindly to finding Carmen's check and she let him know it. "What do you mean he ain't coming?"

"I left his ass."

Kane pushed his mother away. "Wait, wait, hold up. What do you mean you left him? You didn't tell me y'all were having problems."

"I didn't have to. If I need a place to stay, I need a place to stay."

"Well, what about the renovations?" he asked.

"This is the renovation."

Kane became tongue-tied. He stared his mother down, trying to figure out what could have happened. His parents' marriage wasn't perfect, but he didn't recall them ever having a hurricane season. "You don't think y'all could've worked through it?"

"Did you work through your stuff? Shoot, where is she, anyway? I want to talk to Carmen."

"She definitely ain't here," Kane shot back. "I was talking to her on the phone when you pulled up. You could have called her. You have her number."

"She ain't going to answer if I call. You gotta call her. Get her on the phone."

"Mom, look—" Kane heard footsteps joining them outside. He already knew it was Monifah, so he didn't bother to turn around.

"Beverly," Monifah squealed. "I didn't know you were coming."

"Well, I didn't know a stranger was going to be here."

His mother's words had him stunned. She spoke to Monifah as if she didn't know her. "Don't talk to my wife like that."

"Is that what you call her?" She pointed at the U-Haul. "Help the man get my stuff in. We need to get this done. I'm hungry. You're gonna have to get me some food."

"Nothing is getting moved in until you apologize to my wife."

"I told you I wanted to talk to Carmen."

For all his life, Kane had shown his mother the upmost respect. Even when she constantly disrespected Carmen, he told her about herself in the most delicate manner he could. He refused to go through that cycle again especially when his mother was aware of Monifah's presence in his life. Now, he was going to tell her about herself like she needed to hear it. "Carmen and I aren't married anymore. Monifah is my wife. If you wanna talk to my wife, you talk to her. If not, you can get the hell on."

It took a few moments, but his mother's eyes shifted from him to Monifah. "Hello, darling, how are you doing today?" she said in an arrogant voice.

"You are something else," he mumbled. He brushed past her and headed towards the U-Haul. The driver was at the back of the truck, lifting the roll-up door. Upon joining him, he cursed once he saw what she'd pack. She called herself moving in with him, but she only brought furniture. There weren't any suitcases, duffle bags, or boxes. He addressed the driver, "This can't fit in my house. How did you get this on here?"

"One of her neighbors helped."

With an even bigger problem on his hand, Kane scratched his head. "We can't unload this here. All this stuff needs to go back to her house." Kane pulled out his phone to call his father until he heard his mother's voice.

"Where is my luggage?"

Kane ended the call and threw his hands up. "That's what I'm trying to figure out. Why did you bring this furniture when you know my guestroom is already furnished?"

"I didn't tell him to put this stuff on here," his mother yelled. "Who told you to do this?" Her attention was now on the U-Haul driver.

"Ma'am, you did. You said it all had to go. I did what you asked me to."

Beverly was now irritated. "I don't want this crap. I need my clothes."

One glance in the U-Haul driver's direction and Kane saw a man about to lose his marbles. Kane told him to give him a second and he stepped away out of earshot. He dialed his father's number. His father answered on the first ring, which was unlike him. It typically took two attempts before his father would pick up or return a call.

"I knew you would be calling," his father stated.

"I need you to tell me what's going on," Kane replied.

Arnold let out a large sigh. "Your mother is sick. I started seeing it about a year ago. I took her to a doctor, and he confirmed it. She was diagnosed with dementia. We didn't say anything because she wanted to keep it a secret. Some days, I can't control her. I told her not to take our furniture, but when she gets in her mood, she's in it. Just have the man bring the stuff back and I'll pay the neighbor to help him get it back in the house."

Tears wailed up in Kane's eyes. His mother's antics started to make sense. He now regretted what he'd said to her. *If only I had known,* he thought. He exhaled. The problem was bigger than he prepared for. His mother needed special care. He couldn't provide that to her because he had to work. She couldn't move in with him. The last thing he needed was to come home with his furniture missing because she thought she was moving out. *This will show Monifah we need the money. If Carmen gave me the money back, I would have enough to get a bigger place and pay a caretaker to see after her.*

"We're going to bring the furniture back," Kane said, finally speaking. "I'll help him get everything back in the house. Mama is going to have to stay with you, though. I don't have anyone here to watch her. I'll work on getting someone, but for right now, the safest place she can be is with you."

"I know, son. It's not a problem for me. It's just gonna be a problem for her."

"Hopefully, it won't be." Kane looked at his mother who was now in a different mood. She was all smiles, rubbing her hands over Monifah's baby bump. "Hopefully, it won't be," he repeated.

14

Carmen didn't know much about Silvas because the time they spent around each other was limited. She did know him enough to know a shopping spree at Flame wouldn't work. Silvas wasn't a suit and tuxedo kind of man. Or as he was currently telling her, "I need something I can get dirty. I cook and clean all day." They were standing in the middle of The Armoury, on the Upper East Side, and while Carmen thought the fits were perfect, Silvas saw otherwise.

"Three hundred and twenty-five dollars for some pants?" he screeched. "Even if you got it, who said you wanted to spend it?"

A slight giggle escaped her lips. "You have Jay's Black Card. You could buy New York."

Silvas picked up a pair of chinos. "These cost thirty dollars apiece at Pablo's." He held them up by the hanger, examining the quality. "This is too much money to be spending. I wear it once and it'll be covered in flour and bleach."

"Let us worry about that," Carmen suggested. She pulled her phone from her purse now hearing her ringer. When she saw Tiara's picture on the screen, she answered without hesitation. "I hope you have more good news for me."

"I don't have any news," Tiara confirmed. "Where are you? I wanted to meet up to see if we can finalize some things for the photoshoot. You did say King agreed to do it?"

"Yeah, both King and Jay did. I may need to re-confirm with my husband, though. I didn't tell you when we spoke earlier, but Jay and I had an argument last night. I haven't caught up with him to apologize."

"Well, can you do that in like the next twenty-four hours? Tabatha is ready to send out the contracts. We gotta get things booked so we can make our deadlines."

Carmen reassured her she would. "I'll do it tonight."

"Cool. Are you coming in tomorrow?"

Carmen mumbled incoherently. Normally, after the New Year, she would return to work on January 3rd. With a sex tape out, she wasn't trying to show her face anywhere near her building. "I'm playing it by ear," she told her.

"I hear ya. Well, I'll be dropping Robin off in the morning. I'll see you then."

"Sounds good," Carmen replied. They gave each other a quick goodbye before hanging up. She looked at Silvas who now had tons of chinos in his arms. He was holding the pants up one by one like he was still conducting an examination.

"Jay should send one of his men to get my things." Silvas put the chinos back on the rack. "That's what he should spend his money on. I'll write a list."

Another mumble sounded out Carmen's mouth. Her annoyance was growing. If she had known Silvas was that basic, she wouldn't have brought him all the way to NYC. Brookstone didn't have an Armoury, so she was willing to make the trip. In addition, the manager was willing to shut down the store so they could shop without interruption. "I'll take you to a thrift store."

Silvas didn't give it a thought. "He can get someone to get my things. He got me in this mess. It won't hurt him to make sure I'm comfortable." He didn't elaborate, yet he showed her he was ready to leave when he headed for the front door. Carmen followed behind him until he stopped mid-step. When he turned around, they bumped into each other. "I gotta use the restroom. I shouldn't be long. You can meet me outside."

"Will do," Carmen replied. She moved out his way but didn't immediately leave the store. Once a salesperson directed him to the restroom, she walked outside. That was a mistake because she got a quick reminder of how cold it was. About to go back inside, Cesar appeared out of nowhere. Despite being a man who couldn't draw attention to himself, he was donning a top of the line business suit.

Cesar glanced around the area before speaking. "How are you holding up?"

Carmen forgot about the cold. His words reminded her of their secret. "Each day isn't different," she began. "Each part of the day is." She looked behind her as if Silvas would appear that very moment. She spoke freely, keeping her eyes on the inside of the store. "My mother was the first person I ever met. Yet, she was the person I knew the least."

The remark didn't garner a response. She turned back around to see she was alone. She shrugged her shoulders. "Well, that's what he gets paid to do." At that very second, the door to the store opened behind her. When she saw Silvas, she understood why Cesar left. "Well, we're done here," she said to him. "How about we get a bite to eat?"

***

Jay stared at the slip of paper, which contained Carlton's number. The timing of everything made him question Carlton's intention more. It seemed odd he would pop up right when the entire world was talking about his so-called brother. "Fuck him," Jay whispered. He crumbled the paper in his hands before tossing it in a wastebasket. Currently sitting inside his office at Sapphire, he pulled out the USB drive he received from Sanders. With all that happened, he hadn't gotten a chance to look at anything on it. He stuck it inside the USB port right as Gully joined him.

"They're making progress down there," his cousin stated, plopping on the couch.

"We'll be back open on Friday."

"Have you talked to Roman and Linx?"

Jay stared his cousin down. "I was over it, came here, heard those dudes talking, and got mad again. I know they were just being men, but damn, you had to watch my wife get fucked?"

Gully shrugged his shoulders. "I ain't siding with them, but they weren't looking at it like that."

"Well, I look at it like that." Jay explored the drive's files, trying to see how things were organized. There were a ton of folders and not all of them were labeled. He opened one that contained a ton of PDF files. The files were named after his father followed by a date. He picked a random one just to get an idea of what was there. "I'm going to assume you've been talking with them," he said, continuing the conversation.

"Well," Gully stretched the word out. "Linx didn't roll with you yesterday. He ain't with us today. Roman deals with Akaila and the kids so he's straight."

"Linx still has a job if that's the concern."

"He would like to hear that from you," Gully told him.

About to give him a mouthful, Jay was silenced when his phone rung. When he looked at the screen and saw *Silvas*, he picked it up. "Hey."

Silvas was quick with his request. "Can you get one of your muscle men to get my clothes from the house?"

Jay's eyes shifted back to his laptop. A newspaper article was loading on the screen. "Why do I need to do that? I gave y'all my card to go shopping."

"I don't want that rich folks' stuff," Silvas grumbled. "You know that. You don't need to spend hundreds of dollars on some pants I'm only going to drop oil on."

"You're talking about rich folks' stuff like you're not rich. I know you're a millionaire. I saw my father's will. You only work so you can see after me." When Silvas didn't say anything, he continued. "I really didn't want anyone going in the house unless it was the contractors. If it'll make you happy, I'll do it. It just so happens, I have a man who wants an assignment."

Jay looked at Gully. His cousin gave him a half smile.

"Who told you to count my coins?" Silvas joked, responding to Jay's previous comment. "I'm texting you a list. Oh, Carmen and I will be home later. We're on our way to Cipriani's for lunch."

"Y'all eating good. When is she going to call me?"

"That's not a question I can answer. Do you want me to hand her the phone?"

Jay declined. "I'm not going to force the apology. I'll see her when I get to the house." Silvas made small talk for another minute or so before saying goodbye. When they hung up with one another, Jay gave Gully the task of reaching out to Linx and Roman. "Roman can fly Linx to the house. Go ahead and give them the heads up. Once Silvas sends me the list, I'll text it to 'em. They need to get his stuff and come straight back."

His attention went back to his laptop while Gully made the necessary calls. The article on the screen had the headline: *Drugs, Power, Politics, and the State of New York*. He read the first three words before closing the file. The last thing he needed to be doing was diving in his father's Triad file. His time could be better spent with his kids. "Let's go, man," he said, shutting down the laptop. "They got everything covered here." He stood up from his seat, noticing Gully hadn't responded. Earbuds impaired his hearing. Jay picked up a box of Kleenex and tossed it in his direction. It did the trick. "I'm ready to go. What are you watching?"

"It's nothing. Where do you want to head next?"

Jay narrowed his eyes though it would take more than that to intimidate his cousin. They were built the same. "Why can't you tell me?" When his cousin sighed, Jay knew it wasn't good. He saw for himself when his cousin set his phone in front of him. He rewound the video and pressed play. For twelve or so straight minutes, he listened as one of the country's biggest bloggers went in on Carmen's sex tape. He praised both her and Carlos' skills, but it was what he said about him that stuck.

"This is a woman who married a billionaire," the blogger ranted. "She got billionaire dick in her house. The dick can't be that good, she had to go fuck his best friend. Y'all know he was out there selling dope all up and down the East Coast. He gave her that crack dick. I'm sorry, you can't tell me his Dominican-looking ass spent seventeen years in prison and didn't suck any dick. I bet he had 'em lined up outside his cell. He probably was just fuckin' and suckin', fuckin' and suckin'."

Jay pressed pause. He heard all he needed to hear. "We can get this one."

***

Cipriani's looked busier than usual. Most of its guests opted to eat inside although the eatery had heated outside dining. Carmen couldn't blame them as she had chosen to eat in as well. She wanted Silvas to be as comfortable as possible. She had never known him to visit Brookstone, which was why she wanted the city to make a good impression. "So, what do you think?"

"This fancy stuff isn't for me. Give me a good fish and farmers' market and I'm happy."

"A simple guy," Carmen added. "Is that why you hardly visit?"

"I never had to come to Brookstone when Jay's parents were alive. They were in San Juan so much, by the time they would leave, I'd be preparing for their arrival." Silvas took a sip of his water. "There was a time I could've came. Perhaps, I should've." He sighed. "I couldn't see Jay like that. I know I'm not his father, but I raised him, too. I was only twenty-two when I came to work for the Santiagos. I watched Jay grow up. I couldn't see him in prison."

The sadness in his voice struck a chord with Carmen. While he'd always been pleasant with her, a part of her wanted to know what he thought about her. *Does Silvas blame me for Jay's imprisonment? How did he feel about my marriage to Kane?* About to ask, Carmen was silenced at the sound of her ringer. When she saw *Kristian* on the screen, she grabbed her phone. None of her kids had spoken to her since the tape leaked. From what Kane told her, they were all uncomfortable.

"Baby," she greeted. "I miss you."

"Hey, Mom," Kristian replied.

Her voice held a hint of nervousness. Carmen wasn't surprised. She was nervous as well. Their relationship hadn't been the best in the last few years so there was a chance the sex tape had set them back. "I know you have a lot of questions. If you're ready to talk, I'm here."

"I don't even know if the questions are appropriate."

"Any question is appropriate. One of the worst moments of my life is now on a platter for public consumption. The least I could do is be open with my children."

"I appreciate it," Kristian replied. "I'm not ready to talk about it, but I wanted to reach out." There was a bit of a pause as if she were hyping herself up to say something. "I talked to Daddy, and I made the decision to move back in with you."

The news almost made Carmen drop the phone. She wanted her daughter home with her. They could repair their relationship. "I would love that. You didn't have to tell me. Just come home."

"I felt like I needed to say something. I didn't want to just show up. Besides, Daddy's space is about to be limited so it seems like the right thing to do. I moved in with him because we were both going through a hard time. Now that we're better, I feel like it's time for me to move back. Plus, I know you need me."

A tear fell down Carmen's face. "I do need you, baby. I know…" Carmen's voice trailed off. "I know I haven't always been the best mother. I know I said some cruel things and I'm sorry. I love you. I want us to get back where we were. We were always glued at the hip. You were my broke best friend." Her words got a huge laugh out her daughter.

"That, I still am," Kristian said, still laughing. "I do want to take you to dinner."

"All I need is the date and time."

"I'll send some dates your way. Or do I need to go through Cathy?" Kristian joked.

"Chile, I haven't seen Cathy. I'm just paying her."

The two shared another laugh. Kristian followed it up with another reminder she would text her with dinner plans. The call ended right as the waitress approached their table with their meals. With two large entrees in front of them, there was little time for conversation. It wasn't until their plates were empty any conversation started. Nevertheless, it didn't occur between them.

Carmen was wiping her mouth when she noticed the hostess directing Kane and Beverly to a table. She wasn't shocked to see Kane, but his mother was a different story. "My ex just walked in with his mother," she told Silvas. "She hates me. If they come this way, trust and believe, she's going to say something nasty."

"I will kindly let you have the drama."

Carmen looked back in their direction only to meet eyes with Kane. He mouthed an apology as he and his mother made their way to their table. Carmen told herself to remain calm although she knew the fire Beverly was going to bring. She saw the smoke already coming from the woman's shoulders.

"Ooh, look at how God works," Beverly gushed. "I told Michael I wanted to talk to you."

"I bet you did," Carmen replied. The words came out cold, so she gave her one of her warmest smiles. "How have you been?" Her eyes grew big as Beverly pulled out a chair and sat down. Kane remained standing as if he didn't expect to be there long.

"You don't mind if we join you?" Beverly asked. "We need to catch up."

"Well, we're actually finishing *up*," Carmen retorted.

"Oh, you can stay awhile." Beverly pointed at another chair and told Kane to sit down. "I got myself in a little bit of a pickle today. I came all the way down here to move in with my son and didn't bring one ounce of luggage. He had to take me all the way back home."

Carmen shifted her gaze to Kane. When he shook his head at her, she knew there was more to the story. "So, you went home and now you're back?"

"I'm gonna stay with him for a few days."

A single head nod was all Carmen gave. The Lord was on her side if she only had this one opportunity to deal with Kane's mother.

"There's a…" Beverly didn't finish as their waitress approached the table. After drink orders were taken, Beverly continued. "You look beautiful. Motherhood has served you well."

Carmen's eyes went back to Kane. His mother had never told her she was beautiful. If she remembered correctly, she would call Kristian beautiful, but would always follow it up saying, "She gets her looks from our side of the family."

"Oh, don't look at him. He knows I think you're beautiful," Beverly said with a smile. As quickly as it had come, it disappeared. "I know you think I hate you," Beverly continued. "I can understand why, too." Her whole demeanor was changing. The playfulness was gone. "I treated you like I hated you. I made you feel less than."

"Excuse me," Silvas said, rising from his seat. "I'll be in the restroom."

His words echoed in Carmen's ears. *I will kindly let you have the drama.*

"I didn't think you were the best fit for my son," Beverly explained. "I didn't understand why he would want a woman who was carrying another man's child. There were so many other black women out there. I felt like he was selling himself short." She stopped to catch her breath. "I didn't hate you. I only wanted more for my son. Well, I hated you when I saw how happy you were making him. Year after year, you proved me wrong. Oh, why did you do that?" A fresh smile emerged on Beverly's face. "I saw firsthand what a good wife and mother you were. You took such good care of the kids." Beverly grabbed her hands. "I was mad at you because I didn't want to be wrong. I can admit now I was."

Beverly's grip kept Carmen from wiping her tears. Right there, in the middle of the restaurant, she was bawling. It was because her words mimicked what she read in her mother's journal. Her mother loved and despised her all at the same time.

"You slipped up," Beverly was now saying. "I hated seeing my son in pain, but I felt like your wrongdoings put me back in the lead. I could go back to telling him I told you so."

"I'm sorry for all that," Carmen cried. "I'll apologize every day if I have to."

"I don't need the apology. I only need you to accept mine."

When Beverly squeezed her hands, Carmen knew all was well between them. All the cold stares, side comments, disrespect, she would let go. Beverly was willing to put the past behind them, so she could to. "I made a lot of mistakes with you, Carm," Beverly said. She squeezed her hands again. "I don't want to make any more." She used her free hand to touch the side of Kane's face. "I need my family right now," she continued. "I've been diagnosed with dementia."

Carmen's mouth dropped open.

"Sometimes I have it together, sometimes, I don't," Beverly explained.

This time, Carmen broke the hold. "I'm sorry to hear that. Is there a treatment plan? Can it be treated? I'm sorry, I don't know much about this disease."

"I got a few prescriptions that's supposed to help with the symptoms. There's no cure, so I've accepted what's to come."

Carmen placed her hand over Kane's. She did it to remind him she was there. He acted as if he was holding it together, but she knew he was breaking. He would never let his mother see, yet when they met eyes, she could see his vulnerability.

"Before she goes back to Manhattan," Kane began, "we're gonna start looking for a part-time caregiver. Someone who has experience working with dementia patients." He looked at his mother before meeting eyes with Carmen again. "We might need some help there."

Carmen knew what those words meant. *They might need some financial help.* She nodded her head although she couldn't give him a single penny unless she ran it by Jay. Not only that, Kane also needed to run it by Monifah. He was in just as much trouble as she was. Regardless of their spouses, they would find a way to make it work. His mother's care and well-being depended on it.

***

That's all y'all want to do is kill.

Cesar's words played repeatedly in Jay's head like a broken record. The longer he heard it, the longer he paced the floor of his bedroom. *That's all y'all Santiagos want to do. They bred y'all for this shit.* The statements were made because Cesar heard their entire plan to take out the blogger through Gully's earpiece. The levelheaded one, Cesar pulled up right when they were about to walk inside the building where the podcast was taped.

"You're not thinking of your kids," Cesar shouted at him. "You're not thinking of your soul." A quick, painless, punch in the chest came right after that. "You know he has kids," he yelled, now directing his frustration at Gully. "You want to see him locked up again?"

His right-hand made him think about things, but Cesar didn't take away his thirst for blood. The desire was still there, raging through his veins. Jay struggled to control it. It's the reason he came home. He needed to see his children's faces. He needed to feel their hugs and kisses. They would calm the monster. Unfortunately, Akaila had taken them to the Children's Museum in New York City. He returned home to an empty house, which is how he learned Carmen and Silvas were still out.

"You need to get yourself together," Cesar told him when he was in his limo. "That blogger ain't the only one out here talkin'. You can't kill 'em all."

I can't, Jay had thought. *I only want to kill one and you ain't letting me do that.*

He hadn't stopped pacing. He didn't know if he would until his eyes fell upon the bed he shared with Carmen. The answer was right there in the sheets. Sex was his release. While they were still on the outs, Silvas told him an apology was coming. He needed it, plus more. If they were making up, he knew Carmen wouldn't turn him down. She would give him whatever he asked for. They could relive their honeymoon in Saint Lucia.

The fantasy of sexing his wife was enough to tame the beast. Until it could be caged, he needed to get out of New York. All that cost him was one phone call. An hour later, he was joining Linx and Roman on his private plane to San Juan.

15

Carmen heard Jay's footsteps before she saw his face. She had been waiting up for hours. While she could've called him, she didn't want to start the discussion over the phone. Therefore, to occupy herself, she pulled out her bible, picked a random scripture in Jeremiah, and started reading. She was almost finished with the book when he walked inside. Ready to have the conversation, she closed her bible so he would know he had her full attention. The move was pointless because he ignored her all together. He went straight to the bathroom like she wasn't even there. Minutes later, she heard the shower. *Is he stalling?* He knew they had unfinished business.

When he finally emerged, her bible had been replaced with her cell phone. She was browsing Flame's Instagram page, reading some of the feedback regarding the additions to the *Peaches* collection. She looked up from her phone to see him at the foot of the bed. A towel was draped around his waist and his eyes were on hers. It was a clear sign he was ready to talk.

She set her phone beside her on the bed. "I know you've been waiting on this all day," she told him. "I made a huge mistake in what I said to you." She pulled the covers back. "I was wrong. I should've never blamed you for the tape being leaked. I'm sorry. I want you to accept my apology."

To keep the conversation going, she mentioned other things they needed to discuss. "I started the process of changing my name. There's like a hundred things I gotta change it on. I also set up a meeting with Clement so I can update my will."

Jay didn't respond though he moved from the foot of the bed. She could tell he had plans to join her when he went to his side.

"I know the whole 'my money' thing really bothered you. So, I want us to get some joint accounts. That way, you can see every dollar I'm bringing in and taking out. Also, all our household bills can come out one account."

"We'll do it tomorrow," he said, finally speaking.

Carmen stared him down confused why he hadn't addressed her apology. The argument over money seemed miniscule compared to the one over the sex tape. "Kane needs our help," she shared, changing the subject. "His mother came in town today. She has dementia."

"Is that your way of telling me you met with Kane?"

Carmen sucked her teeth. She was trying to keep things on a level ground. "I didn't meet with him. Silvas and I went to Cipriani's, as you know, and he showed up with his mother."

"You're not giving him two million dollars. Let me make that clear," Jay stressed. "I found out why you gave him the money. Lucky for me, Kristian talks to Akaila, Akaila talks to Roman, and he talks to me. Your budget is seven hundred thousand. The house better not cost over five hundred. He doesn't need any more than five or six bedrooms anyway. Buy the house and put it in our names. You can give him the rest as a gift."

Carmen gulped. "How long did it take you to come up with that?"

"Just now."

Jay walked away from the bed. He went in the bathroom and when he emerged, his phone was in his hand.

"I'm sorry," she repeated. He heard her the first time, yet she still deserved a decent response. "I'm sorry for what I did with Carlos, the lying, the sneaking around, all of it. I want to be a good wife to you although I was a fucked up girlfriend."

"I want my name on the house," he said, overlooking her comment.

The request caught her off guard. "You want what?"

"Shit may hit the fan. I don't want you kicking me out."

Carmen made another suggestion. "Let's do a post-nuptial agreement."

"Why do we need that when we didn't do a pre-nup? I want my name on the house."

The ask was a bit much considering he lied about previously owning the property. He also was supposed to be building them a new home. She figured he considered all that and still wanted his name on the estate. Nevertheless, the ask was small if they were putting their money together. He *was* giving her access to his billion dollar fortune. "If that's what you want, I'll do it."

His eyes were on his phone though his mind was on her. "You're not the breadwinner anymore. I can take care of us. We can get the joint accounts, but if you want to keep your money, do it. You can spend mine. Save yours and we'll have it if there's a rainy day."

"You don't have to say that twice." Carmen picked up her phone and set it on her bedside dresser. His eyes were still on his cell, but when she removed her cami, she figured she would make that change. She crawled towards him, hoping her bare chest would make him put the phone away. He set it on his dresser, but without a glance in her direction. "I'm sorry," she told him, grabbing the top of his towel. His eyes traveled where she wanted them.

He outlined her body, a smile emerging to show his admiration. "You like it?" she asked him. His smile got bigger. "Can I kiss it?"

She pulled the towel from around his waist, freeing his manhood from captivity. She needed to make up for lost time. She also needed to remind him of how they were each other's weakness. To their benefit, both occurred. She started out slow, with soft kisses at the tip to get a small rise. Her tongue then licked the bottom of his shaft. She stayed there for a bit, licking him like an ice cream cone. When his fingers slid in her hair, she knew she had him. Full suck mode was activated.

She took as much of him as she could, drenching his dick in her saliva until he pulled it from her mouth. Jay refused to waste his sperm. The only time he ever came in her mouth was if she was already pregnant. If she wasn't, he wasn't cumming unless it was inside her walls. When he made her stop, she knew where they were headed next. She laid on her back and invited him inside.

Jay stared at the pre-cum on her mouth. He'd left his mark, but it wasn't there long. To his enjoyment, he watched as she licked her lips. The move made him lick his as well. Her juices weren't there, but it was on the horizon. He glided his finger up her inner thigh until he reached the lips of her peach. Her panties were still on, so he teased her until her whimpers of pleasure enticed him to remove them. He went further, plunging his fingers inside her yummy while the tip of his index finger touched her pearl. Perfect strokes forced her eyes closed while his licks along her love bud forced her legs over his shoulders.

An act that wasn't new for them, he hadn't routinely started tasting her until their honeymoon. In Saint Lucia, the act was like a daily chore he craved. She didn't have to ask, and he didn't have to offer. He would simply get to work until her body shook with pleasure and he sucked up every drop. Even now, out the corner of his eye, he could see her hands gripping the sheets. She couldn't handle the explosion that was rupturing between her legs. He didn't want her to. He wanted her to break. He needed it. It was like a trophy. A confirmation he exceeded all expectations. Determined to get it, he put intense pressure on her jewel. He ignored the pulsating of his own love muscle as his tongue ran a marathon. Seconds later, he got what he wanted. A shrill cry in his ear and warm liquid in his mouth stamped her first orgasm. He didn't let it slow him. His tongue kept its pace until her legs fell from his shoulders.

Although Carmen was feeling the effects of their tryst, he was ready for the tables to turn. He took full advantage of her lubricated walls. The second he felt her warmth, his dick reacted. He plunged deep inside her, thrusting his erection against her clit. He rocked her like a ship in the worst recorded hurricane. She tried to throw it back, but she couldn't match his speed or momentum. He overpowered her. If anything, he was brutal and relentless.

Time passed. Still, he couldn't let up. With every thrust, the adrenaline was unleashed. With every stroke, the thirst to kill was quenched. Still, he would find more in his veins. Then, he thought she had him. His jewels had been repeatedly smashed against her ass and were wet from her juices. The second she massaged them, he almost lost control. He gathered himself only for her to fall victim. *That's what you get*, he thought. *That was number two*. She squirmed underneath him, but he maintained full velocity.

Nevertheless, it was getting harder to do. He had flipped her over and was penetrating her from behind. She muffled her screams with pillows while he buried his face in her back to censor his. Her pussy was contracting against his dick, yet he still needed more. In one quick move, he slid himself out of her and into her other hole. She wasn't expecting it, which he learned when she shrieked from the pain. He didn't stay there long, giving her only a few short strokes before flipping her back over. He entered her again as his lips smashed against hers. Minutes felt like years as he pounded her. When she came a third time, he let go. His body collapsed on hers, his seed spilling in the place where they connected best.

He pulled out in a matter of seconds. Not a usual move of his, he felt her apprehension when he climbed off her. Her eyes followed him, wondering what he was doing. When he grabbed his phone, he figured that was all she needed to see. Her eyes closed, his dick game putting her right to sleep.

16

Jay's eyes snapped open as the volume in the house increased. He was awake, but his mind was in a state of euphoria. It took a few seconds before his brain registered who was arguing. When he heard Silvas switch from Spanish to German, he threw the covers back. His sudden movement woke Carmen who was now trying to figure out what was going on.

"I thought Fiona was off," he yelled.

"She is." Carmen yawned. "I don't know why she's here. What are they fussing about?"

Jay tried to catch what he could of the argument. "I'm struggling to translate." He looked at Carmen whose eyes were closing back. "You're gonna make me deal with this?"

"No habla español."

Jay squeezed her breast, which sent her eyes back open. "Fiona works for you."

Carmen rolled over. "Nope, we made an agreement last night. She works for you. You're the one who's gonna be paying her." Her words forced Jay to cup her breast. This time, he used it to pull her towards him.

"You're a fuckin' smart ass," he chuckled, kissing her cheek. "No habla español, eh?"

A small giggle escaped Carmen's lips. "No, hoy, no." There was no response as his lips were now centered on her right nipple. He sucked it for a bit until Silvas and Fiona's voices elevated to an even higher level. The bickering sent Jay running in their closet for a robe.

He didn't bother to wash his face or brush his teeth. He realized the error once his feet hit the foyer. Silvas and Fiona were still going at it despite the ringing doorbell. Without looking through the peephole, Jay knew who it was. There was only one person on their property at that hour without a key. Besides, if someone made it that far, they were supposed to be there.

"Oh wow," Tiara shouted once he opened the door. "Should I even leave her?"

"I was getting ready to take care of that."

Jay moved out the doorway to allow her to come in. He rushed to the kitchen. Silvas and Fiona were an inch apart, their index fingers pointed in each other's faces. He had caught enough to know they were arguing over Silvas being there.

"He'll make you get out my kitchen," Fiona shouted. "You don't live here."

"No, I won't," Jay bellowed. "I want to know why you're here."

"I missed my babies. I wanted to make them breakfast."

"I'm making breakfast," Silvas yelled. "You don't know how to make revoltillo."

"I can make revoltillo," Fiona screamed even louder. "I've been making it for years."

"Hold up," Jay shouted, quieting them. "Fiona," he turned to her, "you're not supposed to be here. Silvas is here because we had an incident at my house. He's going to be here for a while. Breakfast is on him."

His words sent Silvas back to the island. Jay saw out his peripheral as his butler resumed cutting vegetables. "You were given time off so you could rest. You watched the kids twenty-four seven while we were gone."

"I did rest," Fiona fired back. "Now I'm home. I live here, too. I have a room."

A part of him wanted to get in the gutter with her. The only reason he didn't is because he wanted to respect his elders. "It doesn't work like that," came out instead. Fiona started digging through her purse. "I know this is your second home. If you want to stay, you can take lunch. Y'all can cook dinner together." A utility knife hit the cutting board. His butler wasn't happy with that arrangement. His reaction made Jay add another one. "Teach her how to make your revoltillo. She's gotta make it once you leave." That request irritated Silvas even more. His butler picked up the knife and pointed it in Jay's direction. Jay was about to tell him about himself until he saw what Fiona had been searching for.

"He was at the big gate. He knew who I was."

He stared at the crumpled piece of paper with Carlton's contact information. *This motherfucker knows where I live. Shit, everyone knows where I live. It ain't a secret.* He thanked Fiona for the information, but once he was out the kitchen, he crumbled Carlton's number in his hand. With all he had going on, he wanted to forget about him. For some reason, he kept popping up. He had gone through Tiara first, only to now end up outside their gated community. *Speaking of Tiara,* he thought as he entered the foyer. She was sitting on the steps with Robin, who was now awake in her arms. "I'm sorry if we woke her."

"Hey, as long as breakfast isn't on the walls, we're good." Tiara stood on her feet.

"Thankfully, it's not. I didn't even need this on my plate."

"And as the Vice President of Flame, I'm going to add to it. Did Carmen talk to you about the photoshoot?"

Jay gave her a devious smile. "Nah, I had her mouth occupied."

Tiara showed a hint of annoyance. "Um, my baby is right here."

"My bad," Jay apologized. "Hey, little Miss Robin." He grabbed the little girl's hand and gave it a soft shake. He then looked at Tiara. "What's going on with the shoot?"

"I want to make sure you're still doing it."

"You have my word," Jay vowed.

"I'll take that, but I really need your signature on a contract. Hopefully, Carmen won't forget to give it to you."

"You know we have a lot going on."

"Y'all always have a lot going on." Tiara set Robin on her feet and grabbed her hand. "I gotta get to the office. One of us gotta work. Tell Carmen to call me once she gets up." Tiara headed towards the dining room.

Shit, it ain't like you had a sex tape dropped on you. He shook his head until he remembered she did. She had to deal with Carlos' betrayal as well. More than likely, she was feeling the same effects of the tape. Sure of it, he dismissed his thought. He headed upstairs with the intention of giving Carmen the message, yet he found her asleep. She wasn't that way for long, though. The second his lips hit her nipple; she was stirring.

"You should've done that last night."

Jay kept at it until it led them to a short round. They were passed out asleep until three giggling voices woke them from their slumber. Nowhere near presentable, they worked double-time getting the sheets and covers changed. They shared a shower and once dressed, headed downstairs for breakfast.

Most of the day was spent with the kids. The only time they stole away was to visit Clement's office and to open their joint accounts at the bank. When they returned home, Tiara was in the kitchen, packing Robin's things.

"The day flew by," Jay told her joining her inside.

"Tell me about it," Tiara agreed. "I feel like I was just dropping her off."

He stared at the island where either Fiona or Silvas had started prepping dinner. "Why don't you and Malik join us?" He took out his phone to send his former right-hand the invite.

"I would love to, but we're having dinner at an exec's house. Give us a rain check."

"Will do," Jay replied. He was about to excuse himself, until out of nowhere, the kitchen became mayhem. A series of high-pitched screams filled the room as Fiona burst through the door. She ran through the kitchen, screaming at the top of her lungs. Nyla was right behind her. He dropped his phone on the counter so he could scoop her up. She was quick so his hands caught Robin who was on her tail. He handed her to Tiara just as Rakim came running through the kitchen. The only one not screaming, he realized why when he noticed something furry in his son's hands.

Rakim wasn't as quick. Jay snatched him up and carried him out the kitchen. Fiona and Nyla were running through the foyer as if Rakim was still behind them. "I got him," he yelled. They stopped in their tracks as he carried Rakim outside. "What are you doing?" He held him in mid-air, trying to figure out what he was holding. "What is that?" he said, shaking him. His son's hands were wrapped so tightly around it, he couldn't tell if he had caught a mouse or a squirrel. Too busy laughing, Rakim couldn't answer him. "Did you kill it?" Jay held him in place to see if the animal was moving. When he noticed it wasn't, he set him on his feet.

He stared at his son, but he didn't truly see him. He saw himself. He saw signs of the man he didn't want Rakim to become. A flashback played in his mind of the first animal he killed. While killing Gully's dog was an accident, it cost him his relationship with his cousin. His killing spree only got worse. He remembered his first victim. Images of various bodies appeared in his mind like one long reel. At the time, he thought death was a better punishment than prison.

He stooped so he was eye level with his son. Rakim's grasp was still tight around the animal like he was choking it. His laughter had disappeared. "Look at me," Jay said. He pulled him towards him. "You can't be like me." He wrapped his hands around his. "You hear me?" Rakim appeared confused. "We're not born to be killers."

Now arose an image of Carlos. He saw him sexing his wife. Tears streamed down his eyes. He was now seeing his bare knuckles as Carlos was bludgeoned. "You have to be better than Daddy."

Rakim opened his hands. A dead chipmunk was inside. "I didn't mean to," his son whimpered. "It was trying to get away."

Jay wrapped his hands around his son's. "Remember when we talked about creation?" Rakim nodded his head. "God made this." Jay could tell his son was feeling the guilt when Rakim's hazel eyes watered. "This isn't an animal we kill for food. We can't harm God's creatures. If we do, we have to apologize and ask for forgiveness." He took his fingers and wiped his son's tears. "You want to bury it?" Rakim nodded his head again. "Okay. I'll let you pick out a space in the garden. We need somethin' to put him in." He needed to take Rakim inside, but he didn't want Fiona and the girls running scared. Just his luck, Carmen was standing behind him. She handed him a box.

He mouthed *thank you*. She gave him a small smile before venturing back inside. Hand in hand with Rakim, he walked towards the garden. By the time the chipmunk was buried, Tiara and Robin were gone.

The rest of the evening went as normal and around nine o'clock, Jay was helping Rakim in bed. He and Carmen would take turns tucking the kids in while some nights they did it together. He was constantly in his son's room, so he didn't know why he never noticed the photos underneath his pillow. Most of the images were of Rakim with his siblings. One photo was not. The photo was a few years old while the wound was still fresh. He stared at the image of Rakim with Kane. If he didn't have two blood tests to prove paternity, he would've thought his son was his. They both shared a deep mahogany complexion, which matched Carmen's, but not his. Why Rakim had the photo, he didn't know. He only knew his son would never see it again.

Jay slid the rest of the photos back where his son had them. The other one he crumpled in his hand. After turning out the lights, he headed to his bedroom. Carmen was in bed with her phone to her ear. He threw the picture in a waste basket right as her conversation caught his attention.

"That's not possible," she was saying. "We never made a tape." Something had changed the mood. "I hear what you're saying, but it doesn't make sense. Look, just screenshot me the messages. I'll contact him." Carmen hung up the phone. Her eyes went to him. "That was my publicist. She got an email from the owner of *Culture XL*."

Jay moved closer to the bed. Culture XL was the blogger he and Gully were going to take out. Carmen was about to give him another reason to go after him.

"He got a tip that I have another sex tape. This time, you're in it."

Jay's forehead furrowed. "He ain't got a tape of us."

A new tear started to run down Carmen's face. "That's what I was trying to tell her. We never made a tape. He told her he was waiting to get the footage. When he does, he's running the story in the morning."

"Doesn't he know we can sue him? We didn't authorize that."

"He's not putting out the tape. He's putting out the story that the tape exists," Carmen clarified. "He knows we can sue him. He has something to lose."

"Me and Gully were gonna kill him today. He said some shit about me on his podcast. Cesar stopped us before we got inside."

"That's disturbing." Carmen shifted her frame in the bed. "Real talk, I don't care about your murder plot. We gotta figure out who taped us." Carmen looked at her phone as she received a text alert. She read the screenshot of the messages, which corroborated her publicist's story. "Where are all the places we've had sex?"

"No one taped us."

"Your office," she told him, her eyes now on his. "Is there a camera in there?"

"Not in the office. There are security cameras in the hallway and downstairs, but none of 'em point to the office."

"Your car," she stated. "We did it there once. Remember?"

"We were supposed to be in the restaurant," he argued. "No one cares about us enough to tape us."

"The boat," she continued. "We did it there when we were sailing to Saint Lucia."

"No one taped us, Carm. There isn't a tape."

Carmen racked her brain. "What if someone taped us when we were in Saint Lucia?"

Jay sat on the bed. "I recently found this out. There were security cameras which faced the entrances. Cesar had men in another villa watching the cameras to make sure no one entered. He made sure we had our privacy. None of the cameras faced the pool or any of the windows in the house." He took her hands in his. "This is a hoax. No one taped us."

Carmen took her hands from his. "If he contacted my publicist, he's not bullshittin'."

"This is bullshit," Jay corrected, his anger rising. "Ain't no fuckin' way they got a tape of us. I don't care if it's from twenty years ago. There isn't a tape."

"He is breaking the story tomorrow," Carmen whispered. "The video isn't going to be that far behind. If that video comes out, everything I worked for is going down the drain." She asked the question again, "Where else have we had sex?" She saw a hint of vulnerability in Jay's eyes. As quickly as it had come, it disappeared. "Your penthouse," she voiced. "My apartment."

"You know there weren't any cameras there."

"Kane was in the closet."

She finally said something that made sense. Jay grabbed her hands and placed kisses on both. "That may be the best guess." He kissed her hands again. "I don't put shit past him." Another round of kisses followed. "Promise me," he demanded, "that if he did this, you'll let me put him down."

The second the words came out, he wished he hadn't said it. The look on her face told him that plan wasn't going to fly. If anything, *he* was about to be put down.

"I heard what you said to Rakim. You don't want him to be you, but *you* still want to be you." She broke his hold. "I would never promise you that. I don't care if he released fifty tapes. Prison separated us because of a murder. It won't take another second."

17

Despite the long flight of steps ahead of him, Kane used the stairwell to reach the executive floor of Flame. He had too much rage to be stuck on an elevator. He needed to move. He needed to push out the anger, the embarrassment, and the jealousy, which consumed him. It couldn't be done standing in one place. He would only be hoarding emotions until he met his target.

When he reached the executive floor, his aggression was full-blown. The door slammed against the wall when he opened it, catching the attention of those in the hallway. They stared at him as he passed, but no one addressed him. He wouldn't have listened anyway. He had enough fury to commit twenty murders. There was only one person he wanted to hear from. Tiara wasn't that person, but he stepped in her doorway when he saw her door was open. She wasn't inside, which made him shoot a glance in Jessica's direction.

"She's in the conference room down the hall. There was an emergency board meeting."

Say less. Kane walked behind Jessica's desk. The door to Carmen's office was closed, but he didn't care. He knew she was back at work when he saw her that morning getting out her limo. That was an hour before one of the security personnel on his team approached him. Also, before he got a three-way call from King and Malachi.

He twisted the doorknob to her office and let himself in. She was where he expected her to be. He slammed his phone on her desk. "What the fuck is this?" he spat. His words shot out like daggers. "What is this shit?" He stepped away from the desk to keep from grabbing her neck. "Another fuckin' tape?"

His vision was blurred. She was sitting in front of him, but he couldn't see her. The anger blinded him. "We got fuckin' kids, yo. Like what the fuck are you doing?" He paced the floor, unable to remain still, as everything inside of him went haywire. He didn't get it. *How could she let this happen again?* His eyes landed on his phone. The video was playing on mute. At the sight of Jay's head between her thighs, he threw his phone at the window.

They hadn't even found out how Lucid got the first tape and a second one had emerged. It wasn't even the entire footage. According to the porn site, it was a twenty minute preview of a three-hour video. "What is this fuckin' shit, Carm? What is this?" The anger was turning to tears.

"You haven't even looked at me," he heard her say.

She was right. He hadn't. He couldn't. It hurt too much. It wasn't the first time he'd seen her and Jay in the act. He caught them having sex before. However, the world didn't have a front seat. This time, everyone was watching with him. They just didn't see his pain.

"Look at me," she ordered.

Kane couldn't do it. If he did, he would hurt her. He never thought she put out the tape with Carlos, but when it came to the new tape, she and Jay were his top suspects. "Our kids gotta see this shit. You're their fuckin' mother." His eyes were on a random spot on the wall. "I want to take your fuckin' head off."

"Look at me," she repeated.

Kane shook his head. Although he refused, he looked in her direction. His heart stopped. The strength he used to see behind her eyes was gone. She looked lifeless. The woman in front of him was broken.

"M-M-Malachi refuses to sp-speak to me." She struggled to get the words out. "K-K-King said he can't get him to go back to school. I, I, I lost a contract I waited years to get. My board is meeting right now to suspend me. Before you walked in, Kr-Kr-Kristian texted me. She's not moving back in."

"Why did you make a tape?"

"I didn't make a tape."

He asked her one more time.

"I didn't make a fuckin' tape," she yelled. "I made love to my husband."

The word husband set him ablaze. He grabbed her laptop and threw it to the floor. He told her on countless occasions that Jay's release from prison was the worst thing that happened to them. There had been nothing but constant problems, threats, and murders. "He did this. Can't you see that?" He could tell she didn't want to believe it at how she shook her head. "I know that room. That used to be our bedroom. Look at the angle. The camera had to be on the wall next to the balcony." He rushed to the window and grabbed his phone from the floor. The video was still playing. He shoved it in her face. She pushed the phone away from her.

"We don't have a camera in our bedroom."

"What do you mean you don't have a camera?" He punched the phone. "What the hell do you think I'm watching?"

"I never saw a camera."

Kane turned the video off. "You're as psychotic as your fuckin' husband. You can't tell me you didn't see a fuckin' camera when you're fuckin' on a camera."

"There was no camera," Carmen screamed.

Kane paced the floor. What she said didn't make sense. *Or was he paranoid?* He knew the latter wasn't it. She was paranoid. She was paranoid and in denial. "It's time," he told her. He looked at her, noticing the fresh tears running down her face. "It's time," he repeated. "You need to file for an annulment." Her face read disapproval. "Or you need to file for divorce. You can't stay with this bastard." She pushed her seat away from her desk as if she were going to get up. "I thought you were over him after he beat you up. I thought you were gonna let him go when Kristian got raped. I thought it would happen when you found out about the house. You didn't. It's like you just won't fuckin' let go."

"We found out about the tape last night," Carmen shared. "Jay didn't think it existed. I don't know what happened. It doesn't make sense."

"What you mean you don't know? You know he did this shit, Carm."

"What they have is from the night before last. Whoever did it was in our house. They were in our bedroom."

When he saw her body drop to the floor, he raced around the desk. He pulled her in his arms. He held her to his chest as she wailed. "He is stripping you of everything. You're losing your kids. Your job is on the line. Your life was never like this until he came. He's never protected you." He closed his eyes at the sound of her tears. He knew she was mourning her marriage. He needed her to grieve. He wanted her to go through all the emotions so she could get out of hell. His comfort worked because minutes later she asked for his help. If there was a camera in her bedroom, she wanted to find it.

***

The door slammed behind her as Tiara fled from the conference room. Fresh tears streamed down her face. The vote was done. Carmen was out. The words didn't even sound believable. At the previous meeting, everyone talked about how Flame's upcoming plans couldn't be accomplished without her. Their publicist said the sex tape was being flagged and deleted. The nightmare seemed fleeting. Overnight things changed. Meetings were canceled. An emergency board meeting was called. Every single person, but her, voted for a one-year suspension. Minutes later, Tabitha called for Jay to be fired from the anniversary campaign. His contract was signed the evening before. The board agreed without a vote. Not even a second later, Tabitha pitched the idea of the campaign being centered around King and his son.

"This isn't all bad," she heard Jerry say. "You're finally president."

"Get out," Tiara yelled. She stared through her tears at him. He looked as if he didn't understand. "Get out," she repeated. "Get out." The words were enough to make him leave. She plopped down in her chair. As if she needed extra noise, her office phone started to ring. She picked it up and immediately hung up. She broke down even further hearing the silence. Her phone rung a second time. She did the same thing again not wanting to speak to anyone. However, when it rung a third time, she answered.

"Is this a bad time?" a voice said.

Tiara checked the caller ID. The phone number showed as Private. "I'm sorry," she muttered. "Who am I speaking with?"

"Carlton Rodriguez," the person replied. "Remember me?"

Tiara almost dropped the phone. His timing was horrible. "I do. How can I help you?"

"I haven't heard from Jay. You did give him my number, didn't you?"

"I did," she replied. "He'll call you when he's ready."

"Well, can you tell him to give me a call?"

Tiara cursed. *This shit isn't important. Why do you even care? Leave his ass alone and live your life.* She slammed the phone down. *I can't tell Carmen this. I can't.* She had to, though. As the new interim President, she had to facilitate the meeting with the board and Carmen. She would have to tell her best friend she was suspended from the company. It was the hardest thing for her to say, but the true blessing was that it wasn't a termination. With Carmen owning eighty percent of Flame, the voting board members didn't have enough power to fire her. Truth be told, if Jerry had sided with her, the suspension wouldn't have been carried out. The vote would've been deadlocked.

Jerry knew if Carmen were voted out, he would take the position as Vice President. Selfishness, narcissism, and greed were all key players in the board's decision. Everyone knew Carmen's character. They knew she didn't release two sex tapes. Nonetheless, Carmen promised them Flame would be international that year. The paperwork was set to be signed that week for their first store to open in Westfield Stratford City, the biggest shopping mall in Europe. The announcement was supposed to be the highlight of the anniversary party. The contract was on the line when the first tape dropped. They got a pass. When the news of the second one hit, the contract was pulled. That was when the emergency board meeting was called.

Now, it was her responsibility to see if she could get the contract back. If it appeared to the necessary powers that Carmen was no longer affiliated with Flame, they could get a new contract drawn. If not, they would have to take their brand elsewhere.

"Are you going to answer that?"

Tiara didn't even know Jessica was in her office until she spoke.

"I'll get it," Jessica offered, reaching for Tiara's phone.

Tiara beat her to it. She picked it up and managed out a small hello. She waved Jessica out the room when she learned Monifah was on the line. "I already know why you're calling."

"Yeah, but I'm not going to rub it in. Are you okay?"

"What do you think?" Tiara's attitude was on full display.

"I think you should take an early lunch. I'm coming to get you."

Tiara rubbed her cheek. "I can't. There's too much work to do."

"Sounds like you have plenty for the rest of the week. Let me treat you to lunch."

A loud exhale came out Tiara's mouth. She knew she needed to stay at the office, but for the first time in the last few days, Monifah sounded sincere. *She lives with Carmen's daughter. She's seeing firsthand what these tapes are doing.* Tiara decided to give her the benefit of the doubt. She accepted the offer. She headed out her office not expecting to see what was before her. It wasn't odd for Carmen and Kane to be in each other's vicinity. It also wasn't odd for them to be boarding the company elevator. The odd part was they did it holding hands.

* * *

When the gates opened to the Santiago estate, Carmen feared the place she called home. For one, she no longer felt safe. Someone with close access to her had betrayed her trust like no other. They had taken a private moment that was undefiled and made it one for public scrutiny. The deception also forced her hand. Whereas she thought Kane would never step foot again in her bedroom, she was about to allow him inside. His investigative skills were a hundred times stronger than hers. If there was a camera in her bedroom, he would be the one to find it.

"This limo right here. Is it Jay's?"

Carmen didn't have to look in the direction of the driveway. She saw the white limo when they first approached the gate. She felt like she was setting Kane up. Jay was still at home, which meant Kane would have to go through him to even get to their bedroom. "It is," she told him. "I was hoping he was gone." She didn't say much else as Kane parked his Jeep. She was now having second thoughts at the situation that was about to arise.

"Look, I can handle him, if that's your concern," Kane said, reading her mind. "We can't let this go. We gotta figure this shit out for the kids. If someone can tape you once, they can tape you twice. We both don't want that."

She placed her hand on the door handle, but that was as far as she got. If it wasn't for Kane getting out and walking up the driveway, she would've still been sitting there. With him that close to the front door, she had to move. She let him inside and just their luck, Jay was nowhere near the foyer. The house wasn't entirely quiet as she could hear the kids talking, but Jay's voice was nonexistent. They made it up the steps without running into him and even inside her bedroom.

Kane didn't waste any time. The second the door closed behind him, he was on the move. He went right to the wall where he believed the camera to be and pointed upward. Carmen's eyes traveled to that spot. She shrugged her shoulders because all she saw was a smoke detector. "That's been there for years. You put it up there."

"I did put one up there, but not that one."

Her eyes lowered as she watched Kane examine the carpet. "Even if that's not the one you put up there, it's still been up there forever." She followed his thoughts by his movements. His attention was now on the dresser underneath the Smart TV. Minimal décor was on it, so he didn't bother to remove the items as he pushed the dresser towards the balcony. He then went back to where the dresser had been.

"It hasn't been up there forever." He waved her over. When she neared him, he pointed at the dents in the carpet. "This one is deeper than that one," he told her. "This one was here the longest. This one is fresh."

"The dresser was moved."

"He had to move it to reach the smoke detector."

Kane stood on his feet. Without asking permission, he climbed up on the dresser. He was inches shorter than Jay, but he didn't need the extra height to examine the smoke detector. With a closer view, he was able to see exactly what he suspected. He tapped the pinhole opening before looking back at Carmen. "This is your camera." With a quick jerk, he snatched the smoke detector off its mount. He then jumped off the dresser.

Carmen remained in place, now speechless. For the smoke detectors to be switched, someone intentionally set her up.

"These things," Kane was saying, the smoke detector in his hands, "are so advance, you can control it by an app in your phone."

Carmen dropped where she was. The move startled Kane and once again, he was on the floor with her. Her head was in her hands, but the tears wouldn't come. Hell fire was oozing through her veins. Jay had been on his phone before and after their sexcapade. The evidence showed everything Kane suspected was true. It didn't necessarily prove that Jay had released her tape with Carlos, but she now suspected him. He would have to admit to it. Once he did, she was drawing blood.

18

A plate of untouched lamb rib chops was set in front of Tiara. The stress of the suspension took her entire appetite. Even the scent of mint gremolata and roasted wild mushrooms couldn't bring it back. Instead of eating, she was spending the afternoon watching Monifah chow down.

"I may have room for it," Monifah told her, cutting into her NY Strip. "This little girl has expensive taste. If you don't want it, I'll take it."

Monifah's intention for lunch was to help her clear her head. Her heart was in the right place, but Tiara's mind wasn't. At some point that day, she would have to tell Carmen she was suspended. *Backstabber, traitor, disloyal,* were words she felt she would be called. She didn't even know if Carmen would give her the chance to say she hadn't voted against her.

"Have y'all learned anything about Carmen's mother?"

The question brought Tiara's eyes back to Monifah. She realized how consumed she had been. Patricia's disappearance hadn't been on her radar. "I haven't heard anything," she admitted. "I'm pretty sure she's still missing." Monifah kept right on eating. It was like she asked a question she really didn't care to have the answer to.

"How is your mother?" Monifah asked, changing the subject.

Tiara shrugged her shoulders. "I haven't spoken to her." While Monifah didn't say it, Tiara knew it appeared as if she was more concerned about Ms. Patricia than her own mom. If that's what Monifah was thinking, Tiara could confirm the thought was true. Her relationship with her mother had been rocky since the day she was born. It grew worse over the years, and she had splashes of time where she forgot her mother existed.

"Tell me about that," Monifah urged.

Tiara cut into one of the lambchops. That first cut made her feel like she was opening a wound. She stared at the meat, watching as the lamb's juices flowed to the other ends of the plate.

"Her boyfriend raped me," she revealed.

Tiara didn't look at anything except for the cut she made in the lambchop. "He was around a year or two before my stepfather. I thought he was nice at first, but he was like the others. He only wanted my mother for the golden prize between her legs. That was all she had to give him. He would come around at night. That's how I knew something was wrong when he showed up during the day. I had just gotten off the bus from school.

"I was barely in the house for two minutes before he came knocking," Tiara continued. "I let him in because I didn't have a reason not to. He told me my mother wanted us to get closer because she was gonna marry him. I didn't know whether to believe him or not. We started watching *Saved By The Bell*. It was the episode where Lisa had her fashion show. I realized I was the only one watching. I stared at the screen until it was over. He told me not to tell my mom. He said she wanted us to be a family and if she knew, it would crush her dream.

"Why do they say that?" Tiara asked. "Why do they tell us what someone else's hopes and dreams are when they've stolen ours? I did tell my mom. She told me he was helping put food on the table. She said I needed to be thankful because other men didn't stick around because they didn't want to take care of someone else's kid. I thought about running away. I thought about slashing her throat."

Monifah grabbed her hand. "That breaks my heart. I'm sorry you went through that."

Tiara made another cut in the lambchop although she hadn't taken a bite. "My mother's relationship with my stepfather and The Bastard, which is what I'll refer to him as, overlapped. My stepfather has always been a respectable man. He never showed up to my mother's house at night. He always came right before dinner, and he would be gone by eight o'clock. After what happened, I didn't trust him either, but over time, I did. All he showed me was sincerity. He earned my trust and a few weeks before I started the sixth grade, I told him about The Bastard."

Tiara made a third cut in the lambchop. "I made him promise he wouldn't tell my mother. Whether he did or not, I don't know. All I know was that, that night, was the last night The Bastard ever came to our house. The Brookstone PD found him the next day when they were scouring Allen's Field for another body."

"Your stepfather," Monifah guessed.

This time, Tiara took a sip of her cocktail. The Black Tie Margarita had previously gone untouched until now. "His name is Tony. He protected me. I protected him." She changed the topic to Carmen. "I met Carm when we started the sixth grade. I didn't think she was perfect, but I thought she had the perfect life. Her parents were well-off, she wore name brand clothes, and she had a mother who loved her. I befriended her because I thought her perfect life could rub off on me. I thought it did when my mother married Tony. He has always been the parent I deserved."

She stopped speaking long enough to finish her drink. When she did, she noticed Monifah's plate was empty. "Carmen doesn't know about the assault. We've shared our lives with each other, but I never shared that. Not even when she had her situation with Pierre." Tiara spoke of an old enemy of Jay's who tried to rape Carmen when they were in their twenties.

"What made you tell me?" Monifah asked. "I've earned enough of your trust?"

Tiara raised her fork to her lips about to take her first bite of the lambchop. "Yes. I also don't want you to ask me about my mother ever again." She stuck the fork in her mouth.

Monifah gave her a head nod. "I understand."

Their waiter approached the table. The check was in his hand, which he set on the table. "I hope you ladies enjoyed your meal," he told them. "The check has been paid in full. The gentleman at the bar covered it."

His words were enough to send their eyes to the bar. To their surprise, no one was there they recognized. Therefore, their eyes went to the bill. Right there on the credit card receipt, was the evidence they needed. In big, black ink was the name *Carlton Rodriguez*. Tiara dodged him when he called, but he was obviously following her. He was using all the available channels to get one thing—Jay Santiago.

***

1, 2, 3, 4, 6, 1, 2, 3, 4, 7, Jay counted his reps as he lifted the hundred and fifty pound barbell overhead. *1, 2, 3, 4,* he paused, skipping the next number as he saw a shadow. He listened hard to see if he heard anyone coming in. Gully told him he was going to join him, but his cousin was running late. *1, 2, 3,* he lost control as the barbell smashed into his chest. Caught off guard, he peered up to see Cesar standing over him. His right-hand held a firm grip preventing him from lifting the barbell up. The extra weight on his chest tightened his airway.

Unexpectedly, Cesar pulled the barbell up. Jay slid off the bench, but his right-hand was quick. Before he was to his feet, Cesar tackled him to the floor. They went blow for blow, scrapping for a few minutes until Cesar slid out his grasp. Gully held Cesar in a chokehold, allowing Jay to take a cheap shot. When he saw he drew blood, he told Gully to let him go.

"I ain't lettin' this muthafucka go," Gully yelled. "We're buryin' his ass."

"Let him go," Jay repeated, collapsing on the floor. He eyed Cesar closely. "I forgot you were a beast," he said, once his breathing regulated. "Thanks for the workout."

"You set me up," Cesar roared.

Gully tightened the chokehold. "What is he talkin' about? Ain't nobody got time for this shit."

"You gonna get some, too, if you don't let him go." Jay rose to his feet. He went back to the bench and picked up the barbell. Once he had it on the rack, he saw Gully as he let Cesar out the chokehold.

After the shootout at his house in San Juan, he and Cesar did a careful review of their security plan. As an addition, he asked Cesar to install hidden camera smoke detectors in both houses. His right-hand wasn't fond of the idea. He argued it was a waste of money considering the current surveillance system in place. After a bit of coaxing, Cesar agreed to do it. He even installed a smoke detector in his bedroom. Nonetheless, Jay didn't tell him when he decided to use it for something other than security.

"You lied to me," Cesar yelled.

"I didn't lie to you," Jay stated, his tone calm. "I made a request. You did your job. Someone fucked me over, too. I didn't give anyone that tape."

"What the fuck are y'all talking about?" Gully yelled.

Neither Cesar nor Jay answered him. They were too busy staring each other down. A short while later, Cesar left the gym, wiping his bleeding lip as he went.

Gully was still confused. "Where is he going?"

"Probably back to Canada," Jay replied. He sat on the bench to gather his thoughts. He knew he fucked up, but he didn't know how. Cesar told him that any footage recorded would stay on the app unless he exported the file. He knew he hadn't. He just didn't know who had. Only he and Cesar had access to the app and neither of them had done it.

"Can you wake the fuck up and tell me what y'all were fighting about?"

Jay would've told Gully if there wasn't another unexpected visitor. When he saw Malik, he dropped his head. Tiara had dropped Robin off earlier that morning, which meant Malik came over to see him. Although his friend hadn't spoken a word, he already knew what the visit was about. He was on the same time as Cesar.

"Y'all look like y'all both been through the ringer," Malik joked. "I'm glad I missed this workout." His gaze shifted to Jay. "Man, come on, you know we gotta talk," he continued. "King called me this morning. The last thing I thought we were gonna talk about is how your dick is all over the got damn Internet."

Gully rubbed his forehead. "Someone put a tape out on you, too?"

The story hit social media before Carmen left for work. From what he and Carmen read, there wasn't a lot of detail for them to narrow down what *Culture XL* had. After Carmen left the house, the video hit. There hadn't been any further communication between them, so he didn't know if she had seen it. However, if it was on Cesar's and Malik's radar she had to know about it.

"Tiara called me when I was pulling up," Malik was saying. "They voted to suspend Carmen."

The news set Jay on his feet. He couldn't hear anymore. Malik's announcement was confirmation Carmen knew. If she saw the footage, she knew it hit close to home. *Not close to home*, he thought, *it was in our home*. He already knew if he couldn't produce a logical explanation, he would be sleeping in a guestroom. Or the worst case scenario, a process server would be in his face.

"Wait, she was in the tape with you?" Gully asked. "Y'all made a sex tape?"

About to leave the gym, Jay placed his hand on the doorknob. He didn't turn it as he heard a ringtone behind him. He learned it was Malik's phone when he told them about the text he received.

"This is from Alec West. He plays for the Knicks. This is an example of the type of shit that's been hitting my phone. *What's up with your man? Did he really go for three hours? What kind of blue pill is that? That shit is crazy.*"

"Three hours," Gully questioned. "What kind of shit are you and Carmen on?"

"We're about to be on some divorce shit if I don't find out how they got that tape."

Jay's words were enough for Gully and Malik to change their banter. His own mindset was changing. It was starting to sink in that he was on the verge of losing his family. Cesar walked out on him, and Carmen was about to as well. All because he couldn't handle Carlos having a one up on him. Even in death, he was still fighting his best friend.

"Give me some time," Jay told them. He walked out the gym. He passed the garden and pool house but stopped in his tracks when he came up on the driveway. He didn't know what to think when he saw Kane's Jeep. He stood there in disbelief, waiting for Kane to show. It took a few minutes, but when he emerged with Carmen, so did the monster within. He contained it long enough for Kane to get behind the wheel. When the engine revved, he caught a second wind. He took off towards the Jeep only to run into an unexpected object.

Cesar.

***

Carmen hadn't reviewed any of her company's contracts in years. Suspensions and terminations never occurred at the executive level. With her board handing down a one-year suspension, she had to find a copy. Jerry was quick to hand it over and she saw for herself how the terms allowed the board to push her out. It wasn't indefinite, but the longest she had ever been apart from Flame was six months. A lot could happen in a one-year span and her fear was returning to a company she no longer knew or even worse, was failing.

She didn't even know what to do once the meeting was over. *Like, am I just supposed to grab my purse and leave?* If so, she wasn't ready to do that. She needed time. That meant spending the afternoon digging through her drawers, collecting sketches, accounting reports, picture frames, and any other miscellaneous items she didn't want to leave behind for a year.

"Can you tell me how this happened?" Tiara asked.

Carmen heard the question, but she didn't give her an answer. She wasn't mad at her friend. If anything, she felt sorry for her. She hated that her past mistakes along with Jay's actions put her in a fucked up predicament. She saw how hard it was for Tiara to tell her she was suspended. Her friend stumbled over the words more than she could count.

Tiara posed another question. "Well, what are you going to do about Jay?"

"What do you think I should do?" Carmen asked, finally speaking. "Kane said I should get the marriage annulled. Should I? Should I even waste my time? Everyone knows our pattern. We break up, make up, only to break up and make up again."

"Are you messing with Kane?"

Carmen dropped the binder she was holding. "Why would you ask me that?"

Tiara sat in front of Carmen's desk. "Because I saw y'all holding hands."

Carmen had to think about it. She remembered. "We were. He was in my office right after I found out about the tape. I couldn't walk. He was helping me to the elevator." She picked up the binder again and dropped it in a box along with some drawings. Once the box was filled to the brim, she sealed it. She then texted Linx to pick her up.

"I'm gonna try to get the contract back," Tiara announced.

"I hope you can get it."

"Do you really mean that?"

Carmen moved the box onto a platform truck. "You're asking me that like I don't want the company to succeed. Yes, y'all kicked me out, but I don't want Flame in the red."

"I'm not part of y'all," Tiara corrected.

"You know what I mean." Carmen looked at her desk. Everything she wanted had been packed aside from a 5x7 portrait of her and Jay. She debated about taking it. His image wasn't something she wanted to see, but she couldn't get away from it. Every time she looked in Rakim's eyes, she saw her husband's. Nyla was the spitting image of him. In addition, she hadn't thought about asking him to move out. With two young children, she wasn't ready to separate them from their father. That meant, picture frame or not, she would still see him every day. It would be impossible to move on.

She saw it for herself when she walked in their bedroom. Everything about the room screamed Jay. From his Gucci flip-flops, which peeked at her from underneath the bed to the cologne he left out on the bedside dresser. They shared the walk-in closet and on the entire right side there was nothing but rows and rows of his suits and shoes. She had built a life with him long before she wore his last name. She even promised her father she would be there for him. She didn't understand why Jay made it hard for her to do. It was like he continuously tested her to see how far she could go. Once again, he had her feeling like she could go no farther.

Or at least that's what she told herself. She practiced saying it to him in her head. However, when midnight rolled around, the words hadn't been uttered. Jay had gone ghost again. No one had heard from him and all she got from Gully was that Jay told him he needed time. She learned from Roman that Jay's Lambo was no longer in the garage. She drew the conclusion he was in it.

That was until he walked in their bedroom. Half asleep, she almost didn't have the energy to deal with him. That changed when she noticed what he was wearing. She hardly ever saw him in a T-shirt and gym shorts. He was the reason the *King* collection was constantly expanding. She had to keep designing suits because he preferred to wear one every day.

His back was pressed against their bedroom door like he expected her to do damage. She only had enough energy for a verbal beatdown. "I want to know why," she demanded. "What did I do to you? I racked my brain trying to figure it out. I mean, we talked about this tape last night. You lied and said it didn't exist. Not only did you know it existed, you knew you taped us. Fast forward to this morning. You woke me up. You kissed me. You told me you loved me. We got the Google Alert about the story. You knew the tape was real."

"You don't know how much I love you."

"So, why do you continuously fuck me over?"

"I—" Carmen didn't allow him to finish. What he didn't know was that everything she was saying was her thought process that led her to an answer. She spoke bluntly. "You're not on your meds."

The accusation made Jay's chest heave. She didn't know what he was on. It wasn't like she was around every time he took a pill. That was something he kept hidden from her, just like his therapy sessions. All she was supposed to know was that he had the tools to control his demons. Whether he used them or not, was his business.

"You've always been an aggressive lover," she continued. "We both know I love that about you. However, that night, that night was something different. You couldn't stop. You didn't see when my pleasure turned to pain. You didn't hear me. None of my tricks worked. I know now you were in the middle of an episode."

"We both know I can prolong a nut."

"You prolonged it for three hours." Carmen sat up. "The most we've gone is thirty minutes. Don't even ask me how I know." She pulled the covers back. "I checked your drawers. All your prescription bottles are full. They should've been refilled by now. Oh, and thank you for making me your HIPAA-approved contact. I called your therapist's office. They said they hadn't heard from you in months."

Jay didn't have a response.

"You thought you were okay. You thought you'd beaten it. You had me fooled. You were triggered. My tape with Carlos opened a deeper wound than you knew."

"I told you that," Jay admitted. "I didn't give them the tape, though. I was gonna give it to somebody, but it wasn't going to be Culture XL. I've been trying to figure out what happened, too."

Carmen was trying to remain calm. If he continued to lie in her face, her own inner demon would be unleashed. "Culture XL didn't put out the tape. Lucid didn't put out the tape with Carlos. Random motherfuckers who we've never laid eyes on is doing this shit. Is it questionable if you gave it to them? Yes, it is, but I know you did. The entire world was praising Carlos and you couldn't take it. You had to change the narrative. So, you waited until I was the most vulnerable to show the world who has the big dick."

She moved across the bed until she was on the side that belonged to him. "Did you get the response you wanted?" She gave him time to answer. When he didn't, she asked again.

"They saw what I wanted them to see."

"A man with a larger than life dick who made his wife cum three times. Did you read that comment?" she probed. "Or what about the one where they were trying to figure out how I'm still able to walk after taking down you and Carlos?" She stood on her feet. "Fuck the comments," she spat, her anger rising. "None of 'em matters. What matters is what I'm going to tell Nyla and Rakim when they're old enough to understand what's going on. What matters is how I'm going to comfort them when someone shoves a video in their faces of their parents fuckin'." Her words were now bringing tears to Jay's eyes. "Did you think about that? Did you think about our kids? You couldn't have." She sat down and took a breath.

"I was this close to signing a contract to put Flame in the biggest mall in Europe," she continued. "They pulled the contract, and it will be by the grace of God if Tiara is able to get it back." Fresh tears were starting to fall. "When I married you, I said you were it for me. I meant it. I took our vows seriously." She took another breath. "God knows I don't want to be with anyone else. I don't want another failed marriage, but I'll take that bullet. We can stay married, but it's only on paper. From this second forward, we are not together. I already told Gully he needs to help you move your things out the room. If you want to stay living with me and the kids, you gotta get back on your meds. You must go to therapy. I need you to do that for the sake of our family."

Jay was no longer at their bedroom door. Her words had brought him to his knees. He wasn't going to beg as her tone told him her mind was made up. It was now on him to do the work. He did the first thing they should've done before a single word was spoken. He prayed for minutes on end for forgiveness, for redemption, and healing. When he concluded the prayer, he looked deep in her eyes though he didn't expect to see a change. "I know you don't believe me, but I didn't give anyone that tape. I know it's just words, but it's the truth. Tomorrow, I'm going to find out how they got it. When I do, and I show you proof, I want you back."

He kissed her hands. She was still wearing her ring, but it didn't mean anything. If she said they were through, they were through. Even if he wasn't accepting of it. When she pulled away from him, he rose from the floor. He went to his bedside dresser and opened a drawer. He pulled out each prescription bottle to show her he was committed. Whatever she asked of him, he was going to do. He didn't care how long it took. All that mattered was that one day she would be his again.

19

Jay did his best to remain quiet as he entered Roman's room. He easily could've woken him with a phone call or text, but he liked to keep him on his toes. He did a decent job of it because Roman didn't stir until he sat on his bed. Jay also wasn't alone. Cesar was in the room as well. After stopping him from confronting Kane, they had a much needed conversation. He gave him the apology he deserved, which brought them to the pool house the following morning. The plan was to take a day trip to Cali as Lucid Entertainment was based in Los Angeles. Afterwards, they would head to the office of *Culture XL*. The podcast taped in the evening, which meant when they landed in Brookstone, Culture XL would be where they wanted him.

"I thought you were gonna start knocking," Roman quipped, his voice hoarse.

"I will when you start paying rent," Jay joked.

Roman shifted his weight. He pulled on the covers, but he didn't get far with Jay sitting on the bed. "What's on the agenda?"

"LA," Cesar replied. "Ready to fly?"

"Always ready to fly," Roman said with a yawn. "Let me jump in the shower."

Jay got up from the bed. He gave a head nod to Cesar to signal it was time to make their exit. They made their way out the pool house right as Tiara and Robin were making their way up the driveway. *Perfect timing.* Jay increased his speed so he could speak with her. Out the corner of his eye, he saw Cesar head in the opposite direction. "You know we gotta talk," Jay called to her, catching her attention. "How did that vote go down?"

"I voted no," she shared, once they were inches apart. "The other board members voted yes. Carmen was the accused. She couldn't be a part of the vote. Not with the way the employment contract and bylaws are written."

"She put those people in their positions," Jay argued.

"People are ready to move up. Jerry has wanted my position for years. I wasn't leaving and we know where Carmen's heart is. This is his chance. Even if it is for a year." She looked at Robin who was now leaning against her legs. "Did you get a call or email from Tabatha?"

Jay pulled his phone from his pocket. He checked his email only to see he had fifteen unread messages. Tabatha's email was one of them. "I got it," he shared, scanning the contents. He stopped at the third sentence once he learned his contract was being terminated. He had signed the paperwork less than forty-eight hours ago. "Anything else you need to share?"

"Yeah, there is," Tiara replied. "Carlton called me yesterday. He hasn't heard from you."

"And he isn't. I threw his number away."

"Well, there goes that." Tiara picked up Robin who was starting to fall asleep. "He's serious about meeting you. He's being sneaky about it, too. He followed me to Capital Grille. I know it's not my business," she said, changing the subject, "but what happened? Like, how did they get the tape?"

Jay shrugged his shoulders. "Your guess is as good as mine." He stared at Tiara, unsure why she asked the question. He figured Carmen had given her all those details. He even assumed Carmen had told her about her plans to separate. "I heard you're working on getting the contract back."

"It's at the top of my list. We gotta let these tapes die down first."

"Well, I'm going to work on it, too," Jay revealed. "The Santiago name holds weight in America. It's time to see if it can hold overseas. If all goes well, I can get the contract hand-delivered."

"What does that mean?" Tiara was confused.

"I got Carmen in this mess. I gotta get her out."

"Did you tell her about that plan?" Tiara now wore a look of surprise.

"She'll find out when I deliver the contract."

"So, that's a no," Tiara said with a smile. "Well, do what you can. I'm gonna do what I can." She shifted Robin's weight on her hip. "Let me get this little girl inside. I need to get to the office before it gets to me."

Jay watched as she continued up the driveway. There was something off about Tiara, but there was something off about all of them. She was dealing with just as much as they were.

"She was with Monifah."

Jay looked to his right to see Cesar approaching him. "You got someone watching her, too?"

"Nah, but one of our ghosts decided to take lunch at Capital Grille, too. He saw her there with Monifah. She shared a lot with her. Stuff Carmen doesn't even know."

His right-hand's words made him look at the front door of the main house. Tiara was disappearing behind it as Silvas let her in. Cesar now had him suspicious. "You know something I don't."

"We need to watch out for Monifah," Cesar proposed. "Tiara is a loyal friend, but with Carmen going on this leave, the vacancy can be a devil's playground."

Tiara walked out the house. She waved goodbye to them, or rather, to him. Cesar was missing in action until Tiara drove her car back through the front gate.

"What is Plan B?" Cesar asked, speaking of their LA trip.

"There is no Plan B," Jay admitted. "We're gonna get what we came for."

In Cesar's mind, there was a possibility they could leave LA emptyhanded. For Jay, it wasn't an option. He wasn't leaving the city without a name and some form of documentation he could show Carmen. He had to prove to her he hadn't sold their sex tape or her tape with Carlos. He didn't care what he had to do to get it. He didn't marry her to be living as a roommate. Those exact thoughts he shared with Cesar.

When they reached the receptionist's desk at Lucid Entertainment, Jay had a feeling something wasn't right. She was juggling several phone calls, had random papers strewn across her desk as well as multi-colored sticky notes. It took her a good five minutes before she even acknowledged them. When he asked to speak with a top executive, she laughed in his face.

"You and everyone else," she told him. "One is on vacation, one is in Vancouver shooting a flick, and the other broke his leg at a baseball game. You'll have to come back in a couple of weeks."

"I got two minutes," Jay stressed.

"Look, I don't know what business you need to handle, but if you need an executive who can make something move, you're not getting one today."

Those were words Jay didn't need to hear. Lucky for her, he had a pill in his system, which prevented him from giving her the typical Santiago reaction. If anything, his mind worked quicker than his anger. He got the receptionist to tell him who was who and after obtaining business cards for each of the executives, he gave Cesar the Plan B he wanted. "The one who broke his leg, let's find out which hospital he's in. If we can't locate him, we might as well fly to Canada. We know one is in Vancouver. We'll have to find the set. I'll check the social media accounts of the one on vacation. Hopefully, he posted where he's at."

Cesar didn't have to verbally agree. When he pulled out his phone, they both went to work, beginning to call the hospitals in the city. Three phone calls later, Jay was able to confirm that Ryan O'Chason was admitted to Cedars-Sinai Medical Center on Beverly Blvd. He asked the operator to transfer him to his room. When the call was transferred, a lady answered the phone.

"Jay Santiago calling for Mr. O'Chason," he told her.

"He had surgery this morning. He's still resting."

"Can you tell him I called?" Jay didn't show the slightest hint he was bothered.

"I can. I'll do it once he wakes up."

Without prolonging the conversation, he thanked her for her time and hung up. Cesar gave him a questionable look as if they reached a dead end. Jay changed his mind. "Let's go wake up Sleeping Beauty."

20

Aside from weekends, holidays, and occasional days off, Carmen hadn't spent full days with Rakim and Nyla since Nyla was three months old. She hated to admit it, but she didn't even know the things they did daily. She did remember asking Fiona to help her prepare them for Pre-K and kindergarten. What occurred was her maid creating a full schedule of classes. Then, when Brookstone University went on holiday break, Akaila created classes of her own. That meant Carmen was now on a full schedule with them. It took some adjusting, but after the first three hours, Carmen wouldn't have it any other way. Not to mention, she received an endless amount of hugs and kisses when her kids realized she didn't have anywhere to be. For the first time, Carmen was seeing the suspension as a blessing.

Currently cleaning up the kitchen from dinner, the silence was short-lived when Kane's name appeared on her phone. She dropped the dish rag she was holding and answered with the quickness. "I just put the food up," she told him. She got a hearty chuckle in return.

"I wish that was what I needed," he replied. "I need a temple rub."

"Uh oh," Carmen responded, knowing what that meant. "What happened?"

"What didn't happen." A loud sigh emerged. "I don't think I'm built for this. I don't know how my father handled my mom. With her and Monifah in the house, I can't deal."

"What happened?" Carmen asked again.

"My mother called her your name."

"Oh, shit." Carmen dropped the phone. She covered her mouth, trying to conceal her laughter. She knew that error sent Monifah through the roof. That was the last thing Beverly needed to do. Still tickled, she grabbed the phone.

"That set off another argument. She started fussing about the lack of space."

The word space reminded her she hadn't told him about her agreement with Jay. "Well, I can't give you a temple rub, but I can give you a house and a check. Jay and I are going to buy a house for you. Our budget is seven hundred thousand with five hundred of that going towards the house. Any money leftover will be given to you." She expected that to give Kane some relief, but he didn't sound any better.

"Monifah isn't going to accept it. No matter how you spin it."

"So, what does she expect you to do? You just got your yearly raise and bonus. You won't get another until the end of the year. You can't pull money out your ass," Carmen argued.

"So, now you understand why I need a temple rub."

"Okay, well, what happened to the millions you got from our first divorce? I know you lived off it. You bought your condo. You paid that girl from the Triad. Where's the rest of it?"

Another chuckle sounded out Kane's mouth. "I transferred most of it into our joint account when we remarried. I didn't think we were going to get divorced again. I did keep some of it in my personal savings, but technically, you have it. You know I didn't ask for anything in the second divorce. I didn't have access to anything when you took my name off the accounts."

Carmen's mouth formed an O. She now understood how strapped he was. "Well, I can't help if she won't let me."

"I know, but are you free? Can you give me a temple rub?"

Carmen didn't hide her laughter this time. "Are you crazy? My temple rubbing days are over. I can't rub your temples. That's your wife's job."

"She can't rub my temples when she's the one causing me stress," Kane shot back. "I need it right now, Carm. You know I do."

"I do know," she told him. She remembered countless nights, lying in bed with him, her fingertips at his temples until his nerves were calm. She would plant kisses on his neck until they were making love. "Close your eyes, take some deep breaths, and relax. Monifah will come around."

"It ain't gonna be today. So, what about that temple rub?"

"And on that note, goodnight," Carmen said with a giggle. She hung up the phone, shaking her head at Kane's request. She picked up the dish rag, but it fell from her hand when Jay walked in the kitchen. She hadn't heard him come in and wondered how much of her call he heard. She learned quickly it was none.

"You already put dinner up?" he asked.

"I did," she told him. She opened the refrigerator. It was the first time she'd seen or spoken to him that day. It was also the first day of them officially being separated. She told herself to remain cordial, as the last thing she wanted was for an argument to spark. "Chicken and dumplings." She showed him the container. He grabbed it from her and set it on the island. Her plan was to put it in the microwave for him, but he obviously wasn't ready to eat.

"I went to LA," he began. He followed the statement with a verbal recollection of the day.

Jay reached for the doorknob to Mr. O'Chason's room only for Cesar to stop him. When he looked at him, Jay saw a concerned look on his right-hand's face.

"We're not going to hurt anybody." Cesar said the words more as an order than as a question.

Jay told him earlier they weren't leaving LA emptyhanded. What he didn't tell him was that they were going to use every means possible to make sure they didn't. The second the hallway was clear, he pulled out a pistol. Despite his order, Cesar followed his lead. They went inside, the door closing behind them. One pistol went up against the temple of a sleeping Mr. O'Chason while the other rested on his wife's head.

"You wanna wake him up, or do you want me to?" Jay asked his wife.

His volume was loud enough to wake the porn exec. The man shook in the bed, alarmed at what was occurring.

"How did you get in here?"

"I ask the questions," Jay fired back. He lowered the pistol only to provide him a sense of comfort. When he looked at Cesar, he did the same. "Do you know me?" he asked, his eyes now back on Mr. O'Chason.

"Why are you doing this? We didn't put out your wife's tape."

"I want to know how you got it."

Mr. O'Chason stumbled over his words. Meanwhile, his wife urged him to tell whatever it is he knew.

"We have a contract, we could get sued," the man argued.

"You could die," Jay proposed, the pistol back at his temple.

A sudden scream sounded out his wife's mouth. Jay shot her a look only to see Cesar's pistol at her head. "Tell him," she begged through her tears. "Tell him who it was. Just tell him."

"I'll tell you," Mr. O'Chason whispered. "Just move the gun away from my wife."

Jay gave Cesar a glance. The gun disappeared. With it now out of sight, he urged Mr. O'Chason to talk.

"Shekinah Graham," Mr. O'Chason revealed. "She works at a CVS in Brookstone. Someone dropped the VHS off at the kiosk and she did the digital conversion. She never told us who dropped it off and it didn't matter. She emailed the footage to us."

The information was enough to make Jay put the gun back in his waistband. He pulled out his phone and did a quick Google search for all the CVS locations in Brookstone. There was a total of four. He called the first one and asked to speak to her. He was told there wasn't an employee by that name. He called the second one. The same result. When he called the third one, he was told she worked there, but her shift hadn't started.

"Was that so hard?" Jay asked, taking a step away from the bed. He looked at Mr. O'Chason's wife to see her tears had dried. "You will never see me again. If you tell someone what happened, you will. If we meet again, I'll be the last face you'll see. Understand?"

Carmen was now sitting on a stool, rubbing her own temples. "Another nobody," she muttered. "I keep getting names of random ass folks I don't know."

"We flew back to Brookstone," Jay told her, overlooking the comment. He knew where the story was going although she didn't. "By the time we were home, Shekinah was at work. She took one look at me, and the bitch ran faster than Sha'Carri Richardson."

Shekinah thought he was a rookie. She ran for her life, knocking over end caps, and slamming into customers as she went. She thought he was solo. He had her cornered. She opened the back door and fell in the arms of Cesar and Roman. Jay joined them less than a minute later.

"We can do this the easy way or the hard way," Jay told her.

"I'll get rid of it," she yelled. "I promise."

"The shit is out now. What good is that going to do?" Jay yelled back.

"Please don't kill me."

"Who dropped off the tape?"

"That's what I want to know," Carmen stressed. "Speed it up."

"She said the name on the order was Monifah Kane."

Carmen swallowed. The name didn't give her the reaction she expected. She wasn't the least bit shocked. Monifah was the only so-called enemy she had. It made sense for her to be the one to leak the tape.

Jay shared a thought. "The only way Monifah could've gotten it is if Kane gave it to her."

"He didn't give it to her." From the way her ex acted in her office when the tape with Jay leaked, Carmen knew he was innocent. "If anything, he lied about having it. Monifah found it and put it out. Either way, it goes, she ain't got shit, I can't sue, and I can't whoop her ass because she's fuckin' pregnant."

"There's more," Jay continued.

"No guns this time," was the first thing Jay said to Cesar once they were outside Culture XL's building. He left his pistol underneath the driver's seat of his limo on purpose. Culture XL was already on his bad side. He had minimal patience for him, which meant he was more inclined to give him a bullet than the others. To keep himself out a murder charge, he had to go in completely naked. Cesar, however, had better restraint than he did. He agreed to not use his gun, yet he chose to bring it inside.

To their advantage, the podcast hadn't started taping. They found Culture in his office, typing two hundred words a minute. When Culture saw him, his reaction was like the others. The only difference was that Culture had nowhere to run. There were only two exits in his office, the front door, and a balcony, where the city served as a backdrop.

"I didn't leak your tape," Culture shouted, already on the defense.

Jay paused when he saw Carmen pour herself a glass of wine. Before she could put it to her lips, he snatched it from her. "What are you doing?"

"I'm stressed," she shouted. "I need something to mellow me out."

"Eat some ice cream because you ain't doing this. You could be pregnant."

There was about twenty minutes of back and forth between them. Culture was determined not to give up the name. About to do bodily harm, Cesar stopped him because he noticed one of the hallway cameras had full view of Culture's office. They were now in a losing situation that even Cesar's pistol couldn't get them out of.

"Do you know what this did to my marriage? You know I didn't give you that tape." Jay was now the one begging. "You talk about me on your podcast. You know what I've been through. This story made you a lot of money, but it's ruining my life. Our kids had to see that shit. All I want to know is how you got it."

His tone got him nothing. Culture wasn't budging. Not to mention, they were running out of time. The podcast was set to start taping, which meant Culture's co-hosts would soon be strolling past the office. For the longest, they had been talking without an audience. "I can write you a check," Jay offered. "Or do you want cash?"

"Your money doesn't spend here," Culture responded. "I told you the deal I made. If I give up the name and something happens, it's all going to come back on me. Yes, they gave me the tape, but I refused to put it out. I was trying to stay clear of getting sued. They put it out themselves."

"They?" Cesar questioned.

"They can be used in place of he or she," Culture explained. "Now, I can call your wife and tell her you didn't give me the tape, but that ain't giving you what you want."

Jay balled his fist as his agitation grew. He strongly believed Carmen knew he didn't leak their tape. She only wanted him to bring home the name of the person who did. "What if I told you there wouldn't be any bloodshed?"

Culture's eyes shifted back and forth between the two. "I'm supposed to believe that from a man whose killed more people than he's had sex with?"

"It's the opposite," Jay admitted. "Have I tried to kill you?"

"You did tell me you would feed my dick to the ducks in the Brookstone City Park."

One of many threats Jay gave him, it wasn't enough for the man to break. He didn't know what it would take. He left Culture's office to think. It was hard to get information when he wasn't using his muscle. Mr. O'Chason was quick to buckle because a gun was at his head. Shekinah was trapped between three men. Culture didn't have that and although he knew his reputation, he wasn't fearful.

"We're not giving up," Cesar told him, now at his side. "Let me watch him for a couple of days. I'll learn his routine and find a place we can corner him." Cesar took his eyes off Jay, looking ahead at the elevator down the hall. "With the right heat on him, he'll budge.

I'll make sure it's a place with no cameras. A place we can really lock down so you can do what you need to. I'll make sure things stay under control. The last thing you need is the Triad on your back. I'll make sure your nose stays clean." Cesar stopped walking when he realized he no longer heard Jay's footsteps. When he didn't see his friend, he broke into a sprint back to Culture's office. He made it to the doorway to find half of Culture's body over the balcony.

A large wet spot covered the man's groin while drool mixed with wet tears slid down his chin. Jay held the man only by his legs. With a murder about to occur in front of him, he rushed to Jay's side. "Monifah Kane," Culture cried. Cesar didn't know what the revelation did to Jay. All he knew was that when Jay's grip loosened, he sprang into action. His hand caught Culture's left pants leg, causing the man's body to slam against the balcony's glass walls. About to lose him, he wrapped his arms around the man's leg, grunting as he struggled to pull him up. His weight was too much to bear. When Cesar felt his own body going over, out of nowhere, there came relief.

In one swift move, Jay grabbed Culture's other leg and pulled him up. He dropped Culture onto the balcony floor, the man crying like a hungry baby. "I want a copy of the email she sent you," Jay ordered. "I also want the security footage from today. Get me that and we'll be good. Fuck up and next time there won't be anyone to catch you."

Carmen stared at the papers now in front of her. There were several pages of email communication between Monifah and Culture XL. With Monifah's email address clearly visible, she had the evidence she needed to confront Kane.

"I told you I didn't do it," she heard Jay say.

She moved the papers aside, giving him her full attention. "You didn't do it, but how did she get your phone to get the video?"

"I'm still trying to figure that out. She could've asked Sanders to hack the app."

Carmen grabbed the papers once again and gave each document another look. "There's no way she could've known you had that app. I mean, this whole thing doesn't make sense." She was confused, but she also was tired of trying to figure it out. "I can't even blame you for this one. I brought this drama to our lives. She did this because of Rakim. She's still upset about him being in love with me. Minister Harrison was right. It's payday someday."

"We've both paid for our sins," Jay whispered. His fingertips touched the edges of the papers. He slid the emails away from her before walking around the island to be at her side. "So, is this over now? Are we back together?"

"You worked quick," Carmen told him. She slid off her stool before saying, "but, we're not together. I still have some animosity and I don't trust you. We gotta rebuild that before I can even think about being with you again. I can't be in a relationship with someone I haven't forgiven."

Her words brought a frown to Jay's face. "What else do you need to see? Do you want me to take down the smoke detector? I'll take it down. You can watch me. Shit, I'll burn it. What else do you need me to do?"

"I need you to give me time. I need us to work through this pain we've both been harboring. You're not over what I did with Carlos. If you were, we never would've seen a second tape."

None of that was what Jay wanted to hear. It wasn't what he deserved to hear. He had spent the day away from her, his children, his businesses, just to sort the matter out and fix his marriage. That wasn't even half of it. In the morning, he had a long flight to London to get her contract back. "Do you really expect me to live like this?"

"I expect you to do what's best for you."

An expletive was on the tip of his tongue. He didn't say it as it would fuel an argument. Instead, he told her he was headed to see the kids and left the kitchen.

In the meantime, Carmen grabbed the papers and her cell phone. She didn't immediately dial Kane's number, choosing to read the emails over and over. After the twentieth read, she called him. He answered on the first ring. "I need to meet with you," she told him, not bothering to greet him. "I got some information we need to discuss."

"If this ain't about a temple rub, I ain't meeting with ya." He chuckled.

"It's not, but this is important."

He responded with a few incoherent words before he told her he wasn't up for the conversation. "I can't take any extra stress right now. I'm on edge. Call me tomorrow. We'll talk."

"What time?" she asked. "I don't wanna bring the kids with me. You know school has started back now that the holidays are over. Akaila can't watch 'em like she used to."

"I don't know. My head is throbbing right now. I'll call you back later."

The last thing she expected to hear was the phone hang up. She was about to call him back when she heard a loud thud in the foyer. It sounded like luggage. It was followed by Jay and Silvas' voices. With the news Jay brought home, she hadn't told him she moved Silvas' room to the den. Earlier that day, she saw his butler struggling to climb the steps. Before he could reach the top, she asked Linx to help her with his things. With Silvas now in the den, the family only had one exit to and from the kitchen. She thought Jay was going to share his thoughts about the arrangement. All he did when he entered the kitchen was throw a box her way.

A pregnancy test was in front of her. Somehow, he thought a test was supposed to be positive after a week of sex.

"You can use the bathroom in the hallway," he told her.

"I'm not pregnant."

"You don't know that. We just started trying," he countered.

Carmen tossed the box in the trash. "I do know," she replied. "My period came on today. For that to happen, we missed the ovulation period."

Carmen could tell he was trying to digest the news. The news was deeper than what was on the surface. It took another minute before *that* news set in. She couldn't tell him they weren't having another baby. Those words would be too harsh for him to bear. With their marriage on the rocks and time working against her, the chances of them bringing a new life into the world was slim. Plus, it could be months or a year before she would sleep with him again.

He wasn't taking the news well, which she could see from the way his chest heaved. Tears were forming in the corner of his eyes. His pain was heartbreaking, but it was the best thing for their family. There was too much going on for there to be a new baby. Their marriage couldn't take anything else and there was no guarantee a new baby could heal them.

"We agreed we would start trying," he cried. "You asked me how many more kids I wanted. You told me you would give me one more."

"You're talking like I intentionally did this."

"If you wanted this baby, you would be crying with me."

"I logged everything correctly in the app. I was supposed to be ovulat—" He left the room before she could finish. He escaped into the dining room, the door swinging closed once he disappeared behind it. Certain he was leaving, she jumped out her skin when something crashed against the wall. It was followed by the sound of splitting wood. She closed her eyes, as he destroyed the room with his bare hands.

The sharp sound of breaking glass told her the centerpiece had been smashed. The floor pulsated under her feet as the dining room table was overturned. She grabbed a hold of the island when she heard the chairs wage war. The designer pieces bounced off the wall like a game of ping-pong. Still, his pain wasn't fed.

Without even being in the room, she could see him clear as day in her mind. She saw him as he picked up a chair from the floor. He held it overhead and then sent it flying towards the window. The glass shattered, the night air receiving an open invitation into their home. Throughout it all, she remained calm. Until she heard the most painful, resounding cry.

Her own tears were coming when the door to the den opened. She blocked Silvas' path when he headed for the dining room. It didn't take much to hold him back as his age didn't leave him with much strength. "Don't go in there," she told him, her right palm resting on his chest. "We have to make sure he's done."

"He's tearing everything up," Silvas barked.

"He needed to," was her reply. Silvas didn't respond and they stood there in silence until Jay's tears ceased. When she heard him leave out the front door, she let Silvas go. One by one they went in the dining room to assess the damage. A cold breeze floated throughout the room. Worse than she imagined, she stared at the chair that was now hanging by a single leg out the window.

"Mi hijo," Silvas muttered. "How did he do this? Birds, possums, and whatever else can come in."

The damage wouldn't have been that extensive if Jay hadn't broken a window. The nighttime air poured through the gaping hole, making the room appear as if it was struck by an earthquake. A clear sign of Jay's pain, she wasn't the least bit surprised when she saw his Lamborghini come flying pass them. He was leaving, which meant the destruction was her problem. She walked back in the kitchen not ready to deal. She dialed Kane's number again. He picked up.

"How about that temple rub?"

21

Carmen closed the door to Rakim's room, a slight smile still on her face. She had gone upstairs to check on him and Nyla, and when she pulled Rakim's covers back, she found them both in his bed. An iPad was in Rakim's hands while he and Nyla were both sharing a pair of earbuds. She startled them when they realized she was there, but she wasn't the least bit upset. *Paw Patrol* had hijacked their attention, so they were unfazed by the incident which occurred underneath them. To show them she wasn't upset, she kissed their cheeks, whispered, "good night," and threw the covers back on them. She didn't even bother to take Nyla back to her room.

Downstairs, Gully and Linx were in the dining room with Silvas. Phones were glued to both their ears, yet Gully hung his up once she entered the room.

"This is *your* husband," he said, pointing at the damages with his phone. "Ain't nobody got time to be dealing with this."

Carmen didn't know how to say they were going to have to. Kane was in a parking deck at Flame, and his Jeep was her next destination.

"Y'all lucky y'all loaded," Gully continued. "I don't know no one who could pay double to get this shit fixed tonight."

Those words made Carmen speak. "Someone is coming out?"

Gully nodded his head. "Jay called someone after he called us. They're gonna be up all night fixing the window, but that noise will be better than some rats running up in your house."

Carmen felt relieved. "So, are y'all gonna stay here until they come?"

"We ain't got a choice," Gully told her. "This is our assignment."

Carmen clapped her hands. "Cool, because I'm on my way out."

Gully probed her. She didn't answer his questions, collecting her things and going out the front door. She wasn't concerned about telling him her whereabouts as there would be someone following her. However, she knew from Cesar, that it wasn't anyone's place to reveal her location unless the matter called for it. If nothing went down, Jay would never know she was with Kane. When it came to her ex, he hadn't told Monifah where he was. His wife would burn his condo down if she knew they were meeting up.

"What made you change your mind?" Kane asked once she made it to his Jeep.

"I need a temple rub," she replied. She studied his face, noticing the vein that was popping out at his right temple. *Damn, you are stressed.* Without him asking, she took her fingers and positioned them on the sides of his forehead. She rubbed his temple for a minute or two until the position became uncomfortable. "Lean your seat back." He did as she asked, and she leaned hers back at well. Her frame became draped over his, their bodies chest to chest as she massaged his temples.

"What has you stressed?" he asked, his eyes now closed.

"Oh, nobody, just the Puerto Rican man living in my house."

A smile flew across Kane's face. It disappeared quickly because he was concentrating on easing the tension in his head. They sat in silence for several minutes until his eyes opened. "I like it when we're like this," he muttered. "We went back and forth so much, I forgot we were ever in love."

"That's why we were arguing," she responded. Their gazes met. "I hated you just as much as I loved you."

Kane closed his eyes back. "Thankfully, we're passed all that."

Carmen felt his arm move underneath her. When it stroked the side of her breast, she knew he was testing her. She didn't say anything, choosing to continue his temple rub as if it didn't happen. She wasn't offended, she just didn't want him to think he was getting something other than the massage. It wouldn't be good for either of them. *He didn't mean to do it.* About to run with that idea, he did it again. This time she said something.

"That isn't yours anymore," she reminded him.

"If it was his, you wouldn't be here."

Carmen pressed her fingertips hard into his temples. The move made his eyes open. They stared at each other until his eyes shifted to her chest. Her cleavage was covered, but if it hadn't been, she could only assume what would've happened. "Close your eyes," she ordered. She massaged his temples once more, neither of them speaking. Minutes later, he fell asleep. She moved off his chest and closed her eyes. She didn't know how long they slept, but when her eyes opened, he was awake and on the phone with Monifah.

"Calm down, baby, I'm on the way," he was saying. "We'll see what's going on."

The word baby reminded her of what she told him earlier. They no longer belonged to each other. She sighed at the thought although she shouldn't have. They may have been feuding with their spouses, but they were still under covenant. That clear reminder was what sent her into action. Before he could say anything, she had her seat raised and was grabbing her things.

"You ain't gotta run outta here." He was no longer on the phone.

"Your wife…" Carmen changed thoughts. "I still need to talk to you. It's about Monifah."

"And it's still not a good time. My headache is gone, but a new one is coming. She's spotting. She wants to go to the hospital."

As much as she wanted to confront Kane about his wife's involvement with her sex tapes, she didn't need to. Not at that moment. The last thing she wanted was to cause any extra stress that could harm their baby. Once Monifah's health was in the clear, she would tell him. "We'll meet up later. I'll let you get to your wife."

She opened the door to his Jeep, but before she could step out, he grabbed her arm. She faced him to see a subtle expression.

"Thank you," he stated, "for being here."

In return, she gave him a small smile. She left his Jeep and got inside her Honda. Not her typical mode of transportation, she drove the car whenever she wanted to be inconspicuous. That was the car's original purpose anyway. She purchased it in Georgia during Kristian's kidnapping. Her plan worked when it came to the public, but not when it came to getting away from Jay's right-hands. When she drove out the parking deck, she saw a black car not too far behind. The driver followed her all the way home until she was behind the gates of her estate.

***

"Gentlemen, we are starting our descent into London. Please make sure your seatbelt is securely fastened."

The pilot's announcement shifted Jay's attention to the cabin window beside him. The city, like most, looked microscopic from where he sat. While it was his first time in Europe, if things worked in his favor, it wouldn't be the last. Cesar had jumped through hoops to find dirt on any of the executives who owned Westfield Stratford City. One of them, the big man at the top, a French businessman by the name of Oliver Beregé, had skeletons that needed to stay in the closet. After writing a large check, Jay had the photos that could help him get Carmen's contract back.

"The window is now fixed," Cesar told him. "Gully confirmed it."

The pain of Carmen's news still hurt him. He wasn't necessarily upset because she wasn't pregnant. He was upset because she lied to him about her ovulation dates. She promised him month after month that the ovulation window hadn't changed. The plan was to start trying for another baby after they were married. He did his part, spilling his seed inside of her multiple times only for her to tell him the dates were wrong. Her lack of emotion told him she didn't want another baby. If she did, she would've called him crying when she saw her period had come on.

"We got the Lincoln House," Cesar was now telling him. "That's the suite at the Rosewood Hotel. That's where Beregé is staying."

Jay was pleased with the news although he didn't verbalize it. His thoughts consumed him. His mood didn't even change when the wheels of the plane touched the ground. If anything, it brought a new thought. The last chance he had to save his marriage was on London soil. In a perfect world, he would deliver the contract to Carmen, she would sign it, admit the error of her ways, and they would move forward with procreating. If the latter didn't happen, he would force it.

"You don't have to talk to me, but can you at least answer your phone?" Cesar said, annoyed.

Jay didn't even realize his phone was ringing. Now hearing it, he pulled it from his pants pocket. About to miss the call, he answered. "North."

"I'm sorry to wake you so early," North greeted. "The matter was urgent."

A slight smile emerged on Jay's face. "You're in luck. I just landed in London. It's about eleven here. Five hours ahead of the U.S."

"I'm the only one who had to get up early?" North joshed. "I'll make this quick. Later today, about seven o'clock p.m., eastern standard time, the President will be addressing the nation to announce the invasion of Kenema."

Jay's mouth tightened. The news was both good and bad. Good because there was a chance the U.S. military would kill his former partner and bad because if they didn't, his entire family was in danger. Either way it went, he had to be prepared. "I'll tune in," he told him.

"When are you returning to Brookstone? I have some business in Manhattan. Perhaps we can link up."

Jay looked at Cesar to see his right-hand's eyes on his. "I don't know. Depends on how fast I work out here."

"I see, I see," North replied. "Well, we'll chat after the address if you're available."

"It's a plan," Jay replied. North ended the call with two words he needed to hear.

God Bless.

God was who he needed. He was who he always needed. God is who he, his family, and his right-hands were going to need once the feet of the U.S. military hit Kenema. He didn't know when retaliation was coming his way, and he had a short time to prepare. "The men we hired for my house in San Juan," he began. "Get 'em to Brookstone. Every inch of my house, the whole community, needs twenty-four hour surveillance. I even want eyes in the sky."

"What was said on that call?"

The wrong reply, Jay made sure to let Cesar know it. "Do what I told you to do and when I'm ready to tell you, I will. You can get me an earpiece, too. I want to know everything you know. I want to hear everything. I don't want Carmen shittin' without me knowing."

"That ain't how this shit works," Cesar told him. "I have to know what you know to keep you alive."

"Just do what I pay you to do. Get on the phone and make it happen." Jay stood from his seat only to hear his phone beep. When he looked at the screen, he saw a reminder of his appointment with his therapist, Dr. Stuart. Just that quick, he had forgotten about it. The office wasn't open; therefore, he set another reminder to call and reschedule. Once his phone was back in his pocket, he looked at Cesar. His right-hand was looking out the window. "You can look at London later. Get me an earpiece."

Cesar didn't budge. Jay had to trust it was for good reason. Within the last week or so, his right-hand had come through for him when he couldn't come through for himself. "Which part do you have a problem with?" The question made Cesar look at him. "They're about to invade Kenema," he told him. "That's what the call was about. Does that settle your nerves?"

"You don't want that earpiece," Cesar replied.

Jay read his expression. A hint of sadness was there. Not only that, his tone was of one who was begging. It was obvious he was trying to protect him from something. It wasn't anything that could cause bodily harm because that was something Cesar would be open about. It had to be something that would hurt him emotionally. He thought of his kids, but he pushed the image of them away when he thought of the woman who birthed them. Without Cesar even saying it, Jay figured it out. *Carmen was cheating on him.*

***

A variety of scents met Carmen in the foyer. She was up early as she didn't want to miss Tiara when she dropped Robin off. Fiona or Silvas was up as well because she could smell the hickory smoked bacon right where she was standing. There was also the smell of fresh paint. The scent led her in the dining room to see the repairs. The room looked better than the night before, but bare. The empty table reminded her she had to replace the dishes and the centerpiece. That part was minimal considering the contractors were able to fix the window without the kids knowing it was broken.

When she returned home from being with Kane, the only person she had to explain things to was Akaila. Her daughter was fond of Jay, but the damage to the dining room didn't sit right with her. Carmen took the blame as she knew things Akaila didn't. Her words soothed her daughter enough that she went to bed without another word about it. The ordeal was something they could soon put behind them.

She couldn't say the same for her sex tapes. When the doorbell rung, she was given the reminder of why she was downstairs in the first place. Before Tiara could ring it again, she ran to the door and opened it. As expected, she found her best friend on the other side with her daughter asleep in her arms.

"We let her stay up late," Tiara explained as she made her way in the house. "There's this new show on Netflix that she loves." She didn't go far, turning around in the foyer as she was unsure of where to lay her.

"Well, her two best friends are asleep, so no need to wake her." Carmen opened the door to the home office and pointed towards the couch. "You can put her there. I want to talk to you about something. I'll take her up once we're done."

Tiara followed her directive and placed Robin on the couch. In the meantime, Carmen grabbed the emails between Monifah and Culture XL. "I'm gonna cut to the chase. Jay found out whose behind the tapes. It's Monifah. This is some of the proof as these emails detail how she tried to give the video of me and Jay to Culture XL." She handed the papers to Tiara, yet her friend only read the first one before dropping the emails at her side. When her eyes became teary, Carmen became confused. The matter was one that called for anger, not tears.

"I should've told you," Tiara said, crying. "She asked me about it."

From the little bit Tiara said, it was obvious her friend had been withholding information.

"She asked me if I knew who had the tape of you and Carlos," Tiara continued. "I told her I didn't know because I don't. I should've told you she was looking for it."

"Ya think?" Carmen shouted. Her anger was building. "You've been sitting up here watching me go fuckin' crazy and you knew what this bitch was doin'?"

When the papers dropped from Tiara's hand, Carmen told herself to calm down. It wasn't like Tiara knew Monifah had the tape. She only knew she asked about it. Still, it was something else her best friend failed to tell her. "I wanted you to know because I know y'all have been communicating," Carmen explained. "I haven't told Kane. My plan is to talk to him after church."

"Can you wait until after the baby is born? Monifah called me this morning—"

"I already know about all that," Carmen interrupted, "which is why I didn't tell Kane." She picked up the papers. "Is there anything else I need to know? I don't want any more surprises." She watched her friend closely. When Tiara's lips parted, she knew another bomb was about to drop.

"Monifah is having a little girl. They decided to name her Isabella."

The news was a relief. While she wasn't one hundred percent content about the baby, she was happy Monifah didn't give him a son. Kane might have considered King his first-born, but he wasn't his birth father. If Monifah was carrying his first biological son, the dining room would've been back in ruins. "I'm actually cool with that," she shared. "Anything else?"

"Carlton wants to talk to Jay. Can you get him to agree to a phone call?"

"I don't even think my husband will agree to a call with me. Last night wasn't good to us. I have no clue where he is."

"You know what," Tiara exclaimed, heading towards Robin. "I'm not even going to ask for those details." She bent down and kissed her daughter's cheek. "I hope the day gets better for us both. Just know, I will be distancing myself from Monifah. We did reconnect, but my loyalty will always be to you."

"I appreciate that," Carmen replied. She met Tiara halfway and they gave each other a much needed embrace. When they broke apart, Robin began stirring. "Let's pray she falls back asleep. Once my kids know she's here, they'll be running all around this house."

They shared a short chuckle as they headed out the office. Silvas and Fiona could be heard in the distance. Carmen invited Tiara to stay for breakfast, but her friend told her she was working on finalizing the plans for the anniversary party.

"You are gonna come?" Tiara asked. "You're not gonna let this suspension stop you?"

Carmen had thought about skipping it. She never finalized the decision, which was why she was continuing to find dresses and suits for the event. Lots of money would be down the drain if she didn't attend. Besides, Flame was her company. She should be there before anyone else. "I'm coming. It'll be uncomfortable, but I've walked into worse rooms."

"That's what I wanted to hear," Tiara shared, now walking towards her car. When she reached it, Carmen didn't move from the front door. Across the street from the estate was the black car. She didn't know who was in the car or what they were reporting back to Jay. What she did know is that she didn't want him to learn anything that could cause more destruction.

22

London, England

Scarfes Bar.

The words echoed in Jay's mind as the door to the master bedroom closed. With nothing but time to kill, he should've been joining Cesar for a drink. Instead, he was choosing to stay cooped up in their suite to further dissect whether his wife had been unfaithful. The second Cesar put it in his head, the opportunity had been there to ask him. He just didn't. Now he was asking himself why. The only logical answer he could produce is that if he didn't know the truth, there was always the possibility she hadn't. *However, if I did know the truth,* he thought, *I would have confirmation she hadn't.*

He walked around the suite he would call home for the next couple of days. The living area had an open floor plan and was outfitted with Italian furnishings. Various works of art lined the walls including a painting of an English woman. An elegant and chic vibe, armchairs and coffee tables decorated the space completing the aesthetic. The feel of the room reminded him of home. The way he exited wasn't fair to his children. While he didn't want to see or talk to Carmen, he had to. The kids were too young for cell phones so if he wanted to speak to them, he would have to go through her. Fiona and Silvas were options; however, they would need Carmen's help to answer a FaceTime call. Akaila wasn't an option because she was in class. From the way he saw it, reaching out to Carmen was the best choice. If anything, he would only have to deal with her for a minute.

While he waited for her to answer, he wandered into the dining room.

"Hey," he heard her say.

His eyes went to the screen. She was sitting on their bed, her hair brushed into a neat bun. "Can I speak to the kids?" He got straight to the point, not wanting to prolong the conversation.

"Yeah, I'll get 'em."

Easy, he thought. In less than three seconds, the thought proved itself to be premature.

"Where are you?" she asked.

She hadn't made it out the bedroom. It was a clear sign the kids weren't in the room. He couldn't even hear them in the background. "I only wanna speak to the kids."

"I'm gonna get 'em. Can you tell me where you are?"

"I ain't tellin' you shit. Get my kids."

He lit the match for an argument. To keep it from brewing, he ended the call. It was a mistake, which was why he called her back. He asked again for his children.

"That's not the problem," she yelled at him. "I'm not keeping them from you. You know where they are. We don't know where you are."

He kept his tone and volume the same. "Can I speak to my kids?"

The question set her off further. She didn't communicate her anger verbally, yet he heard it in her loud stomps down the hall. She then put on an Oscar-winning act.

"Guess what, y'all," she squealed, walking inside Nyla's room. His kids were in the middle of the floor with Robin. They were working on a puzzle, which he learned she wasn't supposed to see.

"You're ruining the gift," Rakim yelled, trying to cover the parts they had put together.

"I know," Carmen told him. "I'm sorry, baby, but look who it is." She brought the phone closer to them. Both Rakim and Nyla abandoned the puzzle, jumping up and down at the sight of him.

"How's my bebés?" Jay yelled. "Tell mommy to go back to her room. It's our time."

Rakim grabbed the phone, already talking a mile a minute. It didn't faze Nyla who started her own conversation, showing him a picture she'd drawn. He asked them about the puzzle, what they had eaten, and even practiced Spanish with them until they were no longer interested. At the end of the call, he broke the news he wouldn't be home.

"Daddy is working," he explained. "Sometimes we have to make sacrifices to get the things we want." They didn't grasp what he was saying. He followed it up with, "I love y'all. Anytime you wanna call me, you can. I don't care what time it is."

"What if you're sleeping?" Nyla screamed. "And you got on your jammies?"

"Even then," Jay said with a laugh. "I don't care if it's the middle of the night."

He stared at them, watching as their attention went back to the puzzle. "Rakim, get your mother for me." He didn't have any intention of having a conversation with her, but he needed her to get the phone. The kids were ready to get back to her gift.

"Daddy wants you," he heard Rakim say once he was in her bedroom.

Jay stayed quiet even when Carmen had the phone. Rakim was still lingering, which meant they would continue their act of a happy married couple until he was gone. Once his son ran from the room, he took a long hard look at his wife. Words fell on the tip of his tongue only to remain unspoken. Questions rose in his mind that went unanswered because he didn't ask. While he was the one who transgressed and filmed their intimate moment, the reason he did it led back to her. The memory of her betrayal brought back the seed Cesar planted of another indiscretion.

"Are you happy?" she asked him.

He didn't know how to take the question. She knew what she had done. She hammered the nail that could break up their family. She was the one who pretended she wanted another baby when she didn't. Still, through his own agony, he showed his love for her by boarding a plane to London. She didn't even deserve it. He wanted to yell it at her, but he couldn't. It was best not to speak on the contract until he had it secured.

"You need to call Silvas," she was now saying. "He wants to know when he can go home." She gave him a chance to respond, which he didn't take. "Can we talk about that? I think it's been long enough. Can you tell me why the house got shot up?" Jay didn't address it although she deserved to know. She also deserved to know there were a slew of people staked out at their estate. "So, you just want to stare at me?" She threatened to hang up. She didn't do it, choosing to stay on the call, waiting for him to say something. When he finally did, he said something she'd heard all her life. Her name. When she looked at him, he summed up his emotions in two words.

"Fuck you."

***

Rakim would never know it, but the best thing he ever asked her to do was leave Nyla's room. By forcing her out, Carmen didn't have to subject him, Nyla, or Robin to her tears. They didn't see her as she punched pillows and cursed about the man she promised God she would spend forever with. They were blind to her hurt as well as Jay's. She knew her husband was hurting. He was grieving a loss that was never conceived. It was the reason she asked him where he was. She wanted to talk things out. Nevertheless, the velocity in which he spoke to her, showed he wasn't going to give her the chance.

He needs time, she cried. *I need to give him more time.*

She had to pull it together. The kids were only going to leave her alone for so long. She hated lying to them, but she didn't want her marital problems affecting their happiness.

"Mommy," Nyla called, running down the hall.

Carmen moved quick, wiping her face again and tidying up the bed. Unlike Rakim, Nyla didn't barge in her room. She knocked on the door and waited for her to open it. Her daughter's thoughtfulness gave her a few extra seconds to change her mood. When she opened the door, all her daughter saw was a woman on top of the world. "Did they send you down here to tell me it's lunchtime?" She scooped Nyla into her arms. "Is my gift ready?"

"Nope, you can't see it." Nyla pulled away from her, running back down the hall to her room. Once she reached her door, she stood in front of it, arms outstretched to keep her from entering. "Can't come in."

"Well, I'll wait a little longer," Carmen replied. She moved from the doorway to grab her phone. The second her fingers touched it, Tiara's name appeared on the screen. She knew she was calling to check on Robin, so she answered. "Right on time," she told her. "I was getting ready to gather 'em up so they could eat. Do you want to talk to your mini me?"

"Yeah, in a minute. I need to give you the heads up on something."

"I'm all ears," Carmen replied. She took her time going down the hall, not wanting the kids to interrupt the conversation.

"This morning I asked you not to tell Kane about Monifah."

"You did," Carmen confirmed. "Did he find out? Did he admit to having the tapes?"

"Nah, none of that. Monifah called me to let me know she was out the hospital. I wasn't going to answer, and I knew I told you not to tell Kane, but I had to confront her."

The news sent Carmen back to her room. She closed her door, desperate to hear what her friend had to say. She was glad Tiara went back on her word because she could get the answers she wanted.

"I didn't ask her why she did it because we know that. I asked her why she didn't think about your kids. Like, we ain't in the streets no more. We're grown women with responsibilities. Shit like this stays with you. It stays with your kids. I asked her why she didn't think about Jay. I mean, he's a patient at her damn clinic."

"Well, what did she say to that?" Carmen asked.

"She said you deserve everything you're getting."

Carmen grimaced. "Her crazy ass. She's a therapist who needs a therapist."

"I said that to her, too," Tiara shared. "Not those exact words, but ya know."

Carmen needed more information. "Did she say where she got the tapes?"

"Nah, I didn't get that far. I planned to ask her, but she told me she had to go. Something about Kane's mama burnin' some rice."

"Oh, Lord," Carmen muttered. She filled Tiara in on Beverly and by the time she was done, she was in Nyla's room. She collected the kids and handed her phone to Robin so she could speak with her mother. After the call ended, she and the kids were in the kitchen. Silvas was fixing the kids' plates while Fiona was pouring their drinks. Carmen went to grab the napkins and silverware only to hear an incoming alert on her phone. When she saw a random number, she figured it was spam until she read the message.

The President will address the nation tonight at 7pm. You need to watch. Cesar.

***

The door hadn't even closed behind him before Jay pulled off his tie. He and Cesar had bounced around the hotel's dining rooms and bars for hours, trying to catch any glimpse of Beregé they could get. The feat was unsuccessful and eventually they ran out of time. While it was nearing midnight in London, it was going on seven o'clock in Brookstone. They were minutes away from the President's address.

"We'll have to catch him tomorrow," Cesar told him, turning on the television. "He's here. I got word he checked in."

"He must've stayed in his suite because he didn't show for dinner." Jay plopped down on the sofa, his jacket now beside him along with his tie. "Hopefully, we'll catch him at breakfast." He pulled out his phone, but he didn't unlock it when he noticed he hadn't gotten a response from Cesar. He looked at his right-hand who was setting the channel to CNN International. "What are they talking about?" he asked him. He suspected something was up only because Cesar had gotten quiet on him. He was obviously listening to a conversation in his earpiece.

"Your wife," was all he got. Before he could probe him for more, the President's image became displayed on the television's 75-inch LED screen. Cesar increased the volume, before taking a seat in an armchair. They listened as the President announced the start of Operation Artemis. He explained the purpose of the attack and how America would be helping to free the people of Sierra Leone. The address was only seven minutes long and once it was over, Cesar retired to his room.

Jay did the same. About to jump in the shower, he changed his mind when he thought back to Cesar's words. *Your wife* was echoing in his mind. Cesar had him curious. Instead of asking for clarification, he decided to find the answer. He grabbed his phone and went to the home security app. The first camera he checked faced the driveway and the front gate. No one was outside. He rewound the footage only to see a black car and then Carmen's Honda. She had left without the kids. The cameras couldn't tell him where she went, but he knew Cesar could. What the cameras could tell him was that she returned two hours later.

Although he wanted to know where she had been, he waited until the following morning to ask. They were walking to Holborn Dining Room when he brought it up. "Carmen left last night," he told him. "Do you know where she went?"

"You know I know," Cesar concurred. "You also know I can't tell you."

They had gone through rules and expectations a long time ago. The agreement was that their location would only be revealed if there was a threat to their safety. Therefore, Jay asked a different question. "What do you think of my wife?" Those words made Cesar stop in his tracks. Jay stopped as well, but neither of them spoke as other guests passed by. Once they were alone, Cesar replied.

"What I think about your wife doesn't matter. You stood in front of God and made a vow. The only vow I made was to keep her alive."

"You've done an excellent job of that," Jay acknowledged.

Cesar continued walking to the dining room. "If you really want to know what I think," Cesar began. He faced Jay. "You got a whole lot more than a lot of men around here. It's all materialistic, though. You got money, but you ain't got no self-esteem. You tore up your house because your wife won't give you another baby. The only reason you want another baby is because you think it'll keep her from leaving you. You still want her to prove she's here for the long haul. She doesn't need to carry another child to show you that." He took a few more steps. This time when he spoke, his voice was much lower. "You killed her fuckin' mother and she's parading around like it didn't happen. She didn't even leave you for that. If it was me, I would've slit your fuckin' throat."

Jay's face remained set as he took in Cesar's words. His wife took what self-esteem he had when she cheated. He questioned everything about himself. While he thought he was the only one who saw the damage, it was obviously external.

"This shit with you and Carmen," Cesar continued, "can be over in the next two days."

He looked past his right-hand to see he was pointing inside the dining room. In clear view, eating breakfast with another gentleman was Oliver Beregé. The men weren't alone as they were joined by two bodyguards who stood on each side of the booth. They didn't intimidate Jay, which is why he approached the table. The bodyguards were quick, both stepping to him to block his path.

"How can we help you, sir?" one of them asked.

Jay spoke loud enough for Beregé to hear him. "Tell Mr. Beregé I need to speak with him regarding Kiyoshi Feng."

Beregé dropped his fork. The French businessman whispered a few words to the man eating in front of him. He didn't hear what he said, but the man collected his things. The meeting was over. Once he was gone, Jay took his seat in the booth.

"Y'all can stand over there," Beregé said to his right-hands. He waited for them to get out of earshot before he spoke. "What do you know about Kiyoshi Feng?"

Jay dropped the name to catch the man's attention. Now that he had it, he pulled out his cell phone to discuss the real topic at hand. "Carmen Santiago," he told him, showing him a picture of his wife. "She's an American fashion designer who was about to open her first store in Westfield Stratford City. She had a couple of hiccups, and the contract was pulled."

Beregé looked flabbergasted. "I don't know this woman. I've never seen her in my life. Besides, I've made too much money to even worry about what stores are going in that mall." He picked up his fork, sticking it in his poached eggs. "Who is she to you?"

"My wife," Jay replied. He grabbed the fork out the man's hands. "This may seem little to you," he whispered, "but it's major. I need you to get her contract back."

Beregé grabbed a napkin and wiped his mouth. "And who are you?"

The question brought a sinister smile to Jay's face. "Death."

"Okay, Mr. Death, you obviously have some information on me. You brought up Kiyoshi Feng. Tell me, why was the contract pulled?"

"A sex tape," Jay told him. "Two to be honest."

Beregé shook his head. "That's not enough to keep her out the mall. If you ask me," he said, tapping the picture of Carmen, "that may be the reason." Beregé grabbed his fork from Jay's hand. "They probably didn't want her there."

"They," Jay questioned.

"The powers that be," Beregé explained. "Look, I don't deal with this. My tax bracket grants me the luxury of not dealing with this petty shit. I would have to call around." Beregé picked up the cell phone and stared at the picture of Carmen. "London is a long way from home. Let me guess, you want me to get you this contract or you'll release whatever you have on me and Kiyoshi Feng?"

"No," Jay said, flatly. "I want you to get me this contract or I'll kill you."

Beregé gave the same reaction most people gave when he threatened their life. Nervousness would manifest, their body would shake, and the fear of death could be seen in their watery eyes. "If you ask me, death is the easy punishment," Jay explained. "It's short and quick. If I release the photos of you fuckin' a fourteen-year-old Asian girl, you suffer. You lose your businesses, money, your family, and you go to prison. You're still within the statute of limitations."

"That was a mistake I made in my past. I could sue you for extortion."

"You can," Jay agreed, "and that is the hard road to travel. With that lawsuit, you'll have to tell a judge what I have hanging over your head."

Beregé picked up the cell phone again and stared at the picture of Carmen. "Give me a few days to look into it. My schedule is packed. I'll see what I can do."

"I'm giving you twenty-four hours."

"Who are you again?"

"Death," Jay responded. He reached inside the pocket of his suit jacket and took out his business card. He set it on the table for Beregé to view. "Google me. It'll help you work quicker." Beregé picked up the card and mouthed his name. "Also," he continued, "here's a piece of advice. Don't try any funny business. I have eyes on you." He pulled his cell phone out Beregé's hands.

"Wait," Beregé shouted once he saw Jay walk from the booth. When he noticed Jay wasn't moving, he pulled out his phone. He went to Google and typed in the name on the business card. Various articles and mugshots came up, which he browsed to get a hint at what he was up against. Murderer and drug kingpin came up more than he wanted to see, but the word that stood out the most was billionaire. "Why do you need me?" he asked, showing Jay the screen. "You've got enough money to buy her a mall."

"Oh, I'm gonna do that, too," Jay admitted. "This store will get our feet wet. Besides, this is what she wants."

"And what do you want?" Beregé asked.

The question brought a smile to Jay's face. "I want her."

23

The Sunday evening sky was grey and dreadful-looking. A vast contrast from the mood on the plane. On a flight back to Brookstone, Jay held a gold-plated, eight-by-eleven box in his hands. The box contained a newly drawn agreement for Flame to be housed in Westfield Stratford City. Also, inside the box was a signed contract between him and his new business partner, Oliver Beregé. The phrase, keep your enemies closer, couldn't rang truer. Beregé knew he couldn't risk having him on the other side of the world with his skeleton. Therefore, he offered him a partnership that would keep them in constant communication. Together, they would build new malls in London within the city's black and brown communities.

The move was major as he was investing a large chunk of money and time. One of the pros of the deal is that Carmen would have business in London, too. Their new business ventures would give him reason to break ground on an estate in the UK. By doing so, he would be fulfilling the promise he made to Carmen of a new home a year ago.

"My laptop died," Cesar told him. "I don't know where my cord is. You got power? The stream is about to start."

Jay set the box in the seat next to him and picked up his laptop. "I forgot about church. This time difference messed me up. It's almost eleven in New York." He watched as his computer booted up. "We missed bible study."

"We can watch the playback," Cesar suggested.

Once the home screen was up, Jay connected the laptop to the plane's Wi-Fi. When he had the livestream pulled up, the congregation was on the second verse of *The Great Redeemer*. "You need to take time off when we get back," he told Cesar. His right-hand was busy humming to the song.

"I can't," Cesar replied. "The anniversary party is this weekend. I gotta meet with the team, get a plan together, learn the venue. More than likely, they'll have a security check. We can't bring any heat through the doors. I gotta find a place to hide our guns."

Jay scratched his chin. While Carmen had talked to him about the party, she hadn't mentioned it in the last few days. He didn't even know if she was going. If she was, he was going with her. The last thing he wanted was her in a room full of backstabbers by herself. "I haven't talked to her," he said, thinking aloud. "The last thing I said to her was fuck you."

"So, you're just going to show up with that box?"

A shrug was all Jay could give in reply. He didn't know what he was going to do. He had plenty of time to think about it, though. He centered his attention on the service, putting all things Carmen on the backburner. It worked for the time being until Minister Harrison gave the invitation. One by one, members of the congregation came to the front, Carmen being one of them.

"For the past week, there has been a dark cloud over me," she was saying. "I was in a space I haven't been in, in a long time. I felt like a failure. I doubted myself as a wife and mother. My darkest sins were shown to the world."

Tears ran down her face. Jay touched the screen as if he could wipe them away. Her pain bothered him, but what brought tears to his eyes was when Rakim ran down the aisle. A soft moan sounded from the congregation as their son grabbed on to her legs.

"I have sinned," Carmen cried. "I've repented of those sins." Her lips were still moving, yet Jay couldn't hear her. His attention was fixated on the arm that was now around her shoulders.

The last person he expected to see at the altar with her was Kane. Yet, there he was, consoling her, as she confessed her sins and cried out to God for forgiveness. To make matters worse, Kane was now carrying Rakim back to his seat while his free hand was entangled with Carmen's. If he didn't know them, he would've thought they were a family.

"If that ain't repentance, I don't know what is," Cesar commented.

"You liked that?"

"She repented." Cesar pointed at the screen. "She made her soul right with God. She did what she had to do. She did the…" He didn't finish. "You didn't like Kane," he said, realizing the problem. "I see." He shrugged his shoulders. "He was being a friend. She needed support and he was there. I mean, I didn't see Tiara or King running to her side."

Jay slammed the laptop closed. The announcements were starting, but he didn't want to hear anymore. He dropped the laptop next to the box and stood from his seat. "He's tryin' to fuck," he whispered. *You ain't foolin' me. You're trying to be a knight in shining armor. I see you. Keep on. I've been waiting to gut your ass.*

***

Carmen's entire mood had changed since morning worship. For one, after service was over, she headed to King's house to have a one on one conversation with Malachi. He didn't show for church, and she learned from Akaila it was because he didn't want to see her.

She didn't like the idea of bulldozing him, but she had to. When she opened the door to his room, he was inside playing a video game. Headphones covered his ears, so he didn't know she was there until she had him in her arms. He tried to break away, but to no avail. She maintained her grip, planting numerous kisses on his cheeks in between apologies. In a short amount of time, she had him hugging her back. That marked the start of a lengthy conversation. At the end of it, they were on better terms. He even agreed to go back to school. She left King's house feeling accomplished, which was different than how she came.

Even now, she felt that way. Dinner was put away, the kitchen was clean, and the kids were in Silvas' room watching TV. She hadn't told them, but she planned to take them out for ice cream. They needed to get out as much as she did. She was on her way to let them know when her phone rung from the counter. She rushed to get it when she saw Kane's name on the screen.

"Hey," she greeted. When he didn't say anything, she checked the timer to make sure it was still going. "Are you there?"

"I need you again," he told her. "I'm sorry to even be saying that."

"What happened?" Carmen asked. She grabbed a stool and sat on it, knowing she was going to be awhile.

"Monifah had a problem with what I did at church. She didn't like that I went up there with you. I tried to explain that you were falling apart, but my wife…" Kane let out a large sigh. "I love this woman, but I want her to understand the place we're in. I swear, it was much easier on my marriage when we were arguing."

"She felt disrespected. You know she doesn't like me. You practically gave her a big 'fuck you,' to the face."

"I wasn't thinking about that," Kane admitted. "You were crying, you were upset. No one was coming to support you. I mean, where was Jay?"

At one point, Carmen didn't know where her husband was. Then, she checked their bank accounts. The recent transactions showed her husband was in London. He spent thousands on the trip according to the numerous charges. Something told her he was there to get her contract back. "Away on business," she told Kane, finally answering. "That's something I don't have to worry about. I'm suspended. I was about to take the kids to Jeni's. Wanna come?"

Carmen didn't see it, but the invitation brought a smile to Kane's face. He accepted and thirty minutes later, she, the kids, and two car seats, were piling into his Jeep. The rest of the house opted not to come but sent her to the creamery with a list of pints they wanted.

The ice cream shop was packed from wall to wall. Despite the numerous people, Rakim was jumping on the glass trying to see the different buckets of ice cream. "I can't see," he shrieked.

"I got'chu." Kane picked him up and leaned him towards the counter. "You see the blue and white one," he pointed out. "That's Rocket Pop. It's my favorite. You wanna try that one?"

Carmen smiled as the two interacted. She could tell Rakim felt more comfortable around Kane than Nyla. He had a bond with Kane that was first established at birth. For more than a year, Kane was the man he knew as his father. With Nyla, it was different. She and Kane separated for a second time shortly after she was born, which didn't give her the chance to know him. "Do you want to see the ice cream, too?" She didn't want Nyla to feel left out although she never asked to see the flavors.

"I want that," Nyla screamed. She ran over to a sign that advertised a big scoop of purple ice cream. "And I want it this big." She held her arms out almost knocking over the sign.

"You can get a pint, but you're not eating all that tonight." She grabbed Nyla's hand, leading her to the counter. Rakim was giving his order to the shop's clerk with Kane interrupting every now and again to help her understand. Rakim was doing so much talking, she looked to see how many people were waiting. To her surprise, a familiar face was there. *This is a coincidence.* The Hispanic woman she saw outside of Flame was standing in line at the back of the shop. Carmen gave her a smile, which wasn't returned. *Forget about her, she's nobody.*

She ordered her and Nyla a waffle cone filled with Wildberry Lavender ice cream. She also got two pints of the same flavor. When she got to the cashier, she whipped out the list she compiled from the rest of the house. It took a minute for the clerks to collect the pints, but once everything was paid for, they ventured outside to eat.

"We can't stay out here long," Carmen reminded them. "Y'all know we got this." She held up the bag of ice cream. "We don't want it to melt."

"Es tan bueno," Nyla squealed, licking her ice cream.

Carmen watched as Kane shot her a questionable look. "She said it's so good," she told him. "Akaila started teaching them Spanish while she was on break. I've learned some of it."

Kane shot Nyla a smile.

They continued eating until Carmen told them they needed to go. She spotted two men taking pictures of them, which meant there was going to be another headline on TMZ. Once word got back to Jay, she would be spending another hour getting cussed out for having the kids around her ex. *If only I didn't have to be photographed doing it.*

"Do you still need to talk to me?" Kane asked once they were back in his Jeep.

"I do." She had almost forgotten about the emails.

"Cool," he said, starting the engine. "This is probably the best time to do it."

Carmen looked in the rearview mirror as he pulled off. She was looking for the black car and sure enough, it appeared. She didn't tell Kane they were being followed, but she did tell him to park in the garage once they were at her house. She took the kids inside, put the ice cream in the freezer then got them settled in their rooms. Her next stop was the home office. She grabbed the papers before returning to Kane's Jeep.

She handed the emails over. "You can read it for yourself."

The papers were in chronological order. She watched Kane closely as he went page by page. He stopped at the third one, now visibly upset. "You're showing me this to prove what?" he shouted. "That I had the tapes and gave 'em to her?"

"No," Carmen corrected. "To show you that your wife was the one behind it all."

"This isn't even her email address. It's her name in the address, but it's not one of the ones she uses. I have her personal one and work one. I use both." Kane went back to the emails continuing to read. "I will say it sounds like her. She does talk like this." He stopped again on the fifth page. "Look, you know I didn't have the tape of you and Jay. I never had the tape with you and Carlos. The Triad didn't collect the tape. I can prove it." He reached in his pocket and pulled out his phone. He handed it to her, which she took. "Call Sanders and have him pull Jay's file. The report is there from what we collected. None of it was a tape. He can email it to you."

"I know you didn't do it," Carmen told him, setting his phone in her lap. "I want you to ask Monifah where she got it. That's all. That's the missing piece of the puzzle. I'm racking my brain trying to figure out how she got close enough to Jay to even get his phone."

Kane arranged the papers in a half-fold and stuck the emails in his glove compartment. He took his phone from Carmen's lap. "Regardless of what she says," he began as the line rung. "Don't say shit."

To show him she would cooperate, she didn't respond. She waited for Monifah to pick up. When she did, she wished she hadn't. The woman was on ten.

"Where did you go this time?" Monifah yelled. "I went to Flame, you weren't there. You found another parking lot to sleep in?"

"I drove around the city," Kane responded. "I'll be home soon." He took a moment to form his words. "You know Carmen still has the investigation open. I told you my friend at the Triad was looking into the tapes."

"She can investigate all she wants. The bitch needed to come down."

Kane didn't look at Carmen as he didn't want to see her reaction. "He sent me copies of some emails between you and Culture XL. According to these emails, you were trying to sell him the tape of her and Jay."

Monifah became even more agitated. "I don't care about that shit. They can have emails, video, the whole nine. I just want her to pay for what she did to us. Did I tell you what Tee told me? She's been workin' with her for almost twenty-somethin' years, and she only owns five percent of Flame. Like, wake up, Carmen. This girl saved your fuckin' life. Your crazy ass boyfriend would've killed you if it wasn't for her. And Tiara's dumb ass doesn't want to say anything to her about it. She's been wanting more." She switched her anger back to Kane. "And you had the nerve to stand next to the bitch in front of the whole church?"

"Let's not start that again." Kane upped his volume. "We've talked about that."

"How? When you walked out?" she screamed. "You got your head stuck up her dirty pussy, too. Admit it. You feel good now that she's smiling in your face. When she was shittin' on you, you couldn't stand her. You talked so much shit about her."

"How did you get the tapes?" Kane asked, changing the subject.

"Fuck you," Monifah yelled. She hung up the phone.

With the line now silent, Carmen let her true emotions show. She was hurt by Monifah's words, but even more hurt at how much she knew. Tiara never expressed any displeasure over owning only five percent of the company. She thought she was fine with the arrangement.

"I didn't want you to hear all that," Kane told her. He placed his hand on her leg, giving it a soft rub. "I did say some things," he admitted. "I was hurt. I lashed out and Monifah was there to listen. You were so caught up with Jay, I don't even think you knew how hurt I was."

"I did know," she confessed. "I was hurt, too, but I had to make the best decision for us. We weren't going to make it." She wore her heart on her sleeve. "You deserve to have a better woman than me." She held her hand up when Kane attempted to speak. "I told you a long time ago I would never let Jay go. I had to face the truth for myself. After Nyla was born, you told me he was going to use her to get back with me. He did. I fought him off. I tried to be faithful, but trying is just that, trying. I couldn't fight him off anymore. I saw it happening before it did. Jay and I had two young kids together. I chose to leave, so I wouldn't cheat."

"We were married for half our lives. How was it so easy for you to walk away from me?"

"That's the thing," she cried. "It wasn't." She didn't speak for a few seconds. "I just knew you had the strength to walk away from me. I can't make the same mistakes and expect you to stay."

Kane sat there in a state of confusion. Carmen was the woman he thought knew everything about him. For some reason, she was showing him she didn't. "You were wrong," he said, slowly. "I couldn't walk away from you. That's why I was begging for you to come back."

Carmen could remember the multiple occasions he asked her to give them another chance.

"I want to make love to you."

She cringed. She wasn't hearing right. It wasn't possible. Kane didn't just say he wanted to make love to her. She heard wrong.

"We can get a room in the city," he was now saying, "just for tonight. I'll pay for it. That way nothing will be in your name."

A slight breath escaped her lips. *How did we get over here?*

"You know we make magic in the bed. Right now is the best time. We're both going through a lot. We need to escape even if it is for a couple of hours."

"My period is on," was the first thing out her mouth. It was her first thought after the initial shock had worn off. Nevertheless, his reply wasn't what she expected.

"We've never done that before," he said with a smile. "Well, there was that one time you said I knocked it on, but you know." He chuckled for a bit. "I'm not gonna let that stop me. You shouldn't either. Now, I won't eat you out, but I'll stick my dick in it."

"Your wife is pregnant," was the second thing out her mouth. "This is the wrong time."

"My wife," Kane retorted, "is driving me insane. From the looks of things, so is your husband." A stretch of silence ensued. "But if it's the wrong time, when is the right time? There is a right time if there is a wrong one, eh?"

At that very moment, she had an angel and a devil on both her shoulders. They were dueling it out. The devil told her to sleep with him. For one, she knew the power in his pants. She needed to get off and the dick was there and willing. Then, the angel presented its case. She wasn't that person anymore. She was married and so was Kane. She had repented of that sin and didn't need to commit it again. "I can't keep doing this," she told him. "I don't want to keep making the same mistakes."

"I don't either," Kane responded, "but we both have a need."

"Is it just sex? Is that all you want? I mean, what if we do it and we can't stop? What if our bodies don't know each other anymore? Like, this can be bad for both of us."

"You know our bodies know each other," he rebutted. "The way you held on to me in your office that day. Or what about the other night when you gave me the temple rub? Like, come on, Carm, I know you felt my dick. I was so fuckin' hard."

Carmen's eyes enlarged. She hadn't felt it. It was because she wasn't looking for it. What she did feel was the wetness now in her own pants. His words were turning her on, sending her down a road of endless memories. Kane had been her partner for a long time. There were nights when she would wake him out his sleep just to feel him inside her.

"Is it just sex?" she asked again. "I need to know. We can't hurt each other."

"It will never be just sex. It will have to be, though. We're married to other people."

Carmen was in a battle between good and evil. If she slept with him, she would be setting off the same bomb that initially destroyed her relationship with Jay.

"I'm begging you."

Those words were even stronger than him saying he wanted to make love. It was too much. It was all too much. She needed a break. "I need to check on the kids," she told him. "Sit tight for just a moment. Let me check on them and I'll let you know. Can I have a few minutes?"

Kane rubbed her leg again except this time he made sure to move his hand all the way up her thigh. "Why are you fighting it? You want it. I can see it."

"I'll be back," she replied. She unlocked the doors and got out his Jeep. He didn't say anything, nor did he follow her in the house. She checked on

Silvas first, finding him asleep in his room. She then went upstairs to Akaila's room. She knocked on the door only to hear a round of giggles. She opened it to find Rakim and Nyla inside. They each had spoons in their hands and were sharing a pint of ice cream. "I told y'all it was time for bed," she fussed. "I also told y'all no more." She went inside and pulled the spoons from them. "Did y'all tell her that?"

"My bad," Akaila apologized. "It's my fault. I let 'em have it."

"Yeah, and you're gonna deal with them, too, when they're jumping off the walls." Carmen pointed towards the door. As expected, both Rakim and Nyla started to whine. "Not tonight," Carmen blurted. "I don't have the energy tonight. You to your room," she said, pointing at Nyla. "And you to yours." She pointed at Rakim.

"I got 'em, Mama," Akaila said, getting up. "I'll tuck 'em in. It's the least I can do."

"No *Paw Patrol*," Carmen yelled. "I gave y'all a freebie the other night."

"No *Paw Patrol*," Akaila repeated. "Y'all heard that."

Carmen giggled at her daughter's tone. In that moment, she sounded like the mother. She shook her head as she escaped to her room. She hadn't thought about what she was going to do with Kane, and time was winding down. Did she want to sleep with him? Yes. She just didn't *need* to sleep with him. *Or did she?* Monifah admitted in so many words that she was the person behind the tapes. Like she said before to Jay, she couldn't sue her, nor did she want to send a pregnant woman to jail. She also couldn't whoop a pregnant woman's ass. The only payback there was, was for her to sleep with Kane. Even if Monifah never found out, it was pleasing to have on the conscience. *One night*, she thought. *We'll do it this one night and be done.*

Her mind now made up, she grabbed a duffle bag from her closet. She tossed in some toiletries, a change of clothes, and undergarments. She also grabbed her phone charger. She snuck back to the garage without running into Akaila. To her dismay, she found Kane in his Jeep with his phone to his ear. When she realized he was talking to Monifah, she dropped the duffle bag.

"I'm on my way. Everything is gonna be okay. I promise you. I'm coming."

Something was wrong. Yet again, something happened. Now, she was standing there feeling like a fool. She made the wrong decision and now it was blowing up in her face. She should've never considered sleeping with him.

"I'm sorry you had to hear that." Kane placed his cell phone in the driver's seat as he stepped out his Jeep. "I wasn't expecting that. Monifah's water broke. I think the stress of everything affected the baby. You know it's too soon. I gotta get to her."

"Of course," Carmen answered, choking back tears. "Your baby is coming."

"This doesn't change what I said." Kane pulled her into him, wrapping his arms around her waist. "I still want us to have our night. It just can't be tonight."

"I get it," she replied, "but this is a sign. We don't need to do this."

"Don't say that to me, Carm." He pulled her in even closer. "Don't say that."

She felt his breath on her neck. The moment was gone. He had to know it. She needed to go inside and tend to her kids while he would be the supportive husband as his wife gave birth.

None of it was going to happen, though, if he kept placing kisses on her neck. "Damn, you taste good," he moaned. He was sucking hard on her skin like he was trying to leave his mark. She let him have his way as it was the only taste of her he was going to get. She fooled herself. When he slipped his hands in the back pockets of her jeans, it marked the start of something greater. They became magnetic. He cupped her ass, pushing her pelvis into his. At the feel of his hard-on, she gyrated. Her right hand held on to the roof of his Jeep while her left hand massaged the back of his neck. Despite the lack of penetration, they grinded on each other like he was going deep.

For seconds on end, his dick pounded against her clit, making her hungry for more. She could feel him, but she was greedy. She reached down between them and undid his belt. Their thrusts didn't cease, merely getting more intense the closer they got to being skin to skin. When she had his boxers down, she stopped him. She had to see him. There was only minimal light, but the vein on his shaft called to her. His penis was so pleasing, a voice in her head told her to taste him. Father Time, however, said otherwise.

She moved quick, undoing her jeans, and dropped them at her feet. She kept her panties on to tell him there still wasn't going to be any penetration. He didn't say anything about it, choosing to accept what she gave him. Their bodies collided up against one another, the friction stronger now that the extra fabric was out the way. The passion increased, almost becoming too much to handle. Both her hands were on the roof of his Jeep as he repeatedly thrusted her against his erection. The volume of her moans sent his hand over her mouth. She muffled his the second he came.

Still in bliss, it took a few moments to come down from the high. Once she had, she separated from him and pulled up her pants. Their bodies showed them that physically and emotionally they were still connected. This also wouldn't be the last time. It was the first. They had walked into Pandora's Box and now they were stuck. She didn't have to say it and he didn't either. The evidence was there. The deed was done.

24

No one in the penthouse spoke a word. Everyone was tightlipped as they watched Kane's Jeep emerge from the garage. *He had to be in there for at least an hour,* Jay thought. *That's how long we've been sitting here waiting.* The Jeep exited the front gate of the Santiago Estate. Jay proceeded to check another camera. He saw Carmen as she turned off the hallway lights. A duffle bag was in her hands. The sight of it made him rewound the footage. He hit play, allowing Cesar and Gully to watch the footage as well.

From what he could gather, Carmen had taken the kids with her and Kane. About forty minutes later, they returned home. That was when Jay clocked how long Kane's Jeep had been in his garage.

"There's no camera in there," Cesar stated. "Don't jump to conclusions."

"You're seeing what we're seeing, right?" Gully gave Cesar a suspicious glare. "You got a wife. What would you think if she were behind closed doors with a man she used to suck off?"

Jay put his hands together as if he were praying. He was on the same page as his cousin. This was the third time he caught his wife with her ex. Something was going on between them and Cesar knew it. His right-hand was the one who put it in his head. "Is she fuckin' him? Is that where she went that night? She went to meet up with him?"

Cesar looked past him at Gully.

"Don't look at me," Gully told him. "Answer the question." He headed in the kitchen. He opened one of the cabinets and pulled out a bottle of vodka. He then returned to the living room. "Here's some medicine." He handed the bottle to Jay.

"He doesn't need that." Cesar grabbed the bottle out Gully's hands. "All I know is what I hear. If I didn't see it with my own eyes, why would I bring it to you?"

"Man, this whole job is built around what we see and don't see," Gully argued. "If you know his wife is playin' him, you, as his man, should let him know."

"I don't know," Cesar yelled. "I'm not about to ruin his marriage over something somebody thought they saw. You don't know either. You heard the same thing I did."

A gun cocked.

Cesar didn't have to look to know Jay had a gun at his head. "That shit doesn't scare me, and you know it." He looked at his friend. "You wanna kill me because your wife may be fuckin' around on you? You dead me and what? You don't know a single ghost. You know names. You wouldn't even know who to trust." Jay pressed the barrel into his temple. Cesar didn't flinch. "Call your wife." He stood there, waiting for Jay to decide. The pistol came down.

"Get my clothes," Jay ordered. He grabbed the vodka and disappeared down the hall.

"Wait a minute," Gully stammered. "He ain't about to move up here, is he?"

"Sounds like it to me," Cesar retorted. "Maybe, you should've taken the medicine."

***

Monday

Carmen was in her foyer waiting on Tiara again. What Monifah said weighed on her mind. It kept her from a decent night's sleep as she tossed and turned most of the night. Not even her tryst with Kane had kept her up. Nothing was going to change her mood until she spoke to her.

Through the windowpane, she saw her best friend's car as it approached the front gate. The conversation was set to happen sooner than later. She reached for the doorknob only to be jerked from the door.

She caught a glimpse of Cesar before he put her in a chokehold. No matter how she maneuvered, he kept the upper hand. They tussled for a bit as he dragged her into the home office. He then threw her on the sofa.

"You make my job very fuckin' hard," he yelled through gritted teeth.

Carmen's eyes bulged. "What are you talkin' about?"

"You know what I'm talkin' about. We didn't make no fuckin' deal. You're holdin' my secret, but I didn't agree to hold yours. That's still my best friend. You ain't gonna hurt him."

Suddenly, Carmen knew the topic at hand. "Nothing happened." She was lying, but only because Cesar hadn't seen what she and Kane had done. There weren't any cameras or windows in the garage.

"What happened at Flame? I heard you were on top of him in his Jeep. He was here last night."

"Heard," she questioned. "I wish whoever told you that *actually* heard our conversation. I question what they saw. If they were really watching us, they would've known nothing went down."

The doorbell rang. Cesar backed away from her, his index finger pointed in her direction. "Stay away from Kane," he shouted. He walked backwards to the door. "If you tell Jay I choked you, I'll tell him what I heard. That's on my wife and kids."

The doorbell rang again. At the sound of it, Cesar ran out of view. Meanwhile, Carmen rushed to the door. She opened it to find a cheerful Tiara on the other side. Robin, on the other hand, was out like a light. She didn't greet her as she was still on ten from her encounter with Cesar. Tiara sensed her attitude and without saying anything, placed Robin in the home office.

"Something is up," Tiara stated once she was back in the foyer. "What happened?"

"I told Kane about Monifah," Carmen revealed. "She admitted to putting out the tapes. She also let it be known that you only own five percent of Flame."

"Wait a minute, you talked to her?"

"Kane talked to her," Carmen replied. "I was in the car when he called her. She didn't know I was there. She said a mouthful. So, tell me, how does she know you only own five percent?"

"I told her. I explained to her how they were able to suspend you."

"You never told me you had a problem with owning five percent."

"Shit, I never told her," Tiara shouted. "Wait, wait, wait," she said, holding her hands up. "Is that what she said? I didn't say I had a problem. All I did was breakdown how you were able to get suspended."

"You need to talk to your friend. She twisted your words."

"Yeah, and I am," Tiara stressed, pulling out her phone. She dialed Monifah's number. It rung twice before Carmen snatched the phone from her. She dropped the call.

"She doesn't know I was with Kane. If you call her, it's only going to make things worse. They're having a tough time right now." Carmen handed the phone back to her. "I believe you. You were about to confront her, anyway. That says a lot."

Tiara was glad Carmen believed her. Unfortunately, what Monifah said wasn't a complete lie. She did want more. However, she only expressed it to Malik. "She's trying to strip you of everything. These tapes took your job, your marriage is on the rocks, and now she's working on our friendship."

"We're not gonna let her," Carmen declared. "We know each other. She's so worried about me when she needs to be worried about herself. She needs to go to counseling. I will never be over what happened to Rakim, but I'm not gonna let it consume my life."

"Same," Tiara agreed. She opened her arms for a hug. Once she and Carmen embraced, she gave her a tight squeeze. "I'm sorry this happened. I'm glad we know each other. We can see through the bullshit. I love you. I'm always here for you. I always have been. I was the one holding you down when you were getting your hair braided in D-Block."

Carmen broke the embrace.

***

From the backseat of his limo, Jay watched as Tiara made her way towards the front entrance of Flame. She seemed to be in a pleasant mood, smiling and waving at several individuals as she made her way inside. He wished her demeanor could rub off on him. What he was currently feeling was something he thought could break him. The idea of Carmen cheating had put the desire for blood back in his mouth. He didn't want to feed it, yet he needed something to calm the thirst. While his last conversation with Kane was cordial, he hoped this new one wouldn't be. He needed to draw blood.

The gag of it all was that Kane didn't know he was coming. In addition, Jay didn't know if Kane had showed up for work. He only assumed he was there because he was a full-time employee. He learned his assumption was right when he walked through the first level of the parking deck. Kane was coming out the security office with another man.

"Congratulations, man, everything is going to be fine," he heard the security guard say.

"Thanks, Bruce. Y'all hold it down while I'm out." Kane gave the man a wave. When he saw Jay, he stopped in his tracks.

"I want to talk man to man," Jay told him. He looked at his left hand and pulled off his wedding band. "You see this?" he asked, holding it up. "You know what this means, right?"

"I ain't got time for this shit. My wife just had a baby."

"Wife," Jay stated, overlooking his announcement. "Carmen is my wife."

"Are you on this bullshit again? What did we talk about on the elevator?"

"Are you fuckin' my wife?"

Kane was at his wit's end. He huffed and puffed as if he was struggling to find words. Jay soon learned that wasn't the case. Kane had too many words.

"You'll never get it," Kane replied. "You don't want to. You want to keep this narrative in your head. You're obsessed with it. Carmen divorced *me*. I had to listen to her tell me she didn't want *me*. I took that bullet. I had to watch her give birth, get pregnant, have babies. A constant fuckin' reminder of what I couldn't give her. You can give her that shit, though. You can buy her the fuckin' world." Kane threw his hands up. "Am I fuckin' your wife? I would love to tell you I am. You were fuckin' her when we were married. You gave her two babies. I would love to dick her down just to see the look on your face. Not the look, the pain. I want you to feel what I felt.

"It ain't going to happen," Kane barked, "because we ain't fuckin'." The conversation had him disturbed. "For the past few days or however long, I've had to sit and listen to her cry over you. I had to hear her talk about how much she loves you. How she wants to make you happy. Do you think I wanna hear that shit? Do you think I care about that? She left me for you." Kane was yelling in his face. "She needed a friend, and I was there. Even if I didn't want to be."

Jay scanned the parking deck as a sign of his discomfort.

"You need to talk to your wife," Kane continued. "Work that shit out. You wanted her, didn't you? Now you got her in the fuckin' palm of your hand. You don't see it, though. Why? Why are you so threatened by me? What do I have that you know you don't?"

Jay slid his wedding band back on his finger. Kane's words echoed the same thing Cesar told him. His self-esteem was shot. It went beyond the physical. Throughout his younger years, he was the chosen one. Women swooned over his light skin and eyes. He thought his features was what initially attracted Carmen. He also thought it was his money. Less than a year into his imprisonment, she married a man who looked nothing like him. Kane couldn't even afford her lifestyle. Those two things didn't matter in Carmen's world. Kane possessed something he did not. He gave her peace.

When she was married to Kane, no one had to follow her. She could drive herself around town. No one was sticking a gun in her face. No one was shooting up her house. She could live carefree. He couldn't give that to her. He brought danger and destruction. It was why Carmen still sought out Kane during their troubles. She was looking for peace. Although he couldn't provide that to her, she still wanted to be with him. That was the revelation Cesar and Kane was trying to get him to see. Carmen loved him. The only person that was a threat to her was him. His lack of belief in her love was tearing them apart.

"Are we done here?" Kane asked.

Jay walked to his limo where Gully was waiting. They were done. He shouldn't have been speaking to him in the first place. Carmen's last name was Santiago, not Kane's. She was the person he needed to be speaking to. It was time he showed her he knew it, too.

25

Tuesday

Years ago, shortly after the paternity trial, Carmen asked Jay to give their relationship another shot. Before telling her he would, he draped a twelve million dollar necklace around her neck. His former business partner had sent it to him after acquiring it from a private collection in Switzerland. The necklace contained seventy carats of all white stones. When he took the necklace off her neck, it remained inside his penthouse apartment until he moved it to his San Juan estate. Now, he was retrieving it so he could drape it around her neck again.

"Cesar told me I can't just show up with a box," Jay told Gully who was in the basement with him. He held the necklace up for Gully to see. "If this doesn't say I'm sorry, I don't know what does."

"That shit will say I'm sorry and give her seventy orgasms," Gully joked.

Jay laughed at his cousin's words. He put the necklace back in its package. He hadn't yet spoken to Carmen although he received a call from Silvas. He was desperate to come home, which is another reason Jay was in San Juan. He needed to see the progress on the house. Things were looking up, but he wasn't ready for Silvas to return. He didn't want him to. Though he been away for most of Silvas' stay, it was warming to know his butler was close.

"Where are we going after we leave here?" Gully asked.

Jay answered the question as they made their way out the basement. "Back to Brookstone. I got an appointment with Dr. Stuart tomorrow. Also, Cesar never brought my clothes. I gotta figure something out. Either I'm going home to Carmen or I'm going on a shopping spree. I'm running out of suits. I don't have Fiona or Silvas around to take my shit to the cleaners."

"That's probably why he didn't bring your clothes," Gully suggested. "He wants you to go home. You know he wants you with Carmen."

"I gotta figure out what to say to her first. I'm sorry ain't gonna cut it. I tore up our dining room, disappeared, and cussed her out."

"Well, shit," Gully muttered. "Ain't that what the necklace is for?"

"I'm giving it to her after the anniversary party."

They made it to the first floor when Jay's phone rung. Before he took the call, he told his cousin to get Roman from the kitchen. His plan was to leave San Juan in the next few minutes. "Hello," he answered as Gully left his side. North was on the other end.

"Are you back from London Town?" North joked.

"I'm on this side of the world," Jay admitted. "Let me guess, you're in New York?"

"I am. Can we meet up tomorrow? I got a meeting in Staten Island and one in Manhattan. I want to squeeze you in between the two. You did watch the address, eh?"

"I did and I'm down. Give me a call and we'll meet."

"I call it a plan. Good day, Mr. Santiago."

Jay hung up the phone to see Gully and Roman joining him in the foyer. "I need to check the mail, and after that, we can get on the road."

They made their way outside. After locking up, Jay went to the mailbox. It was overflowing with mail, so he stacked it on top of the box that held the necklace. Once inside the car, he started the sort. He started one pile for himself, one for Silvas, and another was trash. All was good until he stumbled across a letter from Carlton. The postmark showed it was mailed a couple of days before Carmen was suspended. There also wasn't a return address. He read it in silence, from beginning to end.

Jay –

I have been patient with you. I know you are leery of my intentions. I understand. Please take this final outreach as a peace offering. I only want to talk. I have no ill will. You are the closest living person to my brother. I only want to know him. I feel as if you can give me the closure I need. I'm not trying to stalk you. I'm just a determined man. All I want is a one on one conversation. Tiara has been a tremendous help, but her attempts at getting you to meet with me have failed. I do not want to go through your wife. Please reach out to me. Below is my number and email.

Jay tore up the letter. He put it in the trash pile not wanting anything to do with Carlton. If it was his final attempt, he was now rid of him. He should've stopped a long time ago. He had done absolutely nothing to show Carlton he was interested in meeting him. Unless Tiara was feeding him false hope. If she were, the day would come when she would feel his wrath.

***

Tiara stepped in the hospital room holding a vase of flowers and a greeting card. When Monifah texted her that she had given birth, she felt a multitude of emotions. Happiness was one of them as she knew Monifah was excited to be a mother. At the same time, she was disturbed. Her friend had continued to show herself as a manipulative and jealous woman. For that reason, the visit was bittersweet. Tiara was ending a friendship that never got a chance to blossom. To ease the blow, she brought the flowers and card as part of her goodbye.

"Hey, Tee," Monifah greeted, sitting up in bed. "How are you?"

"I should be asking you that. You just had a baby." Tiara looked for a place to set the flowers. When Monifah tapped her meal counter, she set the vase and card there. "How's Isabella?"

"She's a fighter. Kane went to see her this morning in the NICU. Her organs still need to finish developing. She needs to put on some weight. They also saw some jaundice. Once she's making progress, she'll be coming home."

"That's good to hear," Tiara replied.

"Yeah, I wish I could see her more than I do. Kane took pictures, but I want to hold her." Monifah grabbed her phone from the meal counter as if she were going to share the photos. When she put it back, it was obvious she changed her mind. "I guess Carmen told you what they're saying about me."

"She's my best friend. You know I know."

"You really think I did it?"

Tiara stumbled over her words. "From the emails I saw, yes. Your email address was there. You asked me about her tape with Carlos. What am I supposed to think?"

Monifah shrugged her shoulders. "I don't care. I'm glad it happened. I hate that bitch. Anyway, how is it being president of Flame?"

Tiara gripped the siderail of Monifah's bed. "You hurt my friend. Not just my friend, my sister. I don't feel good about being president. Not with the way I got it. It hurts me to my core." She took a moment to collect herself. "I really wanted this to work. I wanted to bridge the gap between you two. I wanted to be there for you. With all that's happened, I can't. I gotta stand on what is right and you aren't it."

"Wow," Monifah mouthed. "You must be eatin' her pussy, too." She tore open the greeting card. "I would say it's a shock, but it ain't. I can see why you would stick by Carmen. She holds the key to the doors you wanna walk in. If you lose her, you'll have nothing. Who would hire someone who can't draw a circle?"

"I've never had an ounce of artistic skills," Tiara confirmed. "Still, I managed to start Flame and help turn it into a multi-million dollar brand. Don't downplay what I've done."

Monifah read the card. Once she was done, she set it back on the meal counter. "You will always be second as long as you're in her shadow. The best piece of advice I can give you is to keep the bitch out. You have a year to show the board what you can do. Get your money up and buy her shares."

"I hope you get the help you need."

A loud giggle sounded out Monifah's mouth. "Oh, baby, the sentiment is the same."

26

Wednesday

If he had to guess, Jay suspected at least three minutes had passed. He was standing in the office of Dr. Stuart, staring at an empty chair. She gave him an exercise to complete, yet he couldn't find the words to start. Therefore, only time and silence were passing. The minutes prior had been used to catch her up on what had been going on with him. After hearing about his marital problems, she suggested the exercise. It was supposed to provide him with the opportunity to voice his grievances with Carlos. While his best friend couldn't hear him from the grave, he could at least find some closure.

"Can you see him?" Dr. Stuart asked. "Remind me of what he looks like."

Jay didn't see him. He saw an empty chair.

"What does he look like, Jay?"

This time, he shot a glance in her direction. He still didn't answer. Instead, he looked back at the chair. This time, it wasn't there at all. In its place, was his old bedroom. In the early nineties, his house wasn't known as the Santiago Estate. It was Casa de Sangre. His room was covered in posters of famed wrestler, Pedro Morales, while a worn copy of *The Great Gatsby* was always by his bedside.

"Get the bottom ones," his father ordered, buttoning his shirt. "It's your first day and you're already going to be late. I told your mama to take that book from you. You've already read it twenty times. You're too young to even be reading it."

Jay did as his father asked. He only managed to button one as his father was working at lightning speed.

"This school isn't going to be like the one in San Juan," his father was telling him. "You and Carlos are going to have to stick together. There won't be a lot of black boys like you. You understand?"

"¿Qué quieres decir?"

"What do you mean," his father corrected. "Say, what do you mean." His father tucked his shirt inside his trousers. "That's exactly what I mean. Not everyone will understand you." He loosened his grip on his trousers. His father picked up his hand, showing him his light brown skin, which was a few shades darker than his olive one. "There aren't a lot of people at this school who look like you. The ones that do may not understand you. Look at it like this." His father dropped his hand. When he did, Jay buttoned and

zipped his trousers. "School hours are the hours you practice your English. When you come home, tú hablas español." He kissed his forehead. "Got it? You're gonna have a wonderful day. Carlos will be there with you."

Jay recalled the conversation like it occurred that morning. His father had been right. The boys at the private school in East Brookstone didn't look like him or Carlos. They mostly had blonde or brown hair with blue or brown eyes. The boys that did look like them, which were few, gave him and Carlos strange looks when they spoke in the language that was natural for them. It left him feeling like an outcast. Within weeks, both he and Carlos were following his father's advice.

"He's there," he heard Dr. Stuart say. Her voice made him look again in her direction. She nodded her head at him, urging him to talk. "He's there," she repeated." He faced the chair. He found himself face to face with Carlos. His friend was dressed in a gray pinstriped suit, one he remembered seeing him wear before. His jet black hair was closely shaven while his face was free of scars and blemishes. He studied him for a bit, not having seen him in more than twenty years.

"You go first," Carlos told him.

"You go, muthafucka," Jay shouted. He took a step forward only to now see an empty chair.

"He's there," he heard Dr. Stuart say again.

Jay looked back at the chair. He saw Carlos sitting there, his eyes still on his.

"Look at you," Carlos said with a smirk. "You became exactly what I thought you were gonna be. Big Jay motherfuckin' Santiago, still running New York."

"You were supposed to be running it with me."

"Was I?" Carlos shrugged his shoulders. "Or am I where I'm supposed to be?"

"You didn't have to be there." Jay took another step forward. "Why did you do that to me? I'm not talking about the drugs or the diamonds. I can get over that shit. Why did you sleep with Carmen? You knew I loved her. You knew *why* I loved her."

"I knew a lot," Carlos admitted. "I've always been with you." He let his words linger in the air. "Maybe I admired you too much. Maybe that's where I went wrong." He looked up as if he were thinking. "I wanted to be just like you. I couldn't accept that I wasn't. Although I tried to be."

"By taking everything I had."

"You got everything I took."

Jay didn't have a comeback. Carlos spoke truth. He still had Carmen and except for the Pink Sunrise, he had all the diamonds he wanted. "You didn't have to do her like that," he said instead. "She was a good girl."

"I fucked her like I did any broad. She was another name on the list."

"She was on my list," Jay yelled. "She was mine." He was spitting in Carlos' face. "You knew why I wanted her." He broke into tears. He was now seeing his mother. Her image was clear as day, as if she were standing right next to Carlos. "Her skin," he cried. "When I saw her. That dark skin, like my mother's. She was so beautiful. The way she talked, the way she moved. She reminded me of her. You knew that."

"She looked like a lot of bitches we fucked."

Jay grabbed Carlos by the throat. Or so he thought. The chair was no longer on the floor. It was now in his hands pressed against the wall. Confused, he set the chair back on the floor. When he did, Carlos reappeared. "She was pure," Jay replied. "Like my mother. My mother was an angel. She was everything my father wasn't. Carmen was like that for me."

"She wasn't your mother." Carlos straightened his tie. "Yeah, she may have favored her, but she wasn't her. You put Carmen on this pedestal, expecting her to stand on it, and she couldn't even step on it."

His words echoed his butler's. *It had everything to do with a woman who wasn't mature enough to handle what she'd been given.* He put false expectations on Carmen. He wanted her to be like a woman she'd never met. A woman he was longing to have once again in his life.

"I should've never touched her." Carlos' tone now showed regret. "She didn't want to do that shit anyway. She couldn't find a way out. I shouldn't have forced her. Because like you said, I did know. I knew what you were struggling with. I knew you were fucked up over your moms." His eyes were now filling with tears. "I'm sorry."

The apology brought Jay to his knees. It was the one thing Carlos never said. If he had of, he would've thought twice about giving him that final blow. It would've showed him he felt some remorse. "You were my brother," he cried. "You went too far. Now, I can't get you back."

Carlos stood from his seat. "Why do I need to come back? I don't need to come back."

Jay remained planted even as Carlos neared him. His friend knelt in front of him. When Carlos wrapped his arms around him, the embrace caught him off guard. He and Carlos hadn't hugged since they were kids. "See, we settled it," Carlos said in his ear. "I got my brother back."

A thunderous cry roared from Jay's mouth. He was feeling his own regret. He shouldn't have killed him. He should've given him time to apologize. He should've allowed him to see the error of his ways.

"Now I can rest," Carlos whispered.

No matter how hard he tried to control his emotions, Jay's tears didn't cease. He needed to cry. It was time for him to mourn. He needed to grieve so he could start anew. It was the only way his marriage to Carmen was going to work. He had to release what she did with Carlos.

"We got a lot to unpack, but you did good. You did remarkably good."

Jay opened his eyes. Dr. Stuart was in front of him. Beside her was the empty chair.

He had done good.

***

Carmen placed the last decorative pillow on the bed. It was positioned in the same space where Jay used to lay his head. It had been a week since they shared a bed. She was partly responsible, citing the separation. What she wasn't responsible for was his lack of communication with the kids. He hadn't called to check on them. If he did, no one told her. She wondered if he was even thinking about them. She decided to break the ice and send him a text.

I hope you're well.

She wasn't quite sure what to say, but she figured saying anything was good enough. Whether he responded or not was on him. Until he did, she would find contentment in knowing she tried. She would also focus on being a mother.

Her first task was waking Rakim. He was the hardest to get out of bed. It would take minutes of coaxing, pulling the covers back, and tickles before he would cooperate. The only time he didn't put up a fight is if he heard Robin. Her goddaughter's presence told him two things—it was time to eat and play.

"Good morning," she called to him, rubbing his back. When he didn't budge, she pulled his comforter back. "Rakim." In one quick move, he grabbed the comforter and tossed it over his head. It gave Carmen a giggle. "You know I'm not gonna leave you alone. You know you gotta get up."

"I want Daddy."

Those words were new to her ears. "I know you do. I know y'all miss him." She rubbed his back some more. "I reached out to him. Hopefully, he's not working too hard, and can give us a call." She pulled the comforter back only for him to grab it.

"I want Daddy," he yelled. He threw the covers back over his head.

"Well, you gotta get up so we can get to him."

Rakim pushed the covers back. He looked at her, the sleep still in his eyes. "We can go see Daddy?" There was a hint of excitement that Carmen knew was going to disappear. She couldn't pinpoint Jay's location for a trip. While a transaction from Rosewood Hotel had cleared their account, it didn't tell her much.

"I'm still looking into that," she replied.

The answer wasn't good enough. The covers went back over Rakim's head. To show his displeasure even more, he was now kicking against it. "I want my Daddy," he screamed. He kicked the comforter off the bed, but she caught it before it hit the floor. She held his comforter, unsure of what to say or do. She didn't want to sell him a dream. Without saying anything, she threw the comforter back over him. She headed to her bedroom, hoping there was a response from Jay. When she didn't see one, she cursed. Rakim was now having a full-on tantrum. She dialed Jay's number. She put the call on speaker as she headed back to Rakim's room. "Look." She sat on his bed, holding the phone out to him. She wanted him to see she was trying.

The line continued to ring.

"Daddy, answer," Rakim cried.

Carmen hung up the phone the second it went to voicemail. She didn't bother to leave a message as it was pointless. Instead, she went to her photo gallery and pulled up a picture of Rakim and Jay. "Look, baby." She pointed at the picture. "You see how hard he's smiling? See that big grin?" Rakim grabbed the phone from her hand. "I don't want you to think that because your father isn't here that he doesn't love you. He does. See how happy you make him?" She pointed at Jay's smile. "He loves y'all so much. He doesn't like working all the time, but you see all this?" Carmen gestured towards the room. "He has to work so we won't lose it."

"Why can't he work here?"

"He does," Carmen said. "It's just this time, he had to go away. He's gonna come back." Carmen kissed his forehead. "Hey, let's send him a picture." She swiped to her camera and turned the lens on her and Rakim. He covered his face with the sheets at the sight of his reflection. "Come on, Rakim, this is for Daddy." She gave him a nudge, which only sent him into a round of giggles. "You want to look like that in the picture? I'll take it just like that if you want me to." At the sound of the click, he uncovered his face. "Got chu," she said with a smile. She snapped the photo right as Rakim busted out laughing. With perfect smiles captured, she sent the picture to Jay.

Unbeknownst to her, Jay was at the 85th Street train station in Brookstone. He was learning that the subway wasn't a place for him. There was too much noise and too many eyes, especially when your name was Jay Santiago. His presence brought unsolicited stares and greetings as most people had never seen him in person. For most of them, he was merely a fixture on their TV screens, newspapers, and tabloid rags. That day, they were witnessing him in the flesh.

He arrived at the station alone, as did North, which he learned when their paths crossed.

"After you," Jay responded, holding his arm out. North led the way to a pair of empty seats in the middle of the car. The moment they were seated, North spoke.

"Your partner hasn't been located."

Jay strained to hear him due to the noise level on the train.

North repeated his words. "We've captured most of his men," North revealed. "Some were able to flee Kenema. Some have left Africa. Has he been in contact with you?"

"I haven't heard from him." Jay's phone vibrated from his pants pocket. He pulled it out to see a text message from Carmen. Although his expression didn't show it, it made him feel good she reached out. His plan was to head back home once he was done with North.

"Do you know where he could be hiding?" North asked.

The question made Jay shrug his shoulders. "He has millions. Properties everywhere—Colombia, Brazil, Vegas. Last year, he bought something in Singapore."

"So, he could be anywhere?" North proposed. "Anywhere but home."

Jay looked at the palm of his hand as his phone vibrated again. This time, Carmen was calling. He wanted to answer, but the train was too noisy. He could barely hear North. He allowed the call to go to voicemail. North's voice sounded again in his head. *Anywhere but home.* The words stabbed him with guilt. He had been everywhere, but where he needed to be. He also hadn't seen or talked to his kids since Friday. He didn't see it when it was happening, but he had put a lot before them. "Where are we headed?" When North said, Penn Station, his phone vibrated again. He peered at the screen to see Carmen had sent him a photo. When he opened the message, his lips curled into a smile. While seeing her and Rakim brought happiness, her words made him rise from his seat.

We love you. We miss you. I love you.

The subway car came to a stop. "I'm sorry, I have to go," he shouted at North. "I'll give you a call." He rushed to the nearest exit. North yelled for him, but he was no longer the priority. Getting back home was. He made his way through mobs of people until he was standing outside the entrance to the L' Orange Street station. Limo-less, and without a right-hand nearby, he pulled out his phone and called Linx. On the third ring, a continuous rumble almost broke his stance.

Smoke and debris came from all angles, slapping him in the face. A stench of gasoline and gun powder clouded his nostrils. His free hand covered his eyes as he ran from the area while the other held his phone. Screams filled his ears, car horns blared, and bodies crashed into his as people fled. Confusion plagued him even more when he was shoved inside a vehicle. He rubbed his eyes trying to get as much of the pollutants out so he could see. By the time his vision was restored, the car was moving through the chaos. He also wasn't alone. Cesar was beside him.

"What the fuck did you do?" Cesar yelled.

Jay stared at him in disbelief. "What do you mean what the fuck did I do? I don't even know what happened."

"You didn't blow that shit up?"

He looked out the window to see a large part of the ground had been unearthed. Light brown smoke floated through the air. A massive amount of people was running to safety, some falling to their deaths as they succumbed to their injuries.

Jay snatched Cesar up by his shirt collar. "Hijo de puta. Why would I blow up a fuckin' train? I was on that shit. I would've still been on it if…" Jay's grip loosened as he remembered North. He was certain he hadn't made it off before the bomb detonated.

"The way you ran off," Cesar said. "I thought you knew it was coming."

Even more confusion set in. "That was for me." His head fell in his lap as he tried to make sense of what happened. *North, North, North, Andrew North,* the man's name kept ringing in his head. *North, North, North.* He didn't need to receive a text from his former partner to know he was behind the bomb. The timing of it said it all. The U.S. military had disbanded his army.

As the person who gave him up, the bomb was his payback. It was just God's Will for him to survive it.

You saved me.

The amount of noise increased inside the car as the radio came to life. A random pop song was playing until a special announcement took over the waves. They listened as the radio DJ announced there had been a suspected terrorist attack at the L' Orange Street station. The extent of the lives lost was not yet known neither were the suspected number of injuries.

"Fuck," he heard Cesar yell.

Jay didn't raise his head. He couldn't. He didn't know what to think.

"Someone was following us," he heard Cesar say.

The comment peaked Jay's interest. He looked at Cesar and for the first time, he took note of his right-hand's clothes. He was covered in dirt and debris as well. However, he was dressed in rags. "Who is us? I didn't know you were with me. Who is this?" He pointed at the driver.

"Manuel," Cesar told him, "He lives in the area. He works for you as a ghost. I called him when I got off the train. I needed someone on foot. He came with wheels."

Manuel gave a quick wave. Jay became even more confused. "I didn't see you on the train."

"You looked in my direction." Cesar's eyes were frozen on the mayhem outside the car. "I guess you don't notice bums. No worries. You weren't supposed to." He paused for only a second. "You know you don't travel alone. Even if you think you are."

The reality of the situation had stolen Jay's voice. All he could do was watch in silence as police cars, ambulances, and fire trucks passed them. They hadn't made any progress in getting off the street. That part was miniscule, though. He could sit in traffic if it meant he made it home to his wife and kids. The idea of being minutes from death created a desperation in his soul to see them. He peered at his lap to see his hand gripping his phone. It was covered in grit, but he could see enough to get to his gallery. The first picture he came to was of Carmen. God had worked through her to get him off the train. She was the reason he was alive.

You're everything to me. I love you. You saved my life.

27

The kitchen was becoming a fiasco, causing Carmen to see the huge mistake she and Fiona made. Tacos were on the menu for dinner, and due to their simplicity, they thought it would be a good idea for the kids to help. They decked them out in aprons, gave them different responsibilities, only for them to end up all over the place. More time was spent trying to get them back on track than cooking.

"Maybe we should've chosen pizza," Carmen suggested. She grabbed the container of salt from Rakim as he was about to over season the ground beef. "We finished that part, remember?" She set the container on the island. "Why don't we work on the—"

"I got it, I got it," Silvas belched, joining them. He was off for the evening, but it was obvious he heard their struggles from his room. "I'm used to this. I had to deal with it with Jay. He would tear the kitchen up until I figured out how to direct him." He gave Carmen a slight push. "Go set the table or something. You can take her with you." He pointed at her assistant, Cathy, who was on the phone.

With less than three days until the anniversary party, Carmen had put her to work. All her kids except for the youngest two planned to attend the event. That meant it was on Carmen to style them and complete any necessary alterations. Time was of the essence, so despite Silvas' order, she didn't interrupt her. She let Cathy continue with her calls while she headed to the dining room.

It was a wise decision when she saw what awaited her. Jay was in the foyer. His face and clothes gave the impression he'd been rolling in sand. Something had painted him a floury white. He was also bleeding from his forehead. Her eyes traveled all over him, from the soles of his feet to the crown of his head.

Cathy's voice boomed behind her.

"Someone blew up a train at L' Orange."

Carmen waved Cathy away. "Stay in the kitchen. Keep the kids busy." Cathy's mouth dropped open at the sight of Jay. "Go," Carmen shouted. She wanted her out the room as quickly as possible. Cathy followed her directive. Once she was gone, Carmen drew closer to him. Intuition told her he had been on the train. Certain of it, she sniffed his clothes. He smelled like a mix of smoke, gas, and musk. About to touch his shoulder, she decided against it. "We gotta get you out this. Stay here."

She moved quick, running to the kitchen. She grabbed a large trash bag and gloves, then exited before anyone could question her. Once back with Jay, she peeled off his clothes. Everything he was wearing, except his boxers, went in the trash bag. She tied the bag's straps and set it at the front door. "Upstairs," she whispered.

She led the way to their bathroom. He stood in the doorway as she started the shower. Not a word left his mouth, which she believed was a result of the shock. He didn't even speak when she removed his boxers. Now completely nude, she expected a reaction. The only one he gave was when he walked in the shower. The second his frame was under the showerhead, dust and debris fell from his body. She grabbed a washcloth but kept it in her hands as she took off her clothes. Now down to her bra and underwear, she joined him.

There hadn't been a decent conversation or any intimacy between them. Still, as his other half, she did what needed to be done. She shampooed his hair, washed his face and beard, and scrubbed the dirt from every inch of his body she could. The awkwardness didn't come until she washed his penis and it stiffened in her hand. As if that wasn't enough, he moved his hands to her backside. His fingers gripped her ass cheeks as he pressed her frame into his. The position was reminiscent of her tryst with Kane.

The guilt hit strong, leading her to push him away. She even left the shower. It didn't stop there. When she dried him off, a soft peck landed on her cheek. She ignored him until he pulled the towel from her hands.

"Why did you give up the Pink Sunrise?" Jay asked.

Carmen fumbled her words. A question about the Pink Sunrise wasn't what she expected.

"Andrew North was killed on the train," he continued. "He works for the White House. He told me you turned it in. He gave me a reason, but I want to hear it from you."

Carmen grabbed the towel from his hands. She continued drying him, debating whether she would tell him the truth or not. If she did, the conversation could go in one of two directions. Both she wanted to avoid. "What happened at the station?" she asked instead. His harsh expression told her it was the wrong question. "I didn't give it up," she revealed. "I only made them think I did. If North told you I did it because they were threatening to lock you up, well, that's the truth. I wasn't gonna lose you."

"You didn't want to lose *it* either."

Carmen dropped the towel from her hands. "*We* didn't want to lose it."

The statement changed his demeanor. She realized it showed him they were one. He neared his face to hers and kissed her lips. He kept it short, pulling away after only one or two seconds.

"I can finish up."

Jay was dismissing her. She didn't know why, and she chose not to ask. Instead, she grabbed a towel for herself. After they dressed, she told him she would get him some food. He declined.

"Let me see the kids before they go to bed. Don't tell 'em I'm here. Let it be a surprise."

Carmen agreed to the plan. She left the room only to find his luggage outside their door. She brought it in the room right as he was closing his eyes. Due to the severity of the situation, she didn't ask him to move to a guestroom. She wanted him close even if they were separated.

Speaking of separation, Carmen caught wind of Tiara's voice.

"I wasn't expecting you," she heard Tiara tell Cathy. "Did you go on a honeymoon, too?"

"I don't have set hours," Cathy said. "I come around when Carmen needs me. With the party coming up, she needs me a lot. She has to dress a lot of people."

Carmen stayed upstairs not making her presence known.

"You got your hands full," Tiara replied. "Did you hear about the train? The number of deaths is now in the hundreds."

"I was trying to keep up with it. You know they're saying it was a terrorist attack. In Brookstone, though? It doesn't make sense. I had to get on a group text with my family to make sure we were accounted for."

"Me, too," Tiara said. "It doesn't make sense. I thought they would've hit the City. I mean, Brookstone is only famous for two things. Who would attack us?"

"You know Jay is home." Cathy dropped his name on purpose as the Santiagos and Flame were the two things that put Brookstone on the map.

Carmen balled up her first. If Cathy said anything about what she saw, she was firing her on the spot. No one needed to know Jay was at the station.

"Oh, so that's where Carmen is," Tiara said with a grin. "I was wondering why she wasn't with the kids. She missed my calls today."

At the sound of her name, Carmen peered around the wall. Tiara and Cathy were in the foyer. Robin was right beside them, stuffing her mouth with a taco. When she saw Tiara's head tilt towards the stairwell, she took a step back.

"Tell Carmen to call me when she gets done being fast," Tiara joked.

If only you knew. Carmen listened as Tiara left. With the way now clear, she headed down the steps. She used Silvas' room to get to the kitchen where she retrieved her phone. On the lock screen were three missed calls from Tiara. There was also a text message from Kane, asking her to call him. She returned his call first.

For privacy, she had the conversation in the garden. "It's been a day," she told him when he answered. "I know you've been busy." She could tell he was out from the noise in the background.

"It has been a day. I'm trying to figure out where to start."

Carmen remained quiet on purpose. She wanted him to have the floor as he had the most developments. He told her about Isabella, how she weighed in at a little over three pounds. She also learned Monifah had been discharged and his mother was back home in Manhattan. The only thing she didn't expect to hear was that Jay had confronted him at Flame.

"I covered for you," Kane shared. "I told him what you wanted him to hear." The news was pleasing, yet his tone wasn't. He spoke to her like he was aggravated. "Tell him to stay away from me. If he comes questioning me again, I'm telling him the truth."

"What's the truth?" Carmen asked.

"The truth is what you lived," Kane shot back. "You know what we did."

She didn't respond on purpose. They had been in a good space, and she wanted to stay there.

"I'm sorry," Kane said. "I shouldn't have come at you like that. I've just…" his voice trailed off for a bit. "I loved what happened. I needed it. But, when Monifah was pushing our daughter out, all I could think about was how wrong I was. I broke. She risked her life bringing Bella in the world. No matter how crazy she makes me sometimes, she didn't deserve that."

"Well, you know Jay is home," Carmen told him. "I'm feeling some of that guilt, too."

"I know we needed it. I know we love each other."

Carmen looked around the garden to make sure no one was lurking.

"You told me your feelings were gone. Remember that?" Kane asked.

Carmen did remember. She told him that when she learned her tape with Carlos had leaked. "I thought those feelings were gone. I guess hidden was a more accurate description."

"We both said the feelings were gone," Kane continued. "We also said we didn't want to be that person. We slipped, but we don't have to fall. Let's agree. Sunday was our night. From now on, we keep our hands to ourselves."

"Is that what you want?" She asked the question not to get him to change his mind, but to confirm it wasn't going to change.

"No, that's what I need. I mean, what are we gonna do? Start sneaking around?"

"No," Carmen replied. "That would only complicate things. I hear what you're saying. Trust me. We're on the same page."

"I don't want to lose what we've built." Kane sounded hopeful. "I love the place we're in. It's healthy. I can see the change in Kristian now that we're on good terms."

His words brought a smile to her face. "That makes me feel good. It makes me think we have something solid. We don't have to be lovers. We can be best friends."

"As your best friend," Kane dragged the word out, "there's something I need to tell you. I know your big day is coming up, but I decided not to go to the party. I want to spend as much time as I can with Bella. Instead of partying with you at The Ave, Monifah and I will be at the hospital."

"Totally understandable." Carmen looked around the garden again. "Are you gonna give your tickets away? You got two, right?"

"There's no one to invite if I ain't there."

"True, true," was Carmen's reply. "Well, you know the press is going to be there. It'll be all over social media. You won't miss anything."

"Everything is on the Internet these days."

Although she agreed, she didn't voice it. Her mind was drawing a blank. She believed his had as well with the sudden silence. They were only listening to each other breathe. To make some noise, she walked around the garden. She couldn't tell what he was doing, but he did enough for her to know the call hadn't dropped. No words were spoken, which made two things obvious. One of them was building the courage to say something. They also weren't ready to end the call. It took about a minute before she learned which one was true.

"We're gonna fuck, aren't we?" Kane finally said.

His question made her peer at the sky. Despite their earlier agreement, his question didn't surprise her. She knew he was going to circle back to them being intimate. The only reason he told her they weren't, is because he was trying to believe it for himself. Somehow he realized the truth.

"When the time is right," was all she could say. She then dropped the call.

28

Saturday

If anyone asked when he was the happiest, Jay would tell them something about his kids. He had an instant smile anytime he woke up to find them sprawled out all over him. For the past few mornings that was how it had been. He opened his eyes to see Rakim across his stomach while Nyla was asleep at his shoulder. They had been glued to him since they learned he was back home. He made up for lost time, which allowed Carmen to focus more on the anniversary party.

He could tell the event had her consumed when he saw she wasn't in bed. Lately, they had been sleeping side by side. They hadn't talked about the status of their relationship, but he was certain they were still separated. Anytime he would try to get intimate, she would change the subject or move his hands. He was long overdue, which meant he had to get the kids to their beds, so he could get her into theirs. He started with Rakim first and to his surprise, his son didn't put up a fight. He placed Nyla in hers before venturing back to their bedroom to start his hygiene.

An hour later, he found Carmen in one of the guestrooms. It took a moment or two before he realized it was Silvas' old room. The king-sized bed had been replaced with furniture from the den. There were also seven mannequins in the room modeling the family's outfits for the party. The color scheme was blood red.

"That's your suit," she said to him. She pointed to the mannequin behind her. "Cathy picked it up this morning." Her assistant was seated in the room. He gave her a quick hello before checking out the suit. It was pure white, the exact opposite of what everyone else was wearing. The red accents came from the suit's silk tie, handkerchief, and the inner lining of the jacket. "You can try it on," she continued. "I don't think you've gained."

"Why you make it white? I could waste something on it."

Carmen chuckled. "So you won't."

They met eyes for a quick second. She went over to one of the dresses examining the red sequins which decorated the chest area. He looked around the room again, noticing the floor was littered with shoe boxes. It looked as if sixty thousand had been spent in Christian Louboutin alone. "We need all these?" Their eyes met again.

"Seven people do. Y'all need multiples to choose from."

He joined Carmen at the mannequin to see the name "Akaila" had been written at the base of its neck. "Can we talk for a minute?" He didn't expect the surprised look she gave. She knew they needed to talk. They had been running from the conversation longer than he intended. They needed to take a deep dive into what happened on the train and the status of their marriage.

"Look," she whispered, "I know there's a lot we need to discuss. Can we do it after the party? Like, can we forget about everything and have an amazing night?"

Jay took a few steps back until he found the mannequin labeled Carmen. He stared at the dress than at her. The way it hung on the mannequin told him it was skintight. There was also a long split, which started at the bottom of the dress' red sequined corset and went to the floor. "Does that mean I get to take this off?" Her eyes widened, giving the reaction he wanted. He knew the question would make her uncomfortable with Cathy in the room.

"That's my cue," her assistant yelled. She grabbed a clipboard before taking off.

"You and your mouth." Carmen laughed. "You've been wanting to take something off."

"Well, why you ain't let me?"

Carmen gave him a side eye. "You know why." She picked up her phone, giving the impression she was about to exit. "I'm gonna go shower. My glam team is gonna be here around three. Did you make arrangements with your barber?"

"I'll get it worked out."

"Cool."

She tapped his chest before making her way out the room. He knew she expected him to go after her, which he did, but not immediately. He took some time to pick out his shoes. When he returned to their bedroom, he locked the door behind him. His plan was to follow her in the bathroom until he saw her phone lying on the bed.

I logged everything correctly in the app.

Those were the words she said when she tried to explain why she wasn't pregnant. He now had the opportunity to see if she was telling the truth. He picked up her phone and inputted her password. He learned it was King's birthday a while ago. He opened the fertility tracker and went to the calendar for December. *Shit, she wasn't lying.* The app showed she was ovulating during their honeymoon. Somehow, her body didn't accept his sperm.

The proof was there whether he wanted to accept it or not. Truthfully, what he didn't want to accept was that he was the problem. From the way he saw things, getting her pregnant was never the issue. The issue was with her *staying* pregnant. That was the reason the whole thing didn't make sense. He dropped her phone on the bed. *There's gotta be something else.* The shower was still going. He scanned the room until his eyes landed on her purse. *First time for everything.* He found it already open. Her purse was filled with stuff only a woman and mother would need. It also held the key to her betrayal. Zipped inside one of the inner pockets was the explanation he'd been looking for. In his hands was a 28-day pack of birth control pills. Most of the pills were there, but the missing ones was proof she started taking them. It also told him she didn't have any intention of getting pregnant.

You lyin' ass bitch. The pills took him to a place he didn't want to be. With his anger now fueled, he did what he wished she had done. In one of the guest bathrooms, he flushed each pill down the toilet. He went back in their bedroom and grabbed her phone. He scrolled through her text messages until he found an alert from a local pharmacy. The prescription was filled a few days before their wedding. Judging from the date and how many pills were left, she stopped taking them around the time their sex tape leaked. *You didn't need 'em because you weren't giving me none.*

He dropped her phone on the bed. Hurt and anger ran rampant inside him. While the old him would've knocked the bathroom door down, the new him kept it intact when he opened it. Carmen was still in the shower, the steam clouding her naked body.

It took a minute before Carmen noticed he was there. When she did, she jumped as she hadn't heard him come in. She stared at him, hoping he would tell her what he wanted or at least apologize for startling her. She got neither. He stared at her, not in awe, but like he was preparing to attack. His narrowed eyes and gritted teeth reminded her of a lion on the prowl. He stripped himself of his clothes, a sign the lion had found its prey.

Within the last few days, he dropped multiple hints he wanted sex. She would curve him, but now, it didn't seem like an option. She was at her most vulnerable considering they were both naked. His physique was a work of art while his manhood was a blessing and a curse. He knew how to use it to make her succumb to him. Its power gave her three beautiful children. It also caused her to divorce the same man twice who she cheated on him with days ago.

The guilt from that memory made her hesitant to touch him. He was now in the shower with her, his right hand softly caressing the back of her neck. Unlike his facial expression, his touch was gentle. Even the way he brushed his lips over hers was delicate. It wasn't what she was used to.

Everything about him was aggressive. If she had to describe him in the bedroom, she would say he knew how to make love, but he preferred to fuck. That morning, he was different. He didn't rush inside her, taking his time as he entered. She was used to his size, but he was maneuvering like she was a virgin. She didn't quite understand why until she realized how deep the moment was. She had been struggling with forgiveness since the leak of their sex tape. The betrayal also created a trust issue. By letting him penetrate her, she was forcing herself to do both—forgive and trust.

He was aware of it, too. She could see it in his eyes. He was using the act as some sort of call and response. Every time he went deeper, he would stop to catch her reaction. Naturally, her body would respond. He would take another plunge until he could go no further. She matched his grind, their gaze still set on each other. When he increased his speed, she did the same. Her fingertips gripped his shoulder blades to maintain her balance as the intensity of their thrusts increased.

Then, she remembered. Pills, dates, all of it rushed in her head. She tried to count back. Her period started last Friday. She was on day nine of her cycle. They were cutting it close, *oh my*—a loud moan escaped from her lips. The Jay she was used to had taken over. Her thoughts became a blur as she rode the wave of ecstasy. Her legs quivered under the pressure of his manhood. She begged him not to stop, now engrossed inside the high. Until there came the descent.

She hadn't taken a pill in days. There was a possibility he could get her pregnant. She opened her eyes only to wish she hadn't. His stare was a fiery mix of aggression and pain. He knew what he was doing. He tightened his grip around her neck to hold her in place. At that moment, it came. The final thrust in which he unleashed his power inside her. He didn't moan, grunt, or break his gaze. The more she thought about it, he hadn't made a sound the entire time they sexed. It had been all her. She looked between them as he pulled himself out. Every inch of him was at attention.

"Say something," she urged. She needed to know what he was thinking. He knelt his head underneath the shower.

"I just did."

To Jay, it was the perfect reply. Plus she accepted it. They didn't speak again until they were dressed. He asked her if they were back together. Not that sex solved their problems, but it was a step. Besides, he wanted to know before he handed her the contract. She said yes. In reply, he promised that after the party, he would lay everything out on the table. From the shootout in San Juan to what happened on the train, he would tell her everything.

The agreement was sealed with a kiss. She went back to her glam room while he escaped to the home office. He checked the drawer where the contract was hidden to make sure it hadn't been touched. When he saw everything was good, he started to close the drawer until he noticed the USB drive. Despite what he did to get the information, he hadn't given it much of his time. With an hour or so to kill, he grabbed the drive and stuck it inside the USB port.

Instead of searching through his father's files, he went to his own. Everything he saw there, he expected. The folders consisted of various reports, court documents, news articles, copies of tax returns, along with random photos around Brookstone of him, Carmen, and his cartel. There were also pictures of items Kane and his team confiscated from his businesses, homes, and warehouse. A VHS tape was never logged. His findings didn't put Kane off his list of suspects. If anything, he saw how good he was at his job. Kane knew what to document and what to omit.

That was why he was shocked to find a folder labeled Confidential. The word itself would prompt anyone to click on it. The folder contained one PDF document. The file was saved under the name, ITIA_CIA. He knew ITIA stood for International Triad Intelligence Agency. The Triad was in competition with the CIA, so he assumed the acronym didn't stand for them. He learned his thinking was correct when the document loaded. There were over twenty pages in the PDF, the first five being devoted to the Triad's Confidential Informant Agreement. The name on the submission was Malik Tyrone Washington.

You don't want to see it.

In a flash, Sanders appeared in front of him. He heard him say the words again, and again, and again. He tried to protect him. Sanders knew the agreement would be a trigger. He didn't listen and forced his hand. Now, he was learning he'd been backstabbed. Malik laid out his entire operation. He even gave up the address of the warehouse, which is how the Triad knew where to find him. He always thought Carmen led them there when they were following her. According to the documents, Malik agreed to have Carmen visit him there. It would put them in one place for the Triad to make two arrests.

You dirty son of a bitch.

He snatched the drive out the port. For years, Malik visited him in prison, swore he was looking after his businesses, his son, King, and even Silvas. The reality of the situation was that he was a no-good motherfucker who sold him out to protect himself. He pretended he was there for him to keep up the façade. Malik stayed in his corner, working with his lawyer, Gomez, to help find loopholes in his case. The whole time he knew the life sentence was going to be upheld. There weren't any loopholes. Malik made sure of it when he ratted him out.

You said you hid during the raid. That was bullshit. Your ass didn't hide. You knew you were good. Kane made sure of it. All you had to do was be his bible.

He thirsted for Malik's blood. The craving became a throb. Like a vampire, he needed to feed. He raced up the steps almost two at a time, barging into his room. He didn't expect to see Carmen on the bed. He thought she would be in the glam room.

"You ran up here?" she said with a giggle. "What cha got to tell me?"

He closed the door to prep her that the news wasn't good. Her smile disappeared.

"What if this life isn't meant for me?" he asked.

"What are you talkin' about?"

"What if this," he said again, "isn't meant for me? I want this, but is it realistic?"

She stood on her feet. "What are you sayin' to me?"

Jay swallowed. "I need to kill somebody."

She paced the floor, whispering inaudible words. She stopped to look at him. "You're not putting this on me right now. You're not saying that to me."

"I got my file from Sanders. Malik ratted me out."

She took the news lightly. "That doesn't surprise me. I suspected that from day one. I never asked him about it because he always had your back. He struggled to keep your businesses afloat. He was trying to get you out even when he knew it was something I didn't want. He helped me so much with King. If you ask me, he's paid his debt."

"He took seventeen years from me."

"And you should be mad," she exclaimed. "You should be angry, hurt, confused, all of it," she continued, "but you shouldn't kill him. Should you have a conversation? Yes. You should confront him. But don't touch him. Robin needs him."

"King needed me," Jay yelled. "He took my son from me."

"You didn't want your son," came roaring back at him. The wrong set of words, she paced the floor again. "I'm sorry," she repeated several times. "I shouldn't have said that. You were sick then." She took a few seconds to gather herself. "Malik suffered in silence for what he did. He spent years making it up to you even if you didn't know he was doing it. He made a selfish move, but can you blame him? He chose himself, and if you had the choice, wouldn't you choose you?"

"Yeah, if you touch mine," he shouted. He thought of what his African comrade had done to Silvas.

"That is where we agree. Don't," she said, slowly, "touch Malik."

Her words didn't quench his thirst. It was growing. The desire burned, the pain bringing tears to his eyes. "If I kill him, will you leave me?"

"You're set on doing this."

He asked her once more. "Will you leave me?"

Tears streamed down her cheeks. "No," she replied. "Because you're gonna leave me."

He understood her answer. If he did it, and was caught, he was looking at another prison sentence. It was a chance he was going to have to take. It was the reason he kissed her lips, telling her he would be back.

He left without a plan. Neither did he know where Malik was. He simply trusted his gut. He inputted the gate code to Malik's house and watched as the gate opened. One of Malik's cars was in the driveway, which he parked behind. He maintained his composure despite his thirst. Even when Malik answered the door, he didn't drop a hint he was there to kill him.

"I'm glad it's you," Malik voiced, letting him in. "People been running in and out this house. You would think the party is gonna be here."

Jay managed out a grin. "What color Tiara got chu wearin'?"

"It's a black tux. I picked it out."

Jay pretended he cared. He stepped in the foyer to see Robin seated at the stairwell. She was playing with her dolls. A bright pink suitcase was next to her.

"Can you watch her for a sec?" Malik asked. "I forgot to pack some stuff. She's gonna spend the night with Tony. That way, after the party, Tiara and I can be grown-ups."

"Yeah, no problem, I'll holla at chu when you come back down."

"It'll be quick," Malik yelled as he jetted up the steps.

Jay looked at Robin. She was so enthralled with her dolls, she paid him no attention. It was like he wasn't there. It worked in his favor. Without a word to her, he climbed the steps. He took his time so Malik wouldn't hear him coming. He reached the top in under a minute to see Malik walking out Robin's room and into his own. He followed behind him. Once in the room, he slammed the door closed. That was Malik's warning.

"Man, what chu doin'? I was almost done." Malik dropped the items he was holding onto the bed. "Here, you can help me. I didn't even know a little girl would need all this."

"You snitched on me?"

Malik's eyes grew. Jay didn't know if it was because he knew or because he swung. Both caught Malik off guard. When he landed the second blow, Malik's feet flew out from under him. His head hit the side of an oak chest with a thud.

"Kane became your best friend, right?"

Malik held his head as he let out a large groan. Jay showed no mercy, snatching him up by his shirt collar. "Yeah, you were cool with him. He kept you out a cell." He drew his fist back. "You dirty muthafucka." He punched him square in the nose. That blow drew blood. When he saw the red liquid on his knuckles, he ran his tongue over his hand for a taste. He shot Malik a few right hooks before dropping him on the floor. "Get yo bitch ass up." He kicked him in his side. "Get up," he yelled. "You did it, didn't you?" Jay walked past him towards the balcony. He opened the set of French doors, allowing the cold afternoon air to drift in the room. He could hear Malik struggling to get on his feet. Although, he had the upper hand, he didn't strike him.

"Come on," he urged.

Malik stood up, but he didn't swing. He stumbled a bit, holding his hands up to show he surrendered. He started an apology that didn't want to be heard. His words only infuriated Jay. He charged at him and in return, Malik swung. His fist connected with Jay's cheek in the same spot where Carlos stabbed him. The move set off another trigger. Jay became trapped inside a demon. He lost control of his conscience. When he came to, he and Malik were on the balcony. His knuckles were throbbing while Malik's face and neck was covered in cuts and blood. He could also hear screaming from afar.

He raised his fist to deliver another blow, catching a peek at the empty lounge chairs beside him. He saw Carlos. His best friend was shaking his head. Jay blinked his eyes, but the chairs were empty. He looked at Malik. If he killed him, he wouldn't get back the seventeen years he lost. He would also never see the day where Malik made it right. He would lose the moment like he lost it with Carlos. He would make the same mistake again. The fear of that made him stop. It also made him leave the property.

***

Tiara didn't know she was driving past Jay when she did. After meeting with the team to put out some fires, she was returning home for a nap before her glam squad came knocking. Or at least that was her plan. When she arrived home, she found the front door unlocked and her daughter screaming her head off. The bags she was holding fell from her hands.

"What happened, baby? What's wrong? Where's Daddy?" She kissed Robin's cheeks to calm her.

When Robin pointed towards the stairwell, Tiara set her back down. *What is going on? Is someone in our house?* She picked Robin up and set her inside her playroom. She grabbed a knife from a kitchen drawer as their guns were locked away upstairs. All she heard was silence. She climbed the steps only to feel a slight breeze once she reached the top. The tickle of air on her skin sent her gaze to her bedroom. She could see her husband's legs in the doorway of their balcony.

For the first few seconds, she was completely hysterical. She couldn't do anything but cradle him in her arms. "Wake up, baby, please wake up," she begged. She drowned herself in her tears until something told her to call 911. She struggled getting the words out. Eventually, she had an operator telling her help was on the way. "What's going on?" she cried. "Baby, please." She nestled her face into Malik's neck. "Wake up." She kissed his cheek only to hear his voice.

"Jay," he moaned. He repeated the name again.

No, she thought. *Jay couldn't have done this. Malik hasn't done anything to him.*

Malik whispered the name again right as sirens sounded in the distance. *Why did you do this? He's your best friend.* The why didn't matter. What mattered is that it was done. Jay tried to kill her husband. For that alone, she used the only card she had. She dialed Carlton's number. After the second ring, he answered.

"I know where you can find him."

29

The Ave was built for the elite. It was where moneymakers came to play, and starlets came to shine. The who's who of business, entertainment, and sports kept the venue booked. The space served as eight thousand square feet of luxury. Ivy decorated the building's exterior while state of the art lighting systems and fixtures illuminated its interior. New York's major players were guaranteed to show up if an event was at The Ave. That was the sole reason the location was chosen. Flame's executives wanted the party to be memorable. There wasn't going to be a shortage of liquor, glitz, or glam.

From what Carmen was seeing, her team met all metrics. The paparazzi's cameras flashed nonstop as big names arrived. They begged for her time as she stepped out her limo in a white fox fur coat. To the best of her ability, she played her role. Hand in hand with Jay, she stepped onto the velvet crushed carpet. She could feel the scars on his knuckles, but she told herself to ignore them. She was going to follow the plan. They would make the best of the night.

The paparazzi screamed for their attention. She gave them something greater. She slipped her tongue in Jay's mouth as they connected for a kiss. The display of affection sent the crowd into a frenzy. Questions were shouted that went unanswered. Jay led her inside where they were met with even more press. Shots were taken at the step and repeat, some with her and Jay, and others with the entire family. She made her rounds with the media, reciting a rehearsed answer every time the conversation was swayed to her sex tapes. Her least favorite part of any event, she was relieved when the press hour was over.

"Look at that." Jay pointed to the display. They were deep in the foyer of The Ave, underneath the stairwell, where rows of headless mannequins modeled the highest-selling suits from the *King* collection. For Carmen, it was a walk down memory lane. Each design was sketched with her first-born in mind. She created the collection as her prayer to God for what she wanted him to become. Now, King was living her prayer.

Jay led her upstairs to the dining room. Within seconds, she was surrounded by her peers of the fashion world. Conversations with Oliver Rousteing, Dapper Dan, and Kimora Lee Simmons kept her attention. She didn't even notice Jay when he left her side. All she knew was that when she sat at their table for dinner, he was there with their brood. The only people missing was Tiara and Malik. King was the first to point it out. To maintain her image, she didn't speak on their absence. If she did, she would break.

She was saved by the four-course meal. The presence of food meant everyone's mouth would be occupied. The talk switched from Tiara and Malik to the delicious steak on everyone's plate. Thirty or so minutes later, their eyes were centered on Jerry as he presented numerous awards to Flame's top employees. It was followed by a dedication to her in which Jay left her side again. This time, he joined Jerry at the podium, taking the mic. His antics left Jerry standing in front of the crowd like a deer in headlights.

"I saw firsthand the love and dedication my wife has to Flame," Jay said. "When there was only one boutique, she dreamt of having something bigger. She conquered New York, the East Coast then all of America. She sacrificed to make Flame a household name. I feel blessed that she wears my last name. I also feel blessed," he continued, reaching inside his suit jacket, "to announce that Flame will be opening its first store in Europe in Westfield Stratford City." He retrieved a set of papers, which he unfolded. He held them up although the text was too small for anyone to read.

The room erupted into applause and cheers. The sound of it made Carmen rise from her seat. She could hear the cameras flashing behind her as she walked to the podium. She would've had a Halle Berry, Oscar-winning reaction if she didn't know about his trip to London. She did manage out a tear once the contract was in her hand. When Jay handed her an ink pen to sign it, she gave the waterworks everyone expected.

Flame was now international. The news of the company's first store in the UK was reason to celebrate. They migrated to another room in the venue, which reminded her of the inside of Sapphire. The only difference was that the room had a gold tint. It reflected on everything, from the booths to the bottle girls to the DJ. Jay wasn't one to dance, but he joined her on the dance floor. They danced for a good ten minutes until her feet couldn't take anymore. She headed to coat check to grab a pair of flats. Cathy had brought extra shoes over before the party as Louboutin heels were only tolerable for a small length of time.

She was handing her heels to the clerk when she saw Monifah. For a split second, she thought it wasn't her. Kane told her they wouldn't be attending. She hadn't seen him, but there his wife was, in a pearl white gown. *Damn, bitch, you couldn't even let yourself heal.* Although she was annoyed, deep down, she was glad she was there. It was time to end the war.

"Mrs. Kane," she called.

Monifah flashed the same devious smile she'd always seen from her. "It's a little loud in here, don't cha think?"

Her words told Carmen one thing. They were on the same page. "The dining room," Carmen replied. They walked side by side up the steps and into the room where the venue's staff was cleaning up. People were still inside fellowshipping, but she didn't care if they heard the conversation. Her plan was to stay professional. "Congratulations," she told her once they were face to face. "I've been praying for Bella."

Her words made Monifah giggle. "Have you? Come on, Carm," her voice went above a whisper, "I know you weren't happy about my pregnancy."

"Well, I'm sure Kane told you about our issues."

"My husband told me a lot of things."

Carmen noticed how Monifah stressed the word *husband*. "Can we stop all this and have real talk?" Carmen continued speaking. "We both know you're not the devil you portray yourself to be. I understand you're still hurt over what happened with Rakim and for that I apologize. I don't know how to make that up to you. What I do want you to know is that my apology is sincere."

"I didn't want it when we were twenty-one and I don't want it now. I want him."

"I can't bring him back." Carmen stepped away at the volume of her words. "Mo, I'm sorry. I'm sorry I got in between you two. If I could change what happened, I would. I was young, dumb, and stupid. I fucked up a lot of shit. I can admit that. What I don't want is you walking around with this anger. We'll never be friends, but you have a connection to me. Our children are siblings."

"Did you rehearse this?"

"Why are you doing this?" Carmen asked. "Don't you want to be happy?"

"I hate you."

Carmen didn't mean to laugh in her face, but she did. "Okay, Monifah, you hate me. I get it. You can't live the rest of your life trying to get revenge. I mean, what else do you want? When does it stop?" For a quick second, she saw a look of humility in Monifah's eyes. "You hate me, but not enough to put out two sex tapes. You do hate me enough to take the blame for it."

Monifah remained mum like she didn't know what to say.

"If you're not going to do this for me, can you do it for Kane? Shit, can you do it for yourself?"

Monifah wrapped her arms around her waist. She was very post-partum and it showed. Her bump was still visible. "Why would I do anything for Kane?"

Carmen was at a loss for words.

"Do you know how many nights I had to listen to him whine over you? Or what about when Kristian moved in, and she was having those nightmares? We couldn't even fuck without her screaming. I married him for his dick because his personality ain't it."

The urge to punch her was there. Somehow, Carmen managed to keep her arms at her side.

"I'll give him that," Monifah was saying. "The dick is good. I'll ride it out a few more years."

"You gave him a baby."

"I gave him the baby you wanted."

For the second time that night, tears formed in the corners of Carmen's eyes. "You are the devil you portray yourself to be. He loves you."

A sympathetic expression fell over Monifah's face. "No, he doesn't. He loves that I'm there. I'm a space filler. He will never admit it, but I know. We both know who he loves. I can live with it because I don't love him."

"You need help."

"Maybe I do." Monifah shrugged her shoulders. "We all need help."

Carmen didn't know what to think. The conversation revealed things she wished she didn't know. One thing was for sure, she no longer felt guilty for what she did with Kane. Monifah deserved it. She was playing her ex for a fool. "I can see we're not gonna get anywhere. While we'll never be cordial, can you do me a favor? Can you accept my apology? I also would like it if you divorced Kane. Yes, it will hurt him, but I rather him be with someone who loves him than someone who is pretending to."

The request drummed up a hearty laugh. Monifah bowled over in front of her. "I guess Kane didn't tell you I have an egg left. Hopefully, this time, I can give him a son."

Carmen saw herself wrapping her hands around her neck. She saw her fingers choking the life out of her. What hurt more than anything was that the images were only a figment of her imagination. However, the feeling was temporary.

She parted her lips to curse Monifah when she heard an unexpected bang. Monifah fell forward right as the front of her gown became a sea of red. Carmen caught her in her arms while people screamed around her. Across the room, a light-skinned man in a tuxedo held a pistol. Someone knocked her down, separating her from Monifah. The blow felt like a football team had run her over. People ran past her, some falling to the ground, others crawling under tables to take cover.

The hysteria went to another level. An explosion sent gold ceiling tiles raining into the room. Carmen shielded her face from the rubble as a body fell on hers. She uncovered her face to find Jay on top of her, firing at someone she couldn't see. Moments later, she couldn't see him. A woman in a red dress fell on top of her. The woman moved away quick, but Jay's hefty frame kept Carmen pinned to the floor. She caught a peek at the woman and connected the dots. The Hispanic woman from Flame and Jeni's was a ghost. She was the person in the black car. Carmen stared at her as the woman pulled a gun from underneath her dress. The woman made it to her feet, firing at someone she couldn't see. When she ran from her, Carmen peered at Jay. His body was trembling. His white suit was covered in blood.

Although the gunfire hadn't let up, she pulled herself from underneath him. In the process, she saw men dragging the light-skinned man from the room. What she didn't see as she reached for Jay was Cesar firing at them. One of the men fired back, the bullet hitting Cesar in the shoulder. It didn't take him down. He returned fire, the bullet hitting the man in the center of his forehead.

What Carmen did see was the love of her life in a pool of blood. *God, no, God, no.* She struggled to breathe. *Please, God.* Her heart beat out her chest. She draped her body over his, applying as much pressure as she could. She stared at him through her tears, his hazel eyes bleeding into hers. "It's gonna be okay," she cried. He tried to speak. She grabbed his chin to silence him. "I love you. Do you hear me? I love you."

Minutes were passing. *Please don't take him,* she prayed. *God, please. I need him.*

The gunfire had been replaced with sirens. "I love−" she cried out when she saw his eyes close. She panicked, applying more pressure to his wounds. Someone was trying to pull her away. She fought against them. More hands grabbed her. They dragged her from Jay right as a team of paramedics swept in.

God, I'm begging you. Please don't take him.

A bitter cry roared from her lips when they lifted him onto a stretcher. She tried to get to him, but someone held her back. They clutched her to their chest, telling her it was going to be okay. The voice soothed her once she realized she was in the arms of her first-born, King. For the first time, she scanned the rest of the room. Police, EMTs, and paramedics were everywhere. Monifah laid lifeless beside her. Her death brought even more tears. God knew she wanted to make amends. She never had the chance with Tricia and didn't want to make the same mistake with Monifah.

"We gotta get to the hospital," King cried.

Her son pulled her to her feet. Now able to see more, she saw more dead bodies in the room. Most were men in matching black tuxedos. She didn't see her peers until they were outside the venue. They called for her, but King rushed her inside a limo. It was there she learned her children were accounted for. They were on the dance floor when the first gunshot sounded. The Hispanic woman, who was introducing herself as Lia, ordered Roman to get them out the venue. After making it home, King rushed back to The Ave once Roman got word Jay had been hit.

"Gully." Carmen called his name when she realized he was missing.

"He drove Cesar to get help," Lia replied. "Dead men like him can't go to hospitals."

They met eyes in the rearview mirror. Carmen's tears were long gone. What she felt now was fire. A demon she kept buried was awakened. She didn't know the man who shot her husband, but she was going to find him. His last breath belonged to her.

***

The temperature had dropped somewhere in the twenties. If Kane knew it was that cold, he would've spent the night in the NICU. Now that he was outside, it made more sense to continue to his Jeep. Or so he thought. Ambulances sped through the parking lot, catching him off guard. He hopped on a sidewalk to get out their way.

What happened tonight? He figured it was a car accident due to the number of vehicles that were arriving. In the event it wasn't, he pulled his phone from his coat pocket. Although he was no longer a Triad agent, Sanders kept him abreast of certain investigations. He would help guide Sanders if needed even though neither of them could go in the field. He didn't have a text from him, but there were ten missed calls from Kristian, Akaila, and Malachi. He knew something had happened if all his kids called him. He decided to call Kristian first.

When she answered, she sounded frantic.

"Someone started shooting," she screamed. He told her to calm down, but his words were only vapor in the air. "Roman told us we had to go," she yelled. "When we went in the hall, we heard gunshots. Mama wasn't answering her phone. Roman couldn't get ahold of anyone."

Kane looked at the ambulances. Paramedics were running inside the hospital with a stretcher, but he couldn't tell who was on it. "I'm still at the hospital. I'll figure out what's going on. Some ambulances just pulled up."

Her volume increased. "You're not listening to me. I said someone shot Jay."

The news didn't shake him. For half his life he wanted Jay dead. He dreamed of being the one to do it. "Does anyone know about your mother?"

"They took her to the hospital," Kristian cried. "Roman says she's not hurt."

"I'll find her." He ended the call now on his way to the emergency room. He started a new one, this time to his wife. Monifah had been in one of her moods earlier, so instead of joining him at the hospital, she chose to stay home. She wasn't answering, so he figured she had gone to bed. He left her a voice message and sent a text.

The emergency room was packed. He could tell from the way people were dressed they had been at the party. Their injuries looked minor like they hurt themselves trying to get away. Carmen, on the other hand, gave a different impression. Blood was not only smeared across her shoulders, but also on her face and dress. Her hair was all over the place like she'd been electrocuted. King was beside her along with a woman he'd seen around Flame. He knelt in front of Carmen, grabbing her hands. She cried at the sight of him right as an alert sounded on his phone. He peeked at it, assuming it was Monifah.

I'm on my way to the hospital.

The message was from Kristian. He stuck his phone inside his coat. He raised Carmen's hands to his lips, kissing them. "I'm sorry," he told her. He kissed her hands again, not caring about the blood that was on them.

"I'm sorry, too," she replied.

He brought her hands back to his lips. He gave them another kiss. About to address King, he heard a familiar ringtone. "One second," he told him, thinking it was Monifah. He pulled his phone from his coat to see Malik calling. "I gotta take this." He made his way out the ER.

Meanwhile, Carmen sat there, her head now in her hands. She didn't know how to tell Kane his wife was dead. A part of her didn't want to. She wanted someone else to do it. She didn't want to see his pain. It would be unbearable like the pain she felt when she watched Jay fight for his life. She would have to, though.

King got up to check on Coco and Prince. A minute later, Lia stepped away, her hand on her earpiece. They had been gone for a few minutes when Kane came back. He took King's seat right as Kristian came running up to them.

Her daughter collapsed in her arms. An embrace Carmen hadn't felt in ages, she wrapped her arms around her. She held her tightly against her chest. "My baby," she cried. She pushed Kristian away to see her face. "My baby."

"Mama," Kristian sobbed. "How is he? Is he going to be okay?"

Carmen got ready to tell her she didn't know, but Kane interrupted her. In a calm voice, he asked Kristian to take a seat. His eyes were red with irritation.

Kane parted his lips. "Did you know Malik was here?"

Carmen shook her head. She didn't know what Jay had done. She only knew it wasn't good. Her tears became heavier. Never in a million years did she think she and Tiara would have their husbands' lives threatened on the same day.

"Mrs. Santiago?"

Carmen raised her head to see two people in scrubs approaching her. She couldn't read their expressions to know if the news was bad. She rose to greet them. She listened as they spoke, but her mind only received certain words. *Four bullet wounds, one bullet in each leg, two shots to the chest.* Carmen lost her balance. *Those bullets went straight through.* Kane sat her back in her seat but remained standing. *Blood transfusion, still in surgery.* "But alive," Carmen whimpered. "He's alive."

"The doctors are doing their best to ensure he stays that way. Your husband is a fighter."

They told her someone would speak with her once surgery was complete. Once they walked away, she knew it was time to update Kane. She grabbed his hand.

"Monifah," she stated.

"She's at home," he told her. "I called her to let her know I'm still here."

"But you didn't speak to her."

Kane looked puzzled. "No, I didn't. I left her a message. Why—"

The presence of two Triad agents silenced them both. Carmen suspected they were there to question her. She knew very little, but she would cooperate. She waited for them to say something to her, but they never did. They addressed Kane, their conversation starting off informal.

"This is on y'alls desk, ain't it?" Kane asked. "Do you know who's taking the lead?"

"We can talk about that later," one of the men said. "Were you at The Ave tonight?"

"No," Kane said, quickly. "I've been here for the past three or four hours. My wife just had a baby. Our daughter is in the NICU."

A look of compassion fell over the men's faces. It told Carmen they were there to deliver the news. She tightened her grip around Kane's hand.

"I never wanted to say this to anybody," the agent expressed. "I definitely didn't want to say this to you. Fifteen people were murdered tonight at The Ave. There were even more injuries. We believe one of the victims is your wife, Monifah Kane."

Carmen didn't want to react. She held back her tears.

"My wife is at home," Kane stated, not believing their words. "She didn't go to the party."

Carmen let go of his hand. She covered her mouth about to vomit on the floor. She could see Monifah's face, the look of horror and shock as the bullet pierced her.

"I know this is hard," the agent replied. "Do you think you can ID the body?"

"My wife is at home," Kane stressed. "She didn't go to the party. She didn't have a dress. She couldn't fit it. She just had a baby." He looked at Carmen for reassurance. Nevertheless, her face said something different. "Was she there?" The news was starting to set in. "Did you see her?" The beginning of a tear was in the corner of his eye.

Carmen took her hand from her mouth. "She was in all-white."

The agents gave their condolences at her confirmation. It was overshadowed by Kane's howling cry. He dropped to the floor, but Carmen caught him in her arms. Kristian jumped in front of him for support, tears streaming down her face.

"I can't," Kane screamed. "I can't."

Carmen held his face to her chest, rocking him back and forth. "I'm sorry," she cried.

"I can't," he repeated. "I can't." He said the words over and over.

"He can't do it," Kristian told the agents. "I'll ID her."

Carmen continued to rock him, feeling his tears on her wrist. She gestured to Kristian to go with the agents. They made their way out the ER only for King to return.

"I can't," Kane said again. "I can't lose another wife."

Carmen's spirit was broken, but his words shattered what pieces were left. She didn't know details, but Monifah was another casualty of one of her husband's transgressions. The same husband Kane hated. The husband he begged her to leave. The husband whose life appeared to be spared.

Fifteen minutes passed.

"Can you drive him home?" Carmen asked. Kristian was back in the ER. Kane's tears had dried, his body resting quietly against her bosom. Her daughter told her she would. "I love you," Carmen whispered. She kissed Kane's forehead. She felt him touch her hand. It took a few minutes, but eventually, he walked with Kristian and King out the ER. She was left with Lia who returned a short while ago. "I don't know what you have to do, but I'm not leaving the hospital. I want to be here when Jay wakes up."

"We'll both be here," Lia replied.

For the first time, Carmen took a good look at her. She had androgynous mannerisms, which the red dress couldn't hide. Full lips, olive skin, and wavy deep brown hair, made Carmen suspect she had Puerto Rican heritage. Most of the people Jay hired did. "Thank you," Carmen told her, "for everything. I know it's not easy being a ghost."

Lia smiled. "I'm not a ghost anymore. You know who I am. I'm an angel."

30

After Kane left, it took two hours before Carmen saw a surgeon. One came to the ER to tell her Jay was in recovery. The news sent her praising God. An hour later, two nurses crushed her spirit. Jay hadn't woken up. He was in a coma. They broke down what could've caused it, but their words were an unknown jargon. It didn't matter to her anyway. What mattered was that he was still unconscious. They encouraged her to wait it out. He could wake up in the next few hours or the next day. She chose to follow their advice. For hours, she sat at his bedside, her hand around his, waiting for his eyes to open.

When the sun started to rise, Lia told her it was time. The scent of dried blood and sweat was thick. "You should at least take a shower," she told her. "We both need that." Carmen was still hesitant. It took Lia reminding her of Rakim and Nyla for her to consider it. "You've given them a good support system, but Fiona and Silvas aren't their parents. You should be there when they wake up. Nobody should tell them about Jay, but you." Those words made Carmen kiss her husband's hands. "They don't need to see you like this," Lia continued. "You can get cleaned up before they're awake."

That statement was the reason she was now in her bathroom. She cleansed Jay's blood from her skin and washed her hair. Instead of putting on something of hers, she grabbed one of his button-ups. It was big on her, but it smelled like his scent—mahogany teakwood. The time was about nine o'clock. She went to lie down yet a loud thud kept her from her bed. When she went in the hall, a door was open that hadn't been in some time. She walked towards it to find Kristian in her room. Suitcases were in the middle of the floor.

She broke down crying like she'd done several times within the last six or so hours. The only thing that made the tears stop was when a door opened across the hall. It belonged to a guestroom no one was supposed to be in. Or at least not Kane.

"It was my idea," Kristian said, seeing her facial expression. "He broke down when we walked in the house. He couldn't sleep in his room. We tried the living room, but that didn't work either. It was like Monifah was everywhere."

Carmen understood. She wished she had thought about it. It didn't hurt her to see Jay's things because he was alive. If he had died, she wouldn't have been able to walk in the house. "It's okay," she told them. She headed in the guestroom to see Kane was packing his stuff. "You don't have to leave. Jay hasn't woken up yet."

"I got stuff to take care of," Kane expressed. "I gotta call Monifah's parents, her family. I gotta call the funeral home to get her body." He tossed his toothbrush and deodorant into a duffle bag. "I also need to see Bella." He stopped packing when he said his daughter's name. Carmen watched as his gaze shifted to her. "I don't want to do this by myself."

"I know," Carmen told him. "I'll help you."

"I'm talking about Bella. She deserves to have a mother. I didn't agree to have her to do it by myself. I had her so she could have a mother."

Carmen reiterated what she said. "Kane, I'm here. I'll help you."

"I don't want you to help," he yelled. "I want you to be her mother."

A wave of déjà vu fell over her. He asked the same of her years ago when it came to Akaila and Malachi. It took her only minutes to agree to take them in. This time, it would take her seconds. "I'll be her mother. She's mine."

"Don't just say it to be saying it," he barked. "If she's gonna be yours, mean it. She needs to get what everyone else is getting. I don't want her growing up feeling like she was your charity case. Treat her like she came from your womb."

"Isn't that how I treat Akaila and Malachi?"

"You do," Kane admitted. "Shit, they talk more to you than they do to me." He zipped his duffle bag. "Let me take care of some things. I'll check in this evening so you can meet her."

"Seven," Carmen whispered.

"Huh?" Kane barely heard what she said.

"Seven," she repeated. "I have seven kids."

For the first time that morning she saw a smile. It came and went, but it was there. His smile told her he was going to be okay. She excused herself from the room. She got in her bed where she slept until her body woke on its own. It was going on four. She showered again, practicing what she was going to say to Rakim and Nyla. When she went to tell them, she learned Fiona had taken them to her granddaughter's birthday party. Her spirit rejoiced at the news. If it were God's Will, she wouldn't have to tell them. She hoped even now, as she walked in the hospital, that Jay was awake.

To her dismay, he was still unconscious. She sat with him for a couple of hours, but there wasn't a change. She prayed when she headed to the NICU with Kane, that Jay would be awake when she came back. He wasn't. On Monday morning, his condition hadn't changed. She had spent the night and was still in the same clothes from Sunday. She looked at him, his face as peaceful as it had been when she saw him after surgery. She kissed his hands, a form of affection that was becoming common for her. She was about to kiss them again when her phone vibrated. Jerry was calling. She hadn't talked to anyone outside her family about what happened at The Ave.

"Good morning," she said. She braced herself for what he was going to say.

"Hello, Carmen." He cleared his throat. "I know there's a lot going on. I know you're shaken up. We're shaken up, too. It's a lot." Carmen agreed with him, but he didn't give her a chance to voice it. "We don't know what's going on right now. Tiara wasn't at the party. We haven't been able to reach her. The publicist is hesitant to call you because of what happened. She wanted to give you some time, but we need to make a statement. It feels like we don't have a President." Jerry gave her a nervous chuckle.

"I've been at the hospital these past couple of days," Carmen told him. "I still don't know what happened. What I do know is that I need you to step up. I'll call Tiara, but I need you to do what I know you can. It's on you right now."

"You think I can do this?" Jerry sounded unsure of himself.

"I hired you for a reason."

A female voice came out of nowhere. "Is that Carmen? Do you have her on the phone?"

Carmen snickered at Jessica's voice. "Put her on the phone," she said with a smile. She listened as Jerry passed the phone.

"Carm, I'm so sorry, I'm praying for you and Jay. Look, I hate to bother you, but the security supervisor called me. Kane quit this morning."

The only reaction she could give was to tell her she had to go. She needed to get her ex on the phone. He was going through a lot, but he didn't need to quit. "You didn't think they were going to tell me?" she roared once Kane answered. "You should've talked to me. You're already on paternity leave. You didn't have to quit."

Fire came from the other end. "I haven't even made it out the fuckin' parking deck." She heard him hit the steering wheel. "They didn't give me the chance." He hit the steering wheel again. This time, his horn honked. "I didn't quit because of what happened. Shit, fuck it, I did. I got a call from the captain of the Triad. He offered me a six-figure contract."

His words lit a match inside Carmen. "Don't tell me you signed that."

"The captain told me I have a job to finish."

"How much is the contract?" she asked.

Kane sighed. "Eight hundred thousand total. Six hundred of that is the two-year contract."

Carmen made him an offer. "I'll give you a million dollars not to sign."

"I gave the captain my word. I told him I would be at the office at ten."

Carmen gripped the phone. "You son of a bitch." She didn't think she had any more tears. There she was, though, crying again. Their biggest argument aside from Jay was him going undercover. She always feared he wouldn't come home.

"I didn't do this to hurt you. I love you. You and our kids are all I have."

"Do you still want to be buried in the white suit?" Carmen knew the question was out of line. She wanted it to be. She wanted him to feel the pain she was feeling. She had almost lost Jay, now Kane was putting her in a position where she could lose him.

"The rest of the contract is the signing bonus," Kane disclosed. "I get that money at signing if I take The Ave case. He went over some things with me. This is bigger than we thought."

Carmen's demeanor changed at the news. "Why didn't you lead with that? That should've been the first thing you said."

"I'll call you once it's done."

He hung up the phone. The call changed her mood from one of rage to one of relief within seconds. Her mood was about to change again when she saw Tiara walk in the room. She hadn't seen her since Wednesday. Her friend looked just as stressed as her. "I know it's a lot," Carmen said, sitting down. "I know there's a bridge we have to get over."

"He tried to kill him," Tiara said, speaking of Jay and Malik. "That's a freakin' ocean."

Carmen laughed. There wasn't anything funny about what Jay did. What was funny is that Tiara thought she was an innocent party.

"We'll get to that," was the first thing out Carmen's mouth. "You stopped asking about my mom. I'm glad you did. It made it easier to deal with." She grabbed Jay's hand into hers. "Do you remember Cesar?"

"What does he have to do with Malik?"

"Just shut up for a moment," Carmen belched. Tiara made a gesture as if to say continue. "My problems started with my mother. It started on my honeymoon. Cesar found my mother behind the rosebushes at our house." Her friend's mouth dropped wide open. "Jay killed her. Or at least he thought he did. Cesar thought he did, too. He took her to a funeral home so they could cremate her. You know, get rid of the body. My mother is strong, though. She still had a pulse."

Carmen grabbed her purse. She pulled out her mother's journal and set it on Jay's bed. "Cesar let me make the decision. I chose to have her transported to the hospital. I promised him I wouldn't tell Jay she was alive.

Or that he lied. I could explain her condition because my mother was suicidal. She wrote about it in her journal. I knew she was depressed after my father died but not to the point she wanted to kill herself. She couldn't do it, though. She was a coward. Did you know she liked Jay? She did. She liked him more than she liked me. She fucked with his head because he wasn't a coward."

Tiara gripped the rails of Jay's bed.

Tears streamed down Carmen's face. "She made him kill her. She knew his weakness and she played with it. That's why I didn't hold it against him. That's why I could still make love to him. I needed to. He spent most of his life thinking his mother committed suicide. She didn't. My mother killed her." Carmen grabbed her mother's journal. "I was sneaking out to visit her. Then, my tape with Carlos leaked. I blamed Jay. I suspected it was Kane." She slid the journal back in her purse. "My tape with Jay leaked. He went to LA, found out it was Monifah." Her volume decreased. "I thought it was her, too. She agreed to doing it.

"You said something to me one day," Carmen continued. "We were hugging, and you whispered something to me you say all the time." She let out a small giggle. "The whole, 'I've been holding you down since you were getting your hair braided in D-Block'."

"I have," Tiara replied. "I've always had your back."

"You said the same thing to Culture XL in an email." Their eyes were now on each other's. "You were acting as Monifah, and you did an excellent job. I didn't even catch that line. I've heard it so much it's like hello. Monifah hated me, but she was open about it. You hate me, but you do it in private." Carmen ignored the tears falling down her friend's face. "You saved me when Jay beat me up. You were in his house. You took my money. You took my sketches. But for twenty-something years, you never told me you took the tape of me and Carlos."

Tiara whispered her name.

"That's why the Triad didn't find it when they searched the house. It's why Jay never had it after he took it from Carlos. When it comes to the second tape, you have access to us. You're in my house twice a day, five days out the week. You had all the time in the world to grab Jay's phone. It ain't like his password is hard to figure out. It's my fuckin' birthday. You would've gotten that on the second attempt."

"I made a mistake," Tiara cried.

"I was going to award you with twenty percent of my shares at the party. I was waiting for the anniversary to do it. You deserved it. Shit, I thought you deserved more. What you did was fucked up, but the suspension was a blessing. I love waking up to my kids. I love it so much I wasn't gonna come back. I was gonna offer you my job. The truth made me change my mind."

"She got in my head," Tiara argued. "Monifah was asking about the tape. She was telling me I was nothing without you. I felt like I had something to prove."

"You're a multi-millionaire. Your name is said by the fashion greats. They say my name, they say yours. What else did you want?"

Tiara spoke, firmly, "Not to be second."

Carmen exhaled. "I see. Well, you don't have to be. You're fired. Jerry is going to run the company. I'm gonna look for new designers. I'm not even gonna ask the board to lift the suspension. I also don't care to make a fool of you. Yes, I'm firing you, but you can tell the board it's a resignation. You should announce it tomorrow. Make up a reason."

Tiara begged and pleaded. "Flame is my life. It's all I know. We can get past this."

Carmen agreed. "We are gonna get past it. You forgave me for sleeping with Carlos. I've forgiven you for this. You should see it as a time to start fresh. You don't want to be second, right? Now, you don't have to be. Take your money, take your contacts, and start your own company. It doesn't have to be a competition. Start a line for little girls. Flame doesn't have that. You can link up with Kimora. She had Baby Phat Girlz. Put Robin in your ads."

"I don't want to lose you," Tiara cried. "I don't hate you."

"You didn't hear what I said?"

Carmen walked over to her. She grabbed her into a hug. "I'm sure Malik told you he ratted on Jay. We don't need to get into that. That's for him and Jay to work through. It'll be easier on them if they see we worked through our shit." She tightened the embrace. "You can do this. You ran Flame without me, remember?" When Tiara nodded her head, she separated from her. Carmen grabbed her purse as it was time for her to leave. "Tell Malik to call me when he's ready." Tiara nodded again.

They made their way out Jay's room. While they both boarded the elevator, they got off at different floors. Carmen made her exit on the 3rd Floor to access the Trauma Center. Tiara went to the lobby. Now alone, Carmen stood outside her mother's room. She knew what awaited her on the other side. She was ready for it.

She twisted the doorknob and opened the door. Eleise was the first person she saw, loads of tissue in her sister's hands. She went to her first, not acknowledging the nurses and doctors inside. Their embrace was long overdue. "Are you ready?" she said in her ear. She took a step back to see her face. When Eleise nodded, Carmen looked at the medical team who cared for her mother. "We're ready," she told them.

Her mother's doctor was the first one to approach her. She showed her what to do and one by one, Carmen disconnected her mother's life support devices. Seven minutes later, Patricia was gone.

***

Carmen waited until the sun rose at 7:32 to walk in the pool house. She figured Roman would be stirring at that hour versus five o'clock, which was the time she came home from the hospital. She was only on his bed for a second before he rolled over.

"Do you love my daughter?" she asked him.

He pulled the comforter up as he was half-naked. "With all my heart," he replied. "I made the final payment on her ring."

"If you loved her, you would've married her yesterday." Carmen rose from the bed. "Neither today nor tomorrow is promised." She looked back at him once she reached the doorway. "If she'll have you, you have my blessing. You just gotta get Kane's."

"If we get married, will y'all knock?"

"We will if you start paying rent."

Carmen winked at him. She left the doorway still hearing his laughter once she was downstairs. She thought the good vibes had rubbed off on Gully. He was smiling from ear to ear when she got in the backseat of the limo. For the past few days, like most people in the house, he had been in a funk. Today seemed different. "What has you hyped? Excited to groom your cousin?" She chuckled. "I appreciate you doing this for me. Y'all Santiagos grow hair like cavemen. I don't want him lookin' crazy when the kids see him. They already gotta see him in a coma. You know they're meeting Isa—" Her head jerked to the right when the back door opened.

Cesar stepped inside, his arm in a sling. Not able to hold her excitement, she threw herself on him, placing a large kiss on his cheek.

"You know I'm married," he joked.

Carmen kissed his cheek again. "Your wife will understand. She knows what you did."

"I did what God put me here to do—protect." He tapped her hand. "I wanted to see you so I could tell you personally. The Triad is looking for me. There was security footage found at The Ave. They know I'm alive."

Carmen knew Kane had signed the contract to be over the case. He hadn't talked much about it, only telling her he was still completing his paperwork.

"While he's laying low, I'm gonna help with the ghosts," Gully added. "Nicholas is back at Sapphire, so that's covered. Jay's other businesses can run as normal with their managers. Nothing will fall."

Cesar resumed his thoughts. "Until this dies down, I gotta get out the country. Canada ain't safe anymore. My family and I are moving to Abu Dhabi. We'll be there until I can get out these charges. They're still trying to pin the shootout at Blue Magic on me."

"Self-defense," Carmen proposed. "That's what Jay used."

Cesar wished it were that easy. "Jay had the U.S. government. He had a contract that said he would stay free if he delivered the pink diamond. He still gotta go through red tape when he fucks up, but he'll get his freedom."

"I'll get you a good lawyer," Carmen offered. "You can't stay in Abu Dhabi. We need you here."

Cesar shared his wish. "Hopefully, it'll only be for six months."

"Every day you sacrifice your life for us."

Cesar took her hand in his. "We didn't know that was gonna happen. I met with him when y'all got to the party. I told him he didn't need his guns. I gave 'em to him as a precaution. I promised what I always do. I would have his back."

"You need to see him before you leave. He needs to feel your presence."

"A plan is in the works." Cesar touched her cheek. "Be good, Carmen. I'll see you when I see you. Maybe you'll pay me a visit in the Middle East."

Carmen smiled at him. "Te amo," she whispered. Cesar whispered the words back. He said something to Gully, but he did it in Spanish so she wouldn't understand. When he got out the car, she looked in the rearview mirror. She wanted Gully to tell her what he said.

"Is that you or me?" he asked.

Carmen concentrated on the sound. She pulled her phone from her purse to see Kane's image on the screen. "Hey," she answered.

"Can you come by the Triad?" Kane asked.

"I knew that was coming," she said with a sigh. "You have to question me, right?"

"We need to talk," he told her. "Can you come by?"

"I'm on my way." She hung up the phone. "I need to make a pitstop."

Gully was all for it. "He ain't my friend or my enemy," he said, speaking of Kane, "but he got a team of motherfuckers that's going to be looking for the man who shot my cousin. Kane talks to you, you talk to me, we put him down together. Got it?"

Carmen did get it. It was the reason she met with Kane in one of the Triad's offices. The security footage from The Ave was on a large screen. He told her it would put things in context.

"That's the guy," Kane was saying, pointing to an image of the light-skinned man. He was walking towards her and Monifah right as Jay was approaching her from behind. "He didn't have a clear shot because of where Monifah was standing. He shot her to get to Jay."

Carmen squirmed in her seat once the bullet hit Monifah in the back. Kane showed little emotion, which he explained by saying he had seen the tape twenty times. He had become numb to it. Carmen's first-time viewing, she felt every emotion. From the tape, she learned it was Jay who knocked her down. He moved her out the way right as the man fired again. That bullet was the first Jay took to the chest.

"These are Jay's men, right?"

Gully, Linx, and Lia were trading fire with the men in the black tuxedos. More men joined them who she couldn't name.

"You ain't gotta confirm it," Kane continued. "I recognize three of 'em."

She sat straight up when part of the ceiling came down. A gaping hole gave visibility to the third floor. Seconds later, Cesar plunged headfirst into the room. He was on top of another man who he used to break his fall.

The image was paused. "He," Kane said, pointing the cursor at the man who fell with Cesar, "had the bomb. It was similar to the bomb used on the train at L' Orange." Kane moved the cursor to Cesar. "Four things are true here. One, he tried to defuse it. Two, he didn't know what he was doing that's why the ceiling caved in. Three, he did know what he was doing because he kept the whole building from going down." He stopped the tape. "The last thing is self-explanatory. You gonna tell me where I can find this dead man?"

Carmen stuck up her middle finger.

"We can do that right now," Kane joked. He pulled up a picture of the light-skinned man. It was a shot taken at the step and repeat when he entered The Ave.

"I think he's Carlton Rodriguez," Carmen shared. "He's been looking for Jay."

"That's the name written on the ticket."

"He's supposed to be Carlos' half-brother," Carmen added. "Jay never believed it. They never met."

"He would know. That was his best friend." Kane stared at the image of the man. "Jay is smart, I'll give him that. I wonder what would've happened if he met with him. I mean, they both are beasts. Jay was shot and still going." Kane got quiet at what he was about to reveal. "We know the party was invite-only. Each employee got two tickets. Everyone else got one."

"An employee invited him as their plus one."

Kane slid a stack of papers her way. "That's the record of tickets received. Carlton's name was on a ticket belonging to Tiara. A copy of the ticket is there."

Carmen swore she could hear her heart beating. It was about seventy degrees in the room, yet it felt like seven hundred.

"I don't think y'all are gonna be friends after this."

"Look at me," Carmen ordered. She rested her arms on the table. "Women have intuition. My gut is telling me you're about to say something that is gonna make me go to her house. *You* don't think we'll be friends. I'm asking myself if she's gonna be alive."

"I suggest you keep Robin on the forefront of your mind. She already has one parent in the hospital." Kane picked up another piece of paper. He slid it her way. It was a clear photo of the light-skinned man. In the picture, he was dressed like a man of royalty. "A week before the party there was a presidential address. The President announced he was sending military forces to Sierra Leone to overthrow Artemis 66. That's the military group raising hell in Kenema."

Carmen held up the photo of the man. "I watched it."

"He isn't Carlton Rodriguez," Kane said. "There are lots of Carlton Rodriguez's in the world. None of them are related to Carlos. The man you're looking at is a drug dealer. He controls a lot of diamond mines in Africa. Both connect him to Jay. He's the reason our government gave Jay that deal. They told Jay they wanted the Pink Sunrise. What they didn't tell him is that they wanted the identity of this man. He's the leader of Artemis 66."

"I have a strong feeling he was the one who shot up our house in San Juan."

Kane shared more. "The only reason y'all survived what happened at The Ave is because he ain't got his army. The U.S. captured a lot of 'em, but they're still on the hunt." Kane moved closer to Carmen. "He got hit at least five times. Somehow, there's no record of him or a Carlton Rodriguez at any hospital in New York. He gotta be in the states, though. Ain't no way he made it to Africa with those injuries."

"He could be dead. Y'all didn't see where they carried him after they left the building?"

"They got in a sprinter van," Kane shared. "We had eyes on 'em until they hit the Lincoln Tunnel." He took her hand in his. "The captain chose me because I had the most successful run undercover." Kane spoke of an operation he was a part of during the second year of their marriage. For a brief time in Kingston, Jamaica, he was one of the city's most ruthless drug kingpins by the name of Kong. His assignment was to take down the island nation's biggest drug lord, Luck Myers. "My job is to find links that will lead us to this man."

"Does this operation require you to have a girlfriend?"

"Don't even try it. You're not coming with me." He leaned down and kissed her lips. She backed away from him, now uncomfortable. Her reaction triggered his conscience. Moments ago, they both watched their spouses get shot. The timing was off. The kiss was selfish and insensitive.

Carmen didn't speak on it. "So, if he's not Carlton Rodriguez, who is he?" She stuck the picture in her purse although Kane hadn't given her permission to take it.

"He's an Afro-Cuban maniac named Ishmael Dumati."

CPSIA information can be obtained
at www.ICGtesting.com
Printed in the USA
BVHW041225020622
638737BV00005B/64

9 780988 800465